ZACH
Hell's Handlers MC Book 1

Lilly Atlas

Lilly Atlas Books LLC

ISBN-13: 978-1-946068-24-8
ISBN-10: 1-946068-24-1

ZACH
Hell's Handlers MC Book 1

Toni's no stranger to making mistakes. She has experienced firsthand how walking down the wrong path can send life spiraling out of control. Fortunately, she had someone to drag her from the gutter and help set her on the right track. As penance for the poor choices of her past, she pledges to suppress her baser desires and focus on finding a steady, dependable man, even if that means embracing a boring lifestyle.

The last thing anyone would call Zach is dull. As Enforcer for the Hell's Handlers MC, he embodies the outlaw lifestyle. When Toni moves in next door, Zach can't resist the possibility of a quick, hot, fling. But he soon discovers she's not the easy conquest he's used to.

While Zach works to convince Toni she belongs in his bed, a tenuous relationship with a local gang disintegrates and threatens his MC family. Zach's world is turned upside down when he's unable to keep the danger from touching his club.

As Toni fights to resist Zach's pull, her own peace is shattered by demons from her past. With enemies both old and new barreling down, she throws out her rules and turns to Zach for aid. Soon, she finds herself firmly entrenched in Zach's dangerous world.

Is it possible for her to curb her desires, or is she doomed to repeat the mistakes of her past?

None of it will matter if Zach can't keep their enemies at bay.

PROLOGUE

Tennessee 2008

It was finally fucking over.

Or maybe it was just beginning.

Either way, years, *years* of busting his ass, taking shit, and being treated like a worthless maggot were finished.

The vote was unanimous.

He was finally a brother.

Well, he was ninety-nine-point-nine percent of the way in. They couldn't just vote him in and chuck him the patch he'd been salivating over for the past two years. No, they had to throw him one last challenge, and a bitch of a test it was.

A branding. The Hell's Handlers Motorcycle Club emblem. On the left forearm. It was as important as the patches on the leather cut each brother wore. So important, if a man was tatted on his left forearm he couldn't even prospect. No, the emblem had to be seared into clean skin, so anyone and everyone would know who belonged to the motorcycle club.

And if being branded wasn't bad enough, there were rules that went along with the barbaric ceremony.

Every brother had to be in attendance. Heckling, ribbing, waiting to see just how much the new member wanted to be a part of the life. Waiting for them to crack.

1

No screaming.

No tears.

No passing out.

A grunt of pain was allowed, but beyond that, any outward show of weakness would null and void the unanimous vote to end the prospecting period and make him a fully-patched member of the Hell's Handlers MC.

He wouldn't make a peep. They could cut his fucking arm off and beat him with it and Zach still wouldn't utter a sound. That patch was his, and the only way he'd give it up was if some lucky motherfucker managed to pry it from his cold, dead hands. Even then, he'd haunt the bastard and wear the thing as a spirit.

A shrill whistle cut through the raucous laughter and drunken male partying around a huge bonfire. The fire was necessary because the night air was barely butting up against forty degrees. And, of course, the guys made him stand around shirtless while he waited for his fate.

Usually, the sound of fucking made up much of the party's noise, but not tonight. This was just for the men, brothers in all but blood. At least this early part of the night. After Zach got his patch, they'd bring in the club pussy and he'd have his pick of the litter. One, two, hell even three women if he wanted. He'd earned it, watching brother after brother partake in the sweet privilege that was not bestowed on prospects. Club pussy was for patched members only.

And now he was one.

His dick twitched in his pants but died the moment his president spoke. "Okay, fuckers, listen up."

All around him, his soon to be new brothers lowered their drinks and gave their leader, Copper, their full attention. At twenty-nine, Copper was young to be in the role of club president, and since he'd been at it for almost four years, he was officially the youngest leader in the club's near fifty-year history.

Zach

"We're just minutes away from welcoming another brother into the club. Shit, Zach's been one of the best prospects we've ever had. Tough as fuckin' nails, pulls more than his own weight, never runs his mouth, loyal." A puff of steam drifted from Copper's mouth as he spoke to the group.

The prez wasn't one to be fucked with. A good few inches over six feet, with a beard the color of a dirty penny, and plenty of hair to match, he was mean as a starving pit-bull. But Copper had the respect of every man in the club. Not just because he held the title of president, but because he'd earned it, dragging the club from the brink of disaster and making it a thriving brotherhood once again.

Zach blew on his hands, trying to infuse some warmth into the frozen digits. Damn, it was colder than a witch's titty and standing around shirtless for the past half hour hadn't helped anything.

"Just one more test of this asshole's strength before he gets to be one of us. Ready, boys?" Copper waved Zach over to the mountain of wood crackling and spitting sparks. Sticking out of the bonfire, a long branding iron roasted away, just waiting to scorch some of Zach's skin.

Shouts of encouragement and a few hecklers betting on how much of a pussy he was and what octave his scream would hit reached him as he made his way to the fire and his waiting president. Careful to keep his expression neutral, Zach drew up next to his prez and paused. Wasn't that the whole point? Act like he wasn't scared. Wasn't about to shit his pants in anticipation of what would probably be the worst physical pain he'd ever experienced.

Fuckin' Copper's facial hair split and his teeth gleamed in the flickering fire. Prez lived for this bull. And if he didn't, he sure acted like he did with that shitty grin of anticipation. "Anything you want to say first?"

Zach shook his head while he bounced on the balls of his feet, hitting his pecs as hard as he could. Maybe if he could get some pain going somewhere else, the burn of the iron wouldn't be so bad.

"Won't work," Copper said, as though reading his mind. "Tried the same thing when I was in your spot. Ain't nothing gonna make this shit any better." He bent and retrieved a bottle from next to his foot. Zach had no idea what was in it, moonshine probably. "You know the drill. Bottle in your left hand. Ten seconds to drink as much as you can. Hold your arm out straight. I'll mark ya. No dropping the bottle. No spilling. No screaming. No puking. Stay on your feet for two whole minutes. Then you're a fuckin' brother."

Zach nodded. His chest rose and fell in a rapid rhythm as his breathing increased and the blood raced through his veins. After blowing out a breath, he grabbed the bottle and brought it to his lips, tilting his head back and opening his throat as much as he could.

Some of the nastiest hooch he'd ever tasted flooded his mouth and streamed down his throat, burning a path to his stomach. Fitting really, since he was about to be burned all to a crisp anyway. Somewhere in the distance, he could hear his soon to be brothers whooping like a horde of wild baboons, but he managed to drown out most of the noise. All but the sound of Copper counting down from ten.

"Three...two...one...arm!"

Zach tore the bottle from his lips and extended his arm. Unable to look away, he stared in fascinated horror as the glowing end of the iron made contact with the thin skin of his forearm. There was a fraction of a second where his eyes registered the flesh-to-iron connection, but the pain hadn't yet reached his brain.

And then it did.

All-consuming, searing pain like he'd never experienced fired through his nerve endings. Though the spot being branded was no bigger than a silver dollar, agony seemed to encompass his entire being until he couldn't recognize where it originated from.

Zach

Then there was the audible singe accompanied by the stench of melting flesh. He wasn't expecting that.

Blinding pain was a phrase he'd heard before, but in that moment, he lived it. Darkness clouded his vision, and he slammed his knees back, determined not to succumb to the blissful oblivion that hovered just out of reach.

All around him, men screamed and hollered, but he couldn't make out their cries over the rushing in his ears. Nostrils flaring with each forceful inhalation and exhalation, he mashed his teeth together, probably pulverizing the enamel, as he fought to remain conscious.

Then, the nausea hit. Instead of helping to lessen the pain, the damn moonshine sloshed in his gut and started a trip back up his esophagus, just as disgusting the second time around.

His eyes locked with Copper's. The grinning bastard was definitely enjoying it. All the more motivation to remain standing, quiet, and avoid vomiting the moonshine all over.

Copper pulled the iron away and tossed it to the ground, but it did nothing to diminish the agony. After what seemed like an eternity, Copper pulled his gaze away and checked his watch. Seconds ticked by slower than the thickest motor oil dripping from an engine. Finally, he looked at Zach again and this time his smile was genuine, welcoming. "Two minutes, brother."

Brother. Sweeter fucking words had never been spoken.

Copper grabbed him by the elbow and lifted his throbbing arm. The pain was still there, but now the rush of excitement at achieving his two-year long goal overrode the worst of it. That, and the moonshine was kicking in.

With a loud cry of triumph, Copper held up Zach's branded arm. "Say hello to your newest brother, men." Cheers rose up all around.

Zach swayed on his feet as pain and nausea still warred for victory over his consciousness.

Copper whistled, reigning in the crazy. "He's now to be shown the same respect any other brother receives. He's going to make a damn fine addition to the club."

Zach's chest constricted as pride surged.

"Proud of you, brother," Copper said, for Zach's ears only. "You were one hell of a prospect, and you'll be one hell of an addition to the club."

"Thanks, Prez."

Raising his voice again, Copper turned to the rowdy crowd. "Now someone get Zach a beer and some pussy. The man's waited long enough."

They wouldn't be giving him any pain medication for the burn, but losing his dick in a club girl should take care of the last of the discomfort.

Brothers converged on him from all angles, slapping his back and welcoming him. Not only would the moment be burned into his skin forever, but it was seared into his brain as well.

Best night of his life.

He was in.

Now it was time to set his sights on an executive position.

Enforcer would do quite nicely.

CHAPTER ONE

Tennessee Present Day

Toni trailed her hand along the sparkling clean counter top as she strolled the length of the diner. Spotless. Always clean to the point of sanitized. The health department had nothing on her parents.

All her life, their family-owned diner had done well. Their baby. More so than their flesh and blood child. A fact that had messed with Toni's head growing up, but she'd long ago come to terms with. Or so she liked to think. Some people just weren't meant to be parents.

The diner had been a thriving business from the moment Lucy and Roger Jennings hung the first open sign in the window.

Location, location, location.

They'd always had it going for them. The town itself was itty bitty. A true American small town where neighbors borrowed a cup of sugar, citizens were all up in each other's business, and gossip spread like a fiery line of gasoline lit by a match.

Townsend, Tennessee just happened to be one of the gateways to the Great Smoky Mountains. Fortunate for business owners because throngs of tourists, campers, and hikers shuttled through the area year after year. Summertime never failed to be packed with visitors from all over, eager to spend time in one of America's most beautiful regions.

Closing down the diner would be a tragedy. It was iconic. A landmark in their little slice of the world. Some of the regulars had been enjoying the cooking here almost daily for thirty-plus years. As a child, Toni used to imagine owning it all by herself. Having everyone in town swing by to chat with her as much as to eat the food. The diner had been home to her more than her actual house had. Especially as she grew into her preteen years, and her relationship with her parents deteriorated.

The chatter of the townspeople. The smells of frying bacon, brewing coffee, and cinnamon rolls. Even the heat of the kitchen after hours of cooking comforted her. The sights, sounds, and smells of the diner were so burned into her sense memory, it was difficult to think about parting with it forever.

But now Toni lived in Chicago. Had a job in Chicago. A boyfriend in Chicago. A life in Chicago. One she wasn't willing to give up to run the diner her deceased parents left in her care. Especially given the fact that she hadn't spoken to her parents in over five years.

Really, it was a wonder anything had been left to her at all. Her inheritance came down to one of two things. Either Lucy and Roger hadn't gotten around to changing their will before their untimely deaths, or they just figured screw it, Toni was their only child. Who else would they leave their legacy to?

So, she inherited a diner.

And a house.

Two things that were now solely her responsibility. Two responsibilities she didn't want.

The plan was to find a buyer for the diner as well as the house. The money she'd receive would go a long way toward purchasing her dream home in Chicago.

Selling the diner would be the best decision all around. She could vet the new owners. Choose someone who would continue to run it as a diner so she didn't feel like she was selling off the one good thing from her childhood. No matter her fondness for the establishment, she didn't want it. It wasn't part of her life plan.

For some reason, she had to keep reminding herself of that. The idea of someone else owning and operating what her child-self had imagined running put a bad taste in her mouth. Even if a buyer planned to run the diner exactly as her parents had, some things would inevitably change. And something about that had her heart aching.

The last piece of her childhood, last good piece anyway, and she was selling it off like a fatted calf bound for slaughter.

From the booth closest to the entrance, her phone chirped. She'd dropped her purse there when she arrived, because it would be hard to forget on her way out. After digging the phone out of her giant bag, she grinned at the display. "Hi, Uncle Mark," she greeted her favorite person in the world.

"Hi, sweetie. How're you holding up? I'm so sorry I had to jet five minutes after the funeral."

"I'm good, Uncle Mark. And I think I told you the last four times you apologized, to knock it off." She sighed. "Let's be real here, no one would have held it against you if you hadn't come at all."

He snorted. "Not to speak ill of the dead, but I didn't do it for them. I did it for you."

Warmth filled her chest. "I know." And she did. Her mother's brother was more of a father to her than her own had been over the past decade.

One week ago, a drunk college kid flying down the mountain switchbacks like some kind of wannabe NASCAR driver lost control on a near ninety-degree turn and careened head-on into her parents' Honda Accord. All three lives were lost instantly. Toni wasn't heartless, she felt sadness over her parents' passing, but their relationship was so strained, she felt somewhat dissociated from true grief. As though it was the death of some distant relative, rather than the people who'd created her. She'd mourned the loss of her family years ago when they broke contact.

They'd been the people who were supposed to love and support her, no matter what.

No matter how bad she rebelled.

Or screwed up.

But they hadn't. They'd turned their backs on her when she'd needed them most. Old hurts she barely visited any longer, but now she'd inherited everything they owned including a hopping business. And all the damage from the past had been a constant in her mind since she received the call from the police.

"Toni? You still there?"

With a shake of her head, she pushed the old ghosts to the background for the time being. Later, they'd probably creep back up on her, as they had been since she returned to her hometown, but she didn't want any of her pain to bleed into the conversation with her uncle. He'd be on a plane in a heartbeat, showing up to battle her demons. "Sorry, I'm here. What did you say?"

He chuckled in her ear. "I asked how things were going at the diner?" Fifteen years her mother's junior, Mark was closer in age to Toni than he'd been to his sister. Toni had worshiped him like a beloved older brother her entire life. A life that she pretty much owed to him and the fact that he loved her just as much.

"We re-open tomorrow." She huffed. "It's only been closed seven days for the funeral and everything, and you'd think the apocalypse was upon this town."

"People like their pancakes."

Even though he couldn't see her, she shrugged. "I guess they do."

"Say what you want about your parents, but they knew how to run a business and they knew how to hire a damn good chef."

"That they did." She glanced around the pristine diner once again. It was a fifties style diner with a long-curved counter running the entire length of the restaurant. The fifteen bolted down chrome stools with teal seats were always occupied as were most of the teal and coral booths against the windows. A black and white checkerboard floor covered the entire establishment. As a kid, she used to start at the black square that butted up against the entrance and see how far she could jump. Whenever Mark visited, he challenged her to a contest, seeing who could hop the farthest. They'd measure based on how many squares they leapt over.

Toni heaved a heavy sigh. "Can I ask you something that might make you want to commit me?"

"Sure, kid. You know you can ask me anything."

"Am I crazy to feel a little bit like I don't want to sell this place?" She chuckled. "You know what, don't answer that. The answer is yes. I'm crazy."

The silence that greeted her seemed to last forever. "Uncle Mark? You still there?"

"I don't think it's crazy, sweetie," he finally said. "In fact, I always thought you'd do an amazing job at running the joint. I still think that."

Toni couldn't help the laugh that bubbled out of her. "Me? Run this place. Now who's crazy? First off, I know nothing about running a business and, more importantly, I haven't stepped foot in this place in over six years. I don't have a clue how things are run anymore. Just because I wanted to own it as a child, doesn't mean I could actually do it now."

"Oh, please, that's such bullshit."

Toni pictured him waving his hand as he dismissed her statement. No one talked with their hands more than Mark did, something he had to work to curb when arguing cases in a courtroom. "You grew up in that place. Worked there since you were old enough to toddle a menu over to a table. It would come back to you in the blink of an eye."

"Working the counter and waiting tables aren't exactly the same as overseeing the business. Besides, Mark, I'm a guidance counselor in Chicago, remember? I have responsibilities. Remember Christopher? My boyfriend?"

"Ugh, as if I could forget that asshat." Mark had been near hostile toward her boyfriend, Chris, ever since Chris stood her up for a date. It had been a miscommunication, and she'd never held it against him, but Mark had a long memory and wasn't big on second chances. For anyone besides her, anyway.

Despite the insult to her boyfriend, Toni laughed. Her uncle wasn't one to censor himself. "Nice, Uncle Mark. Real sweet."

"Look," he said, "Oh, hold on a moment." The sound of a murmured greeting was followed by an audible smooch that brought a wide grin to Toni's face and made her forget a few of her worries.

"Ooo, Mark and Andrew sitting in a tree. K-I-S-S-I-N-G," Toni sang.

Both men's laughter could be heard through the phone. "You're such a little shit, Toni," Mark said.

"Tell your hunky husband hello for me."

"He is hunky, isn't he?"

Toni laughed. "Damn straight. You picked a sexy one there." Andrew was definitely classifiable as a hunk. But then so was Mark. And therein lay the reason her borderline bigoted parents had nothing to do with her favorite uncle. They just couldn't accept the fact that he was gay. It rocked their perfect little, ultra-conservative, close-minded world.

Mark hadn't come out to the family until Toni was twelve. Right around the time her relationship with her parents began to crumble. It was part of the reason. One of many parts, but their reaction had affected the way she viewed her parents. Her mother especially. The idea of them writing someone, family, out of their lives boggled her mind. Little did she know, only a few short years later, she'd be the ostracized one.

"Andrew says hi back. Now shut up and listen to me. I want you to consider something for me." Mark paused.

"Okay, counselor" she said, mostly because she felt he was waiting for confirmation she was listening.

"You have six weeks until school starts again. How about, instead of hiring a temp manager to keep the diner running until it's sold, you do it yourself?"

"What? Me? Why would—"

"I said listen. I did not say speak." He used his sternest attorney voice, which was pretty much ineffective on her.

"So sorry. My ears are wide open." Her tone said she was anything but remorseful.

"Always a smartass. Anyway, run the place for six weeks while you look for a buyer. Either you'll be itching to dump it on someone else by that time, or you'll fall in love and keep it for yourself."

"You make it sound so simple." She ran a hand through her hair and stared out the front window into the parking lot. Her rented navy Ford Focus was pulling into the empty lot, driven by Christopher.

"It is simple."

"Uhh, hello? Job? Boyfriend?" A boyfriend who'd traveled with her and helped her through this entire week of funerals, sorting through her parents' belongings, will readings. A boyfriend who was striding from the car to the restaurant in an immaculately pressed suit. She'd left early in the morning, catching a ride with the diner's chef, Ernesto. Chris had still been in bed when she left. Ernesto had been kind enough to spend his morning showing her the ropes. Payroll, inventory, ordering. All sorts of fun, business owner tasks.

Why was Chris wearing a suit? It had to be eighty-five degrees. She was in cutoffs and a tank top. A far cry from the preppy skirts and button-ups he usually saw her in.

"A job you're frustrated with and a man that's a dud," Uncle Mark said. "Come on, girl, you're in a rut and you know it."

He may have had a small point, about the job anyway. She'd become a guidance counselor to help kids like herself. Rebellious kids one bad decision away from wrecking their futures. Kids she could relate to because she'd made so many of those poor choices in her own teenage years. Lucky for her, Uncle Mark had stepped in and dragged her out of a life that would have chewed her up, spit her out, and left her for dead on the side of the road. And that wasn't an exaggeration.

Once she'd gotten her act together, she completed her GED, went to college, and set out to help those just like her. But it wasn't working out that way. After a few weeks at her first school, she realized her ability to do much of anything impactful was hobbled by privacy laws, state regulations, and those damn standardized tests. Most of her days were spent helping kids and teachers prepare for those exams and helping seniors plan for college. Worthwhile, yes, but she'd wanted to focus on the kids slipping through the cracks, and that just wasn't happening.

As Christopher's long legs ate up the distance between the car and the door, she said, "Stop ragging on Chris. He works for your law firm, for crying out loud. I met him because of you. Doesn't that mean you like him, at least a little bit?"

"I like him fine as an attorney. As an employee of my law firm. But he's just not for you."

"Well, that's not your decision now, is it, Uncle I-have-the-best-man-ever-so-I-look-down-on-all-other-boyfriends?"

"Aww, you're so sweet, Toni." Andrew's voice sounded like it was at the end of a tunnel.

She laughed. "Am I on speaker phone?" Chris waved as he caught sight of her through the window. His smile was wide and welcoming. A nice, handsome smile full of straight, white teeth.

Seriously? Straight teeth? That's what she noticed?

Her heart didn't even pitter let alone patter.

"Yup, you are definitely on speaker."

"Well, I gotta go, you two. Chris is here to pick me up."

"Think about what I said," her uncle ordered.

"I will. Love you both. Bye!"

She hung up before Mark could provide any additional words of wisdom but had to admit her interest was piqued. It was summer. She didn't have to work. She could use this time to reconnect with people she hadn't seen in years. People she knew as a kid but were now strangers. Maybe it would be good for her to spend some time in the place where she'd made her biggest mistakes. Cathartic. She wasn't a careless teen anymore. She was a respected member of society. Plus, she had a place to live. Work to keep her busy.

Hmm. Maybe Uncle Mark was on to something.

"Hey, sweetheart," Chris said over the jangle of bells as he walked into the diner. He came straight to her and dropped a quick kiss on her upturned lips.

No zip.

No zing.

No wham.

No pow.

Not even a flicker of excitement or arousal.

Damn it. And damn Mark for making her face what she'd been ignoring since…well, basically since her first date with Christopher.

He was a dud. A nice man who had a stable job, good apartment, fine family, enjoyable friends. A good-on-paper man who just didn't get her motor revving.

"Hi, honey," she said, giving him what she hoped was a happy-to-see-you smile. "Let me grab my purse and I'm ready to go. You pick up something for dinner?"

His eyebrows drew down and a frown marred his face. "What's with the outfit?"

As Toni slung her handbag over her shoulder she glanced at her clothes. "You've been here a week. This is how everyone dresses here. It's a very casual town. No one puts on airs." Her parents had, but that was a separate issue.

"Yeah, but that's not how you dress. I've never seen you in anything that didn't scream of preppy." Chris winked. "It's one of the reasons we fit so well."

Huh. Is that how he saw her? It certainly wasn't what she felt represented who she was. Wasn't who she used to be. Ugh. This damn trip was making her delve way too deep into her psyche.

"It's hot. You're the one who looks out of place here." She grabbed his hand and tugged him toward the door. "Come on. I'm hungry."

When they reached the exit, Chris held the door for her. Impeccable manners ran in his blood. Just as she was about to step into the warm evening, a sign in the window caught her attention. "Wait one sec."

She peeled the sign down, leaving two sticky squares of tape behind.

We reserve the right to refuse service to anyone. No Bikers Allowed.

Under the text was a circled motorcycle with a line through it. Her whole life she'd hated that sign. There wasn't a person in town who didn't know some member of the Hell's Handlers Motorcycle Club, and while they weren't exactly on the up and up, they deserved to be able to eat where they chose.

Perhaps it was juvenile, and perhaps it was wrong to ignore the wishes of the recently deceased, but removing the sign made her feel lighter. Her final act of rebellion against two people who'd never understood or accepted her or so many others.

"Why are you taking that down?" Chris asked. "Are you going to allow those lowlifes to eat here?"

Toni smiled. "Yes. Yes, I am. It's a breakfast joint. I lived next door to a biker and his family my whole childhood and nothing bad ever came of it. What's the worst that could happen?"

Chris shot her a concerned look just as the roar of a motorcycle filled the quiet evening air. The setting sun glinted off a black and chrome beast of a bike as it slowed passing the diner. The rider turned his head and stared straight at the empty spot in the window. Between the helmet, riding glasses, and

Zach

bandana over his face, she couldn't make out a single one of his features, yet somehow, she knew he was smirking.

CHAPTER TWO

"You wound me, Bill," Zach said as he leaned against the man's silver BMW. He folded his arms across his chest, making sure to keep the Louisville Slugger—who he'd named Louie—on full display.

From his spot on the ground, in the driveway of his isolated three-million-dollar mansion, Bill groaned. He was curled up in the fetal position after Louie had made contact with his rich-guy soft gut.

"Fuck you," Bill coughed and groaned again.

With a chuckle, Zach bent forward until he was just a foot away from Bill's grimacing face. He tapped the bat against Bill's leg and couldn't hold back a laugh when the man jumped like a skittish little girl. He was typically more about the intimidation than actually beating on people, but Bill had been a thorn in the club's ass for months now.

"Okay," he said around a smirk. "Maybe you're a little bit right. I do get some pleasure out of this, but what you seem to forget, Billy-boy, is that I don't have to be here. I don't seek you out to get my jollies by beating your ass. You're the one who keeps crawling back to my club, begging for money so you can feed the slots. Or is roulette your game of choice? Craps?"

The MC had a very lucrative loan sharking business, fueled by idiots like Bill who couldn't seem to get a handle on their vices. At a fifty-point vig, the money their clients owed added up fast,

Zach

especially if they missed the fourteen-day payback timeline. In that case, the fifty percent interest was added to the original loan and recalculated. After another two weeks, Zach came by for a little visit. Just a gentle reminder of the contracted agreement.

"I asked you a question, Billy." Zach stood and swung the bat like he was chasing a home run ball. The wood whizzed through the air at least three feet above Bill's head, but he still curled tighter with his head cradled in his arms.

Pussy.

Like Zach would actually bash the man's head in. Men with splattered brains couldn't pay back their loans. But men with broken kneecaps sure could. And usually did, very fast.

Those results were why a hefty bat was Zach's motivator of choice. He could show up at a client's house with a gun, but then he'd have to shoot sometimes, and that was undesirable for a number of reasons. First off, it was messy as hell. Who had time to clean blood anyway?

Then there was the bullet, which if removed and collected for evidence, could be traced back to Zach and the MC. Exactly the opposite of what Copper wanted from him in his job as enforcer for the club. And lastly, there was always the chance he'd miss the mark and kill some poor schmuck that owed them money.

And again. Dead men couldn't pay.

For the same reasons, he stayed away from knives. His own fists would work just fine, but then he'd be walking around with permanently bruised knuckles.

So, a bat it was. Clean, effective, untraceable.

Good stuff.

"You pussing out on me here, Bill? Come on. Tell me what you blew my club's ten grand on."

"P-poker." A nasty cough followed a wheeze as Bill struggled to a sitting position. Sweat dotted his receding hairline and his skin took on a grayish pallor.

"Deep breaths, buddy. Got your diaphragm good there, didn't I." Zach laughed. "Damn, man, I guess I really do enjoy this shit.

19

Hey, Bill, anyone ever tell you that you suck at poker? Now, I shouldn't be giving you this advice since I'll be eating a nice steak dinner on you soon, but you might wanna find a new hobby."

"Th-this is the last time," he coughed and groaned, clutching his portly stomach. "I s-swear it."

"Well..." Zach spun the bat like a baton twirler. He'd spent so much time with it over the last few years, he'd mastered some fancy tricks. "Don't quit on my account. As we've just learned, I seem to enjoy coming 'round and busting kneecaps. Which reminds me. This is your last warning. You're up to twenty-two thousand, five hundred now. I'll be back in two weeks. You don't have it, I take this as collateral." He rapped the bat against the tire of the man's fancy ride. "I suggest you march right in that big old house you can't afford and start crying to your wife. Maybe she'll take pity on your pathetic ass and crack into her trust fund."

Zach started down the driveway then spun and pointed the bat at Bill who was still on his ass in the driveway. "Oh yeah. Almost forgot. I'll break a bone too. My choice."

That announcement drew a sharp gasp from Bill. He'd always cut it close in the past, but this was the first time he'd been late to repay a loan. Zach shook his head. Loan sharking was one of the club's most lucrative businesses. And Zach's baby. Well, at least the bone crushing side of it. Jigsaw, the club's treasurer, ran the financial side of things.

Copper was the brains behind the entire operation. About fourteen years ago, when he was voted in as prez, the club was a fuckin mess. Drugs and weapons trafficking were the main sources of income, and for a time, it looked like the club wasn't going to survive. Cops were sniffing around. Wars with other MCs and a local gang over turf almost destroyed the entire operation.

Copper hauled the club away from that shit. He opened a few legitimate businesses, a garage, a bar, a strip club, and eventually

Zach's gym. One of the guys even owned a private security gig. Of course, as an outlaw MC, they didn't do everything on the shiny side of the law. Loan sharking, money laundering, and a fair amount of muscle for hire kept the club lubed with plenty of cash.

Done with his work for the evening, Zach stuffed the bat in his saddle bag and mounted his bike. The warm night was still young. Most of his brothers would be at the club's bar, the Double H. After drinking for a few hours and collecting women, the party would move to the clubhouse where it would become much more R and even X-rated in some cases.

Zach wasn't one to pass up an opportunity to drink with his brothers and find a willing woman to kill a few hours with, but tonight he pointed his Harley toward his house. An uncomfortable restlessness crawled through him. Maybe it was letting Bill off with little more than a whack and a warning. Zach hadn't had time to work out that day, either, too busy helping Prez with a problem.

Someone had roughed up a few of their strippers after hours behind the strip club, which was what had tied up most of Zach's day. He'd worked to coordinate increased security while Copper and Maverick worked to discover who it was. Man, Zach wouldn't want to be those assholes when the Hell's Handlers caught up to them. And they would. Maverick could follow a trail better than a bloodhound.

When he was about five minutes out from his house, his Bluetooth chirped in his helmet. He tapped the button on the outside of the helmet, activating the phone. "Hey, brother, where the fuck are you?" Speak of the devil. Maverick's voice filled his helmet. They'd prospected together for a about ten months until Maverick was voted in. He'd joined the club about a year before Zach.

"I just left Bill's."

Maverick laughed. "You leave any of his bones intact?"

With a snort, Zach hit the throttle and flew toward a yellow light. It switched to red about one second before his wheel hit the intersection. Eh, close enough. "Yeah he's fine. Louie gave him a warning shot and I offered up some friendly advice. Dude can't take much of a hit though. He was down and sniveling after just a love tap from Louie."

"Sounds about right. That man's softer than your mama's tits. You meeting us at the Double H?" Maverick's slurred voice sounded distracted. "Hold your fucking horses," he whispered.

A feminine whine had Zach laughing. "What the hell do you need me there for? Sounds like you got yourself a plaything for the night."

"Eh, she's all right. A bit clingy, but, man, what an ass. We're about to take off. Just wanted to let you know I wouldn't be here in case you came 'round."

"Thanks, brother. I'm heading home, anyway. Feel like I need to beat on the bag for a while, get some tension out. And watch out for the clinger. You might wake up tomorrow handcuffed to the bed with a marriage license waiting for your signature."

Maverick snorted. "Like I'd stay till morning. You know, pounding pussy is better stress relief than pounding on a heavy bag, right?"

Most of the time Zach would agree, but for the past few weeks he'd been edgy. Bored, maybe. Suffering from same shit, different day syndrome. Sure, the pussy and tits might be new, but the air between their ears was the same. And it was getting routine. Maybe skipping a few nights of partying would get him back on track.

Or at least have him horny enough not to give a shit if he was bored.

"Not tonight, bro. You go enjoy your new toy. I'll catch you tomorrow." Zach coasted to a stop in his driveway. A man and woman were just climbing out of a car in the driveway next door. Dressed in a pair of tiny cutoffs and a fitted tank top that hugged her generous breasts and the gentle swell of her stomach, the woman shut her door and waited for the man to lock the car. Had to be the daughter of his next-door neighbors. Or former neighbors. They'd died in a wreck a few days ago.

"Your loss, brother." Maverick disconnect the call.

Zach's gaze drifted back to the neighbor. What was her name. Trisha? Tori? Something along those lines. They'd grown up next door to each other, but seeing as she was a handful of years younger, they weren't exactly pals. He'd left for the army before she'd even been in high school, if he recalled correctly.

One thing was for certain, she'd sure grown up to be a looker. Big round eyes, the color of emeralds, had watched him coming and going a few times over the past week.

What he knew of her was based on a few flinty memories. She'd often sat in the bay window at the front of her parents' house watching him and his friends make jackasses of themselves in high school.

Both her parents were prejudiced assholes who rarely let their daughter out of the house to have any fun. She was either at school, home, or working at the diner. Those green eyes had captivated him, even as a kid, but for a different reason than he was drawn to her now.

Back then, they held sadness and longing. Poor kid was probably starved for affection and friendship. Now, they made him imagine her down on her knees gazing up at him while his cock disappeared between her full lips.

One time, when he was home on deployment, he recalled his mother talking about the wild girl next door who'd gone into full-on rebellion mode in her teens. No surprise there. Most animals didn't like to be kept in captivity and would tear their chains off for a bit of freedom.

She hadn't made a move to walk up to the house yet but spoke in the driveway with the guy who'd driven her home.

Boyfriend? Husband? Who knew? What Zach did know, was that the guy looked like a giant snooze fest. He wore a perfectly pressed suit and had posture that spoke of money and a proper upbringing.

Snore.

The pair climbed the three steps up to the porch with the suit's hand resting on her lower back. What a waste. If she were Zach's woman, he certainly wouldn't be taking a slow journey into the house, lightly touching her back. No, he'd have her thrown over his shoulder while he rushed them to the bed. Or better yet, he'd hold on to her ass while she wrapped her legs around his waist. Then they wouldn't even have to make it to the bed; he could prop her right there against the front door and make her shatter the quiet night with her screams.

Damn, maybe he should have gone to the bar.

Trisha/Tori glanced over her shoulder as the dud unlocked the door. After scanning across her property, her gaze locked with Zach's. Maybe she'd sensed his attention.

Even from yards away, the connection was like a punch to the gut. A little taste of what he'd given Bill a short time ago. She didn't turn away, and his cock hardened under her watchful stare. Damn those intoxicating eyes. The rest of her made for an enticing package as well. Her hair was brown, or maybe blonde, he wasn't sure. Maybe brown with blonde streaks, highlights or whatever chicks called that shit.

She wasn't tiny, perhaps a smidge under five and a half feet, but at six one, he'd still tower over her. He'd always liked being with women significantly smaller than him. She wasn't a twig, nor was she overweight. Just kind of soft and feminine. The kind of soft that would absorb a hard fucking very well.

Zach yanked his helmet off and hung it from the handlebar. He wanted her to know he was staring at her. Wanted to see her reaction when she realized where his mind had gone.

It didn't disappoint. If she'd sensed his original gaze, she also sensed that his interest turned toward the erotic, because those beautiful cat eyes flared and she jerked her attention away.

Zach

As he dismounted his bike, Zach smiled. Suddenly, he didn't feel so restless. But he did feel hot and bothered. Instead of spending time with the bag, it looked like he'd be hitting the shower for a little hand-to-cock action.

Maybe the neighbor girl would stick around for a while. She may have a boyfriend, but at the very least, she'd fuel some damn good fantasies.

CHAPTER THREE

A dull throb bloomed directly behind Toni's eyes as she stared at the fifteen people she was now responsible for paying. Their livelihoods depended upon her ability to keep the diner afloat. Successful. If she failed, they wouldn't be compensated. They wouldn't be able to pay their bills. Clothe their children...

Okay, maybe that was a bit dramatic considering the diner pretty much ran itself like a well-oiled machine. Her parents hadn't marketed in years. Just wasn't necessary. Regulars and tourists flocked to the joint. Top it off with the fact that she still planned to sell the place, and she only had to keep it running a few weeks. Long enough to find a buyer.

Actually, not even that long. Next week she had two applicants for a general manager position coming in for interviews. So, one week. She had to keep her head above water for one week before she could hopefully pass the torch to someone better qualified and more willing.

As she looked into the faces of her parents'—her—employees, the magnitude of what had changed in her life finally hit.

Both parents gone in one terrible instant.

Never would their family have the chance to reconcile their differences and forgive each other. Wiped out in the blink of an eye. Viewing their differences from an altered position, from hindsight, made them seem less significant than they'd been all those years.

Zach

Falling into a pit of regret and shame would be easy. But Toni wouldn't allow that. She'd atoned for the mistakes of her past. With Uncle Mark's help, she'd pulled herself from the gutter and made something of her life. Years ago, she'd asked for forgiveness, but her parents wouldn't grant it. They were unyielding in their disapproval. Didn't matter that she'd worked her ass off to become a better person. Lucy and Roger weren't fans of forgiveness.

So, she could spend the next few years questioning whether or not she did all she could to mend their relationship, or she could accept life for what it was. A series of tests and hurdles with the newest upon her. She didn't have time to bemoan the past and wish she could fix situations that were no longer changeable. Because she was now a homeowner, a business owner, and an employer. Not to mention, all of these new roles existed states away from her real life, where she had an apartment, job, boyfriend, even a betta fish being watched by a neighbor's kid.

Geez. One could easily collapse under the sudden weight of such heavy newly acquired responsibility.

"Everyone's here now, Miz Jennings," a high school senior named Danny announced in his slight southern twang. From what Toni had observed so far, he was a great kid. A hard worker who bussed tables on Saturday and Sunday mornings. Supposedly saving up for a "sweet ride."

"Holy hell, please call me Toni," she said, then smiled as the group chuckled. "I'm not old enough for a Miz, or a ma'am, or anything besides Toni. Except maybe Your Highness. That would be okay." Everyone laughed again and warmth stole through Toni.

They liked her. She'd wondered how they'd feel, considering she was the daughter who had nothing to do with the place or her parents. She had to admit, part of her assumed her folks would have poisoned their employees against her. Especially the few who knew her way back when.

Michelle, the last to arrive, dropped into a vacant seat and shoved her untidy hair out of her eyes. A year or two younger than Toni, the busy mother had faint circles under her eyes, some kind of stain near the collar of her uniform top, and a messy bun with loose tendrils tumbling out in all directions.

Toni had only met the server for the first time at the funeral, but if she had to describe Michelle in one word, it'd be exhausted. Rumor had it, she lived alone with her three-year-old daughter and worked her ass off at two jobs to provide for the kiddo. Hopefully, Toni could find a few minutes to chat with Michelle at some point throughout the day. She seemed friendly, outgoing, and kind. Toni could sure use a female friend, especially if she was planning to stick around until the end of the summer.

Wait.

What?

Where the hell had that thought come from? Damn Uncle Mark and his advice. She had no plans to stay in Tennessee. None whatsoever.

"So sorry I'm late," Michelle said in a breathless voice. "My mother had some car trouble and was late to come babysit."

Toni waved the woman's concern away. "Please, don't worry about it. It's just six now. You're right on time." She addressed the group seated in booths along the front windows. "Okay guys, thanks so much for getting up crazy early on a Saturday morning to indulge me. Especially those of you who don't normally work Saturdays. But I wanted to chat with you all before we re-open at seven."

Murmurs of "no big deal" rose up from the team.

"Let me ease your minds by first saying that you all still have jobs and I do not plan on that changing. Since I don't live here, I'm going to be looking for a buyer for the diner with the stipulation that everyone remains on staff, barring any issues. And I don't anticipate any issues because I've heard nothing but amazing things about you guys from pretty much anyone I've talked to since I've been here."

Smiles popped up on each and every face. Huh, look at that. She was rocking her first staff meeting.

"Are we going to stay open until you find a buyer?" Ernesto, the head cook, asked. He was quite the head-turner. Time had been good to him. Fifty-something, dark hair speckled with gray, dark eyes, trim build, bit of an accent. Toni remembered customers swooning over him back in the day. She'd been thrilled to find out he still worked there.

"Yes, absolutely. I have a few interviews for a general manager to handle the day to day until it's sold, since I have to go back to Chicago."

You don't have to go.

Ugh. Why the hell was her inner voice getting all sassy now?

She heard at least four sighs of relief, and a wave of guilt washed over her. "Oh gosh, I'm sorry guys. I should have met with you all earlier to ease your worries."

Michelle's face showed the most relief. Must be a tremendous challenge having to provide for yourself and a child without any assistance from the father. "None of us expected that, Toni. You were planning a funeral for crying out loud. We're all just glad to still be employed."

Toni chatted with her new team for a few minutes, getting caught up on any changes in the diner since she'd last been there, years ago. Turned out, much was exactly as she remembered, which would make slipping into her role as owner a breeze.

"Okay, last thing before those of you not working today can head out and those on schedule can get ready to open. I'm going to make a few changes around here. Changes I hope will be positive."

Fifteen pairs of eyes blinked at her, waiting for the news.

"Does this have anything to do with the sign not being in the window this morning?" Michelle asked. After speaking, she pressed her lips together and twisted the hem of her shirt around her hands.

Interesting. Was she hoping the answer would be yes or no?

"Yes, but I'll get to that one in a minute. First is the dress code. The khaki skirts and pants my parents had you wear are gone. The T-shirts will stay for now, maybe we'll rework the logo or something in the future, but you guys can wear jeans or shorts if you'd like."

"Oh my God, really?" Danny bounced in his seat. "No offense to your parents, but we all *hate* wearing the khakis. This town is so casual no one will ever care if we're wearing denim."

Nods and whispered assent had Toni grinning.

First managerial decision was a success.

"No offense taken, Danny. I hated them too, when I worked here, and I'm much more laid back, so let's ditch the Dockers. And to address Michelle's question, yes. The sign is gone as are any restrictions on who we will serve. It was discriminatory, and I won't tolerate that kind of thing. So, anyone and everyone may eat here…bikers included."

"That's great." A hard swallow moved through Michelle's throat and her face blanched, in direct contrast with her agreeable statement.

Very interesting. Hopefully, Michelle didn't have some kind of issue serving the men of the MC. Toni would hate to lose her. But her decision was final and firm. As long as no trouble was caused, anyone could patronize the diner.

"One last thing. For real this time. I'd like to open myself up to any suggestions you guys have for updates or improvements. You know this place far better than I do, and I'm sure there are some things you'd all like to see change. And I mean anything from décor, to menu ideas, to scheduling. My door and my ears are always open."

Well that last part was straight out of a Hallmark movie, but her declaration was met with happy faces and nods, so at least they didn't seem to mind her cheesiness.

Zach

After the meeting concluded, the staff got busy prepping the diner to open. Ernesto came over to her before making his way to the kitchen. "Proud of you, chica," he said, using the nickname he'd called her when she was eight. "You've really stepped up to the plate here."

Toni shrugged. "Not sure if they'd be so proud of me."

"Eh, I worked with them for over twenty years. Knew how they were and what they did to you. They weren't the type to wax on about being proud." He patted her shoulder. "Always thought you'd be good for this place. Like that you're letting the bikers in. My nephew's in the MC. They're good guys. See? You're already rocking it, chica."

Warmth flooded her. It was nice to have a connection to the past. A person who was able to see beyond the dumb kid she'd been and to the responsible adult she'd become. "Thanks, Ernesto," she said, smiling to mask the lump in her throat.

At exactly seven a.m., Toni unlocked the door, and a flood of hungry townspeople piled in and filled almost every empty seat.

Time flew faster than Toni could ever remember. The wait staff were so busy, they were practically jogging between tables and behind the counter to keep up with the demands. Toni appointed herself in charge of coffee; brewing, filling, and refilling both black and a few fancier coffees. The task turned out to be perfect, because she was able to visit each table and chat with customers. People of the community couldn't have been nicer or more welcoming. Many remembered her from her youth, but quite a few new faces were committed to memory as well. Before long, she felt like she'd never left, either the town or the diner.

Ernesto was never without a spatula in hand; flipping pancakes, scrambling eggs, and shaking his hips to music while he worked. At one point, he pulled Toni aside and asked if he could run some new, trendier menu ideas by her, but they'd grown so busy, neither had any time. She made a mental note to seek him out after closing at one.

About forty-five minutes before close, it happened. Two bikers strolled in. Each wore a Hell's Handlers cut and a healthy layer of badassery. A woman was with them as well. One who seemed to fit right in with their motif of leather, tattoos, and intimidation.

A hush stole over the crowded diner, but it didn't last for more than thirty seconds, because an older gentleman seated at the counter took a giant bite of Ernesto's famous blueberry pancakes and let out an orgasmesque moan. After that, laughter ensued and chatter resumed once again.

Look at that. No one really gave a crap who ate in the diner.

Just her very narrow-minded parents.

"Which section is Shell's?" The largest of the bikers asked. He had dark auburn hair and a beard to match. No smile, no friendly hello, just tough-guy macho-man vibes. Actually, he had a strong resemblance to Tormund Giantsbane from Toni's favorite show, *Game of Thrones*.

"Shell?" she asked, the full coffee pot testing the limits of her biceps. She hadn't worked this hard in years.

"Michelle," the woman said. At least she smiled. As she spoke, the brown haired, blue eyed biker she was with circled her shoulders with his muscled arm. He also had a beard. Was it a requirement to join their MC?

No, it wasn't. The biker who lived next door to her had a face as smooth as silk. A face that had appeared in more than one spicy dream the previous night. The gaze he'd ensnared her with had been intense and stuck with her for hours, heating parts of her that had no business getting hot. Especially since she had a boyfriend. A boyfriend who'd never gotten her as fired up as one smoldering stare from a man she didn't know.

That was a problem.

"Oh, yes, sorry. I didn't realize she went by a nickname. You can grab that empty booth right over there." She pointed toward Michelle's section with the coffee pot. "I'll let her know she has another table."

"Thanks," the big one said. The couple had pretty much disappeared into their own world, whispering and stealing kisses. The man murmured something in the woman's ear, probably something dirty, because her eyes heated and she wrapped her arms around his waist.

The pang of jealously that hit Toni was unexpected. Not that she wanted the biker, but their connection was so obvious, no one would miss it. Neither seemed to mind public affection. Toni's boyfriend would barely hold her hand. He said it looked common, whatever that meant.

Uncle Mark was right about him. He was a dud. They had no chemistry. No fire. No passion. Toni had been ignoring it since... well, since he first kissed her. It was getting harder to ignore by the day.

When they'd gotten together, she'd thought she was making a smart choice in a companion. A responsible choice. Choosing a man who had a stable and lucrative job, goals for the future, one who was dependable, and reliable. Chris wasn't a bad guy. In fact, quite the opposite.

He'd treated her well throughout their relationship. Hell, he'd even dropped everything and come to Tennessee with her for her parents' funeral. He just wasn't a panty-melter. And while she'd tried to tell herself it didn't matter, it was starting to matter.

Problems for another time. Toni started to turn toward the kitchen, but a large hand on her arm stopped her.

"Like what you're doing here, lady. Always wanted to eat at this place. Got a lot of growing boys in my club," the copper-haired giant said with a smile she wouldn't have thought possible until she saw it with her own eyes. A smile that made him look less fierce and more attractive. "We'll bring you some good, steady business."

She met his gaze and saw the unspoken words. *And we won't cause you any trouble.*

With a nod she said, "Enjoy your breakfast. I'll grab Michelle."

Toni found Michelle in the kitchen, leaning against the walk-in refrigerator with her pad and pen in hand, her head tipped back, and her eyes closed.

"Hey, hon, you okay?" Toni asked.

Michelle's eyes popped open and she sighed. "Just taking a minute to catch my breath. Busiest day in a while. Guess that's what happens when people can't get their breakfast fix for a week, huh?"

"Well don't stab me with that pen, but you have another table. It's, uh, three of the Hell's Handlers."

Half of Michelle's mouth moved up in a chagrined smile. "Yeah, I saw them come in."

"Ahh, might that have anything to do with your sudden need for air?"

"Could be." She chuckled and said, "Thought I found the one place I wouldn't have to see them."

Toni sensed she hadn't meant to say that last part out loud, so she let it go, though it had her very curious about Michelle's life. "The big one called you Shell. Seems pretty familiar with you. You okay serving them?"

A very unladylike snort came from Michelle. "Trust me, you don't want to tell those guys they can't get what they want. I'll be fine."

"You sure? I won't have anyone making you feel uncomfortable."

Her blonde curls bounced as she shook her head. "It's nothing to worry about. Just a lot of complicated...ness."

"Complicatedness, huh? I may have some experience with that." Toni flexed and straightened her right elbow a few times. She'd only been holding the coffee pot for about five minutes and the bicep was already screaming. Another few hours and she'd have a dead arm. Time for a gym membership. "Maybe we should grab a drink while I'm here and compare stories."

Michelle smiled. "I'd love that. I've only been back in town a few months, and it's been hard finding girlfriends, since I'm either working or mothering. I could really use some estrogen time. I'm trying to remember you from when you were a kid, but I'm drawing a blank."

"Most of my time was spent here until I was in my teens, then my crowd was mostly out of town kids." That was as much as Toni would be telling anyone about what she got up to before she left. Some things were better left unsaid.

Shell nodded. "And I was the daughter of a biker, so we weren't exactly eating in here."

"No offense, but I'm surprised my parents hired you." She put the coffee pot on the counter and almost sang for joy at the relief in her arm.

"I was too, actually. My dad died about ten years ago. Lung cancer. Anyway, I applied kinda on a whim when I returned to town, and I don't think your parents realized whose daughter I was."

"Makes sense. Well, go give those bikers a run for their money, and we'll plan a night out soon. I'm going to refill everyone's coffee, then I'll be in my office for a while if you need anything. A few staff members have given me some great ideas for some updates to the place."

"Hmm," Michelle said, tapping her pen against her pursed lips. "You know, you sure don't sound like someone who is about to pass the restaurant off to an outside manager, then sell it." She winked. "You sound more like someone who's excited about a new opportunity." With that parting shot, she spun on her sneaker covered heel and left the kitchen.

Well, shit. Toni blew out a breath and sagged against the walk-in, in much the same pose she'd found Michelle in. Her employee was right. She sure didn't sound like a woman ready to turn over her business.

Didn't feel like it, either.

Instead, she felt a renewed excitement. Ideas flowed through her head on ways to make the place even better than it already was. It was an old, dormant feeling coming to life. Remnants of a time when she was happy. Before it had all gone bad.

She'd loved working the floor that morning, chatting with customers, bustling around.

Shit.

She wasn't going to find a manager for the diner.

She was staying.

But just for six weeks.

And now she had to spring that surprise on her boyfriend. The boyfriend she was also pretty sure she should dump.

CHAPTER FOUR

"You can't be serious!" Droplets of Chardonnay and spittle spewed from Chris's mouth and dotted the deck of the wraparound porch outside Toni's new/old house. "Shit, Toni, warn a guy before you pull something like that."

He coughed again and Toni whacked him on the back. Clad in a tailored shirt and slacks, Chris was dressed about as casual as he got, at least when there was a chance of someone beside Toni seeing him. At least he'd lost the tie and jacket.

Had he always been so stuffy? So formal? Judgmental?

Maybe she was being too hard on him. So he was more conservative and close minded than she was. Different ideas and opinions on life were what made relationships interesting. Weren't they?

Toni shot forward in her seat and squeaked.

Holy crap. It hit her like a lightning strike.

Chris was her parents.

She was dating her parents.

Everything she'd rebelled against.

She'd come full circle.

"What's wrong with you?" Another cough shook Chris's body. "I'm the one who's choking over here."

They were lounging on her porch, much to Chris's chagrin. He was much more an inside kind of guy. In the ten days they'd been there, Toni had taken to sitting on the porch and watching the sun set each evening with a glass of wine. The house had woods behind and a view of the Great Smoky Mountains from the front.

Beautiful sunsets. So focused on education and forming a life she could be proud of, Toni had forgotten how wonderful being still could be. She'd forgotten so many things about the sleepy town she grew up in. Especially the sense of community. In Chicago, in a building with fifty apartments, Toni had only spoken to one of her neighbors, and that was because she'd accidentally gotten some mail for the tenant above her.

"Nothing's wrong. And I am serious, Chris."

His wineglass hit the side table with a clunk and he shot her an incredulous glare. "You're going to stay here and run a diner. For six weeks? Here? In this shit town." He snorted. "If that's not a joke, I don't know what is."

Frustration rose and she stood, jamming her hands on her hips. "Why is that so funny? I grew up here. In this town. In that diner."

Chris stood as well, damn him for being so much taller than she was. He was handsome in a very Wall-Street-investment-banker kind of way. Or an attorney way, which made sense because that's what he was. Polished, coiffed, expensive. Good on paper. Everything she'd be smart to want. So she'd tried to force it.

But she'd always been one to go for a man who was more tarnished.

And look where that had gotten her? Girlfriend of an asshole gangbanger by the time she was seventeen. Passed around to his friends like some kind of live sex toy. Drugged-out and a hot fucking mess.

Once Mark literally dragged her wasted ass away from that life and cleaned her up, she'd vowed to never make those mistakes again. To never be led around by lust, hormones, and anger. So, she steered clear of anything resembling a bad boy.

And now she was coasting along in a bland, boring relationship with a man who didn't really know her. Not deep down.

Not his fault.

She'd hid herself from him. Hell, she hid herself from herself the past few years. And now she had the opportunity to rediscover who she was over the next six weeks. To really determine what she wanted to get out of her life. An opportunity she couldn't pass up.

"You're a city girl, Toni." He waved his hand around as though the beautiful nature around them was a steaming pile of garbage. "You wear J Crew, drink cosmopolitans, and get your nails done every two weeks. You do not belong here in hick town."

Was this guy for real? "Wow, Chris. Snobby much? That's me, huh? Summed up in three insignificant details."

With a snort, Chris threw his arms in the air and paced the length of the porch. "That was just an example. You're different here. Look at your outfit for God's sake. Your pockets are longer than your shorts. I've seen the little sluts at your school wearing the same outfits."

Toni's blood was a few degrees from boiling. "You did not just call me a slut," she shouted.

From opposite sides of the porch, they stared at each other. Toni tried to steady her breathing, tried to calm her anger, but it wasn't working. This was a side of Chris she hadn't known existed. She'd never slapped anyone before, but there was a first time for everything.

Chris on the other hand deescalated much faster. After stuffing his hands in his pockets, he focused on the setting sun before facing her. "Look, I have to go back to Chicago tonight because I have a deposition in the morning. I don't want to fight with you. You're grieving over your parents' deaths and you're lost right now. How about this, you stay here this week and I'll fly back out on the weekend. We can sort everything out then."

Such a sensible, rational, adult way of handling their conflict when Toni wanted to rant and rave at him. Maybe being back in her hometown was throwing her off her game.

Not off enough that she didn't realize this relationship was quickly coming to an end.

Instead of reacting on instinct and emotion, she dropped her hands from her hips and rolled her shoulders. Tension had her upper back muscles protesting the movement. "Maybe we should take a break," she said.

Chris nodded. "I'll go back, and we'll talk next week after we've each had some breathing room, okay?"

She could try that, but would she feel different in a week? Probably not. Really, she shouldn't have been with him in the first place. He'd have every right to be pissed at her. In a way, she'd used him. Not with poor intentions, but to try to wedge herself into a specific kind of life. A life that didn't seem to fit who she was, unfortunately. Maybe she just needed to steer clear of relationships altogether.

"No. I mean break like break up. I don't think this is going to work, Chris."

His face fell, and guilt hit her hard. Just because he wasn't for her, didn't mean he was a crappy boyfriend. And if the look on his face was any indication, he was crushed by her declaration.

Townsend was screwing with her head, big time. Perhaps this wasn't the time to make a decision about the fate of her relationship, but even though she felt guilty about hurting Chris, it felt right.

Zach splashed cold water on his overheated face, then braced his hands on the sides of the sink. He let his head drop down as his breathing slowly returned to normal. For the past hour, he'd pounded the heavy bag like the sack of sand personally disrespected him and everyone he gave a shit about.

If the throb in his shoulder wasn't enough of an indication he'd overdone it, the ache in his knuckles was.

Zach

Fucking gangbangers.

The club's board was meeting in two hours and Zach had bad news for Copper. Bad news for the entire club. Shit news, really.

As enforcer for the Hell's Handlers MC, Zach had contacts with MC's, gangs, a few dirty cops, and various lowlifes for hundreds of miles around. He'd collected quite a few favors over time and made sure everyone knew not to fuck with him or his MC. For years, they'd run their club and conducted business without competition or threat of a turf war.

Until now.

Until the fuckin' Gray Dragons gang decided to get greedy. Now, he had to tell Copper that some two-bit gangbanger and his band of merry assholes was coming for the club. They wanted to steal the Handler's business, sure, but mostly it was a power play. Show of force. Flexing muscles.

Drive out the local outlaw MC and become top dog.

The Gray Dragons had been around for over a decade. Small time gang nonsense, mostly. At least, in the beginning. Selling weed, pimping girls, petty robberies. They operated about thirty miles out of Townsend and had mostly kept to their side of the proverbial tracks. Apparently, they'd grown over the years. Gotten their dicks hard over a little extra cash and, suddenly, they wanted a larger piece of the pie.

Namely heroin. And since the MC stopped dealing in that shit before Zach prospected, the Gray Dragons didn't view them as competition. But, apparently, they did view Hell's Handlers' territory fair game to distribute their garbage.

It was a problem.

A big, fucking problem.

Heroin could bring cops, Feds, and all sorts of shit to Townsend. Beyond that, it was Hell's Handlers' town and that should have been enough to keep the Dragons out. They wouldn't stop at peddling heroin through Townsend. In fact, that was the really bad news he had for Copper. The Dragons were slowly buying up debts owed to the Handlers. A way to gain support and cut the MC off at the knees. And they'd been the ones responsible for the attack on some of the girls who worked at the club-owned strip joint.

Worry tightened Zach's worn out muscles. A turf war between the Handlers and the Dragons wouldn't end well. He could feel it in his bones.

"Fuuuck," he yelled as he clenched the edge of the counter until his fatigued joints screamed in protest. He needed a distraction, something to take his mind off the fact his MC's world was about to be blown to bits. Maybe he should wander next door and introduce himself to the pretty little lady who'd inherited his neighbor's house. Staring at her lush hips and tits should take care of distracting him.

Zach lifted his head and stared out the kitchen window which had a straight-shot view of the neighbor's house. Sure enough, she was out on the porch with the twiggy suit who was staying with her.

Boyfriend? Husband? Didn't matter. All he wanted was to ogle her for a few moments, maybe make a few suggestive comments and find out if she was a blusher or not. Pissing off the walking, talking stick in a suit would just be icing on the cake.

Decision made, Zach jogged to his room and tossed on a plain black T-shirt. Sweat still coated his body, making the cotton stick to his chest and back. After stripping his workout shorts off, he found a pair of jeans on the floor and slid them on. As he left, he grabbed his cut from a hook by the front door and shrugged into it.

No member of the Hell's Handlers went without their cuts unless they were riding in a cage or through another MC's territory. As a sign of respect. And they never tossed them on the floor in heap, no matter how tired, how wasted, or how hot the pussy they were about to dive into was. Respect for the club was number one. Each man worked their ass off to earn it and that leather represented the club and everything that was important to him and his brothers.

Thirty seconds later, Zach's large stride had eaten up more than half the yard separating the two houses. The suit noticed him before the neighbor's daughter. The man looked like someone had kicked him in the nuts, and the tension surrounding the couple was so thick he could almost see it part as he walked up to them. When Zach reached the steps leading to the porch, the suit straightened and stepped out in front of the neighbor, blocking her from Zach's view. Like he could somehow keep Zach from getting to her if harming her was his end goal.

He almost laughed out loud. Zach ate guys like him for a snack.

"Chris, what are you doing?" she asked, sidestepping around him. "Hey." She lifted a hand and sent Zach a wave.

The suit, Chris, apparently, sputtered and tried to wrangle her behind him once again, but she resisted. Jesus, the man couldn't even wrestle one slip of a woman. He'd be no match for Zach even on his worst day.

"We don't want any trouble. Why don't you head back to your side of the property line, man?" Chris kept his hand around the woman's upper arm despite her frown and attempts to wriggle away.

"Chris, seriously? He's not doing anything wrong. He's my neighbor. And not to be mean, but he could probably kick both our asses in his sleep."

Whether she'd meant the words to be heard or not, they were. Loud and clear. Zach laughed and rested his hip against the stair railing. "There are plenty of hours in the day for kicking ass. Wouldn't waste my sleep on that. There are a few other things I could do in my sleep." He winked at her. "Especially if I had someone as hot as you keeping my bed warm."

Well look at that. No blush. No prudish little gasp. Just a sassy smirk and a delicate grunt.

"Are you hitting on her?" Chris released her and started toward Zach, but the woman stopped him with a hand on his chest.

"I'm Toni," she said, holding out her manicured hand.

Tori, Toni. He'd been close. "Zach." He grasped her hand and gave it a squeeze. Her hand shake was strong, confident, and soft as fucking handwoven silk. Christ, that feminine grip would feel fantastic about a foot and a half lower.

"I remember," she said.

Before he allowed her to withdraw her hand, he met Chris's gaze.

The man was pissed. Looked as if he was trying to melt Zach with the heat of his shitty stare. There was probably more of a chance of that happening than him actually beating Zach in a fair fight.

Poor little soft man.

"Figured it was about time I did my neighborly duty. Seen you coming and going for the past week or so. Can't say I'd have recognized you on the street. You did a damn good job growing up."

She laughed. "I'm glad you popped over. I've heard your bike a few times, but it was always late so I never bothered to come say hello." She pushed a lock of shoulder-length hair behind her ear. Definitely brown with blonde highlights. It suited her and made her green eyes even more obvious.

She was one hell of a looker. Curvy hips, large tits, round ass, small waist. If he'd closed his eyes and described his fantasy woman, Toni would have easily slid right into the mold.

"Hey douche bag, her eyes are about ten inches higher."

Busted.

Zach just smirked at Toni. He wouldn't apologize, because he wasn't sorry. Not for one second. The outfit she had on did nothing to hide her figure and that included the breasts he'd love to bury his face between. A woman couldn't wear a top with a low neckline and a necklace that ended an inch above her cleavage and not expect men to look.

Again, she didn't blush. Just raised an eyebrow and placed one hand on her hip.

"Hope the bike's not too loud for you," he said.

"Nope. I kinda like it, actually. That deep rumbly sound is comforting in a way."

Holy shit. If he was interested in tying himself to a woman, she just might be the perfect one. "A woman after my own heart," he said at the same time Chris snorted.

"Can I get you a beer or anything?" she asked.

He'd love a beer, but that would mean she'd walk away and he didn't want to stop staring at her, nor did he want to be alone with her asshole boyfriend. Not that the guy intimidated him, but because he wasn't in the mood for a pissing contest. This visit was supposed to be a fun distraction, not an annoying whose-dick-is-bigger contest.

It was so obviously Zach's there was no point in even measuring.

"Nah, I'm good, thanks. So, you guys sticking around town for a while?"

"I'll be here for the next six weeks or so," she said. "Chris was actually just leaving. He's got a flight to Chicago this afternoon. Right, Chris?" Her tone was soft but brokered no argument. Like she was trying to gently prod him along.

"I do." He slid his arm around Toni's waist and dropped a kiss on her cheek. "Walk me to the car, baby?" he not-whispered in her ear.

Zach fought to hold back his laughter. If the suit was trying to stake his claim, it didn't seem to be working too well. Toni's eyes narrowed and she slipped out of his hold. "Sure," she said, though the word sounded forced. She gave Zach a strained smile. "I'll be just a second."

"No problem, beautiful." If Zach was a better person, he'd make an excuse and hightail it back over to his house. Leave these two to sort their shit in peace. But he'd never claimed to be a good man. In fact, he was an outlaw. And sticking around to watch the uncomfortable goodbye between Toni and the suit seemed exactly like something an outlaw would do. So, he climbed the steps to the porch and took a seat in one of the side-by-side rocking chairs.

And the goodbye was awkward. Zach couldn't make out what was said, but if Toni's flailing arms and Chris's deep scowl were any indication, it wasn't a lovers parting. After about three minutes, Chris climbed into the car, slammed the door, and peeled out of the dirt driveway engulfing Toni in a cloud of dust.

"Trouble in paradise?" Zach asked as she ascended the three steps back to the porch.

"You could say that." She grunted. "I'd actually broken up with him about five seconds before you wandered over here. Wasn't too well received." She sighed and shook her head. "Sure you don't want a beer? I could use a few myself."

Broke up with the boyfriend.

Only in town for six weeks.

Jackpot.

"Sure, I'd love one."

CHAPTER FIVE

The man was sex in jeans. And leather. And a tight T-shirt that almost looked a little damp as it stretched tight across a seriously impressive set of pecs. The thick head of blond hair was so coiffed she wanted to run her fingers through it and muss it all up. Zach's smooth face resembled a model from a new Ralph Lauren ad she'd seen in a magazine on the plane ride to Tennessee.

Flawless skin, sharp jawline, piercing blue eyes. If it weren't for the tiny slant to his nose, he'd be model material for sure. The nose looked like it'd been broken in the past.

Interesting.

The rest of his body, though, well it wasn't exactly model worthy. No, it was too hard, too bulky to fit with any of the preppy clothing ads she'd seen. No, Zach's body was made for snug jeans, T-shirts, and leather.

Convenient, since that seemed to be his outfit of choice.

Yes, she'd gaped at the man while mid breakup with her ex standing right behind her. What she hadn't meant to do was come across as flirtatious. Just friendly. Neighborly. But then he'd scanned her with those ocean eyes, and she'd felt as though her clothes were invisible to him. When his heated gaze lingered on her breasts she'd been tempted to grab him, run inside, and tackle him to the bed. It had been a long time since a man looked at her with such blatant interest and desire.

Chris never had. And at the start, it had been tolerable. Passion and fire weren't what she was looking for from him. Dependability, stability, long-haul potential, crash proof. Those were the qualities she'd admired in Chris.

They were also the qualities families looked for in a minivan.

Not sexy.

But she didn't know how to combine sexy and a solid relationship. Actually, she wasn't convinced it could be done. Not with the type of men she truly found attractive. Men like Zach. Hard, dangerous, and players.

So, she chose the complete opposite to protect herself.

And was unfulfilled.

Breaking up with Chris was the right move. And long overdue. He'd be upset for a while, but in the end, it wasn't fair to string him along in a relationship she wasn't fully invested in.

"I was sorry to hear about your parents," Zach said as he accepted the beer she offered when she returned.

"Thanks." She lowered into the empty rocking chair adjacent to Zach's.

He planted his booted heel against the porch railing and set his chair in motion. The muscles of his thigh stretched and bunched under the denim as he rocked. "Never spoke to them much, despite living next door to them my entire life. They were assholes."

Surprise had Toni sucking in a sharp breath and a mouthful of beer. She sprang forward and coughed as the liquid burned a path down the wrong pipe. Zach's large hand pounded her back, forcing the beer from her lungs. "Shit." She gasped for breath.

"Christ, babe, I'm sorry."

Unable to speak due to a spasming diaphragm, Toni waved away his concern. "N-no worries," she said after another cough. "Whew. I was not expecting you to say that."

He grimaced. "Yeah, sorry, guess that was kinda a dick thing to say about your family who just passed."

Zach

She swiped her hand back and forth again. "Really, it's okay. It's honest. They could be assholes. No one knows that better than me." A weird emotion she couldn't identify settled as an ache in her chest. "I stayed away for a long time for a reason. And now I'm left with this strange mix of sadness, regret, some anger, and indifference." Oh, my gosh, had she really just laid that on the near stranger from next door? "Wow, a little heavy, considering we barely know each other. I'm sorry. Just ignore me."

Zach chuckled then flashed her his perfect toothpaste-ad smile. "Doesn't bother me."

As though he sensed she needed a minute to get over Chris's departure and talk of her complicated relationship with her parents, Zach fell silent. It was nice. Sitting on the porch with a beer, watching the sun dip behind the mountains, not feeling the need to fill the silence.

"So," Zach said after a few moments. "I hear scoundrels like me are now allowed at your diner."

The laugh that bubbled out of her felt great. Hot, funny, wasn't scared of serious talk. Zach should come with a flashing neon danger sign, because he was hell on the ovaries. Just what she did not need. She was not staying in Townsend for a man. She'd gotten rid of a man two minutes ago. She was there to figure out her life and sort her parents' affairs. That's all.

Zach would just have to be the nice eye candy next door whom she drooled over from afar. Like he'd been when she was in late elementary and middle school and he was the cool high schooler next door.

"So, you're a scoundrel, huh?" Ugh. It came out way too flirty but, come on, what sane woman could resist flirting with a man who looked like Zach?

Not her.

He waggled his eyebrows. "Been accused of it a time or two."

"I'll consider myself warned. And yes, you and all your scoundrel friends are welcome in the diner. My first executive decision as owner. Never agreed with the restriction."

He grunted his understanding. "Well, I have to warn you that you're going to have hordes of bikers falling to their knees and professing their love to you. Shell used to bring us some takeout on occasion and those pancakes are fuckin' orgasmic."

Ahh, so there was some kind of connection between Michelle and the bikers. Interesting.

"I'm sure Ernesto will be thrilled to find out he's given you orgasms."

Zach barked out a laugh. "I think I'm gonna like you, babe."

Danger, danger.

They chatted for about an hour. Zach filled her in on changes in town since she'd left, all while looking so hot she could barely stay in her seat without squirming. He was funny, flirty, and had a way of looking at her that set her ablaze.

Damn man.

Eventually, he begged off, having to take care of "club business." Man code for things he wasn't going to talk about and a reminder of exactly the kind of man Zach was. The kind she needed to stay away from because he was involved in activities he couldn't even speak about.

"So," he said as he rose. "I'll give you a week."

"Huh? A week for what?"

"A week to get over that sad excuse for a man who just left."

Oookay. Where was he going with this? "What happens after a week?"

He winked and swallowed the last of his second beer. "Then I'm coming for you, Toni. I want to fuck you, and I go after what I want. I'm not that damn suit. Seven nights of lying in my bed and stroking my cock while picturing your gorgeous fucking eyes, sexy tits, and that ass I want to bite will be all I can take."

Zach

Holy. Shit. Who said things like that? To someone they hadn't seen in years and barely knew? Her eyes opened so wide, she worried they'd get stuck.

"So, sweetheart, one week. Then I'm coming for you." With that, he jogged down the steps and stalked back toward his house.

Toni was left speechless in the rocking chair, her nipples hard as stones and her ass stuck in panties wet from arousal.

That man was going to be very hard to resist. Because as crude and shocking as his offer was, she wanted it and him. But she'd find a way to resist him because she'd made the mistake of thinking with her horny parts before. And it had nearly destroyed her.

A few minutes later, Zach caught her attention as he emerged from his house again. She watched him out of the corner of her eye in a lame attempt to disguise the fact she couldn't help staring at the man. He mounted the giant motorcycle parked in his driveway and revved the engine, biceps bulging as he squeezed the throttle.

With a growl of self-disgust, Toni rolled her eyes and looked away.

She was in so much damn trouble.

CHAPTER SIX

There was nothing worse than riding his bike with a rock-solid dick. The tight fit of the denim. The hard seat. The vibrations of the machinery. A ball-crushing combination that turned his second favorite activity into a miserable experience.

It didn't seem like he'd be getting a chance to engage in his first favorite activity any time soon. He'd probably have better luck sticking his dick in his bike's tailpipe than trying to get it into Toni five minutes after meeting her and interrupting her break up with the suit.

But it was going to happen. Club pussy was getting stale, as were one-night stands, though if asked, he'd deny that to his death in front of his brothers. A real relationship was also out of the question. Having a woman for the long haul held no appeal to him. His priority was his club and a permanent ol' lady would only detract from his obligation to his brothers. But a six-week fuck fest with a woman who'd be leaving the state? That was a golden situation all around.

The fifteen-minute drive to the clubhouse was one of the highlights of Zach's day. Winding mountain roads led to the sprawling cabin the club had purchased over fifty years ago. Connected to the building was the Double H bar, owned and operated by the MC. It wasn't the club's biggest money maker as far as businesses went, but it stayed busy and attracted a steady stream of both locals and tourists looking for a bit of wild.

Zach

Anyone was allowed to drink at the bar, but to pass through the doors that connected the Double H to the clubhouse, visitors had to be invited and accompanied by a club member. Most nights started out with drinking in the bar, then the brothers and whatever women they'd gathered for the night would mosey on over to the clubhouse side for a more private party.

Well, sometimes private. Sometimes on full display of the entire club. To each his own. Zach wasn't much of an exhibitionist, preferring his entertainment to be for his eyes only, but he didn't mind watching. Could be a nice way to get the evening rolling. Especially if he'd found a woman who also enjoyed a little visual stimulation.

"Hey, Z, 'bout time you got here, asshole," Maverick hollered as soon as Zach's boot cleared the doorway.

"I'm ten minutes early." He accepted a beer from Carli, one of the club girls who'd been hanging around for years, before making his way over to Maverick and the pool table.

Handlers' Honeys, Double H girls, or just the Honeys, they'd come to be called. Carli also happened to work the pole at the club's strip joint. And she was one of the unlucky girls to have been on the receiving end of some man's fists a few days ago.

The right side of her pretty face was covered in a thick layer of makeup, but no amount of goop could hide the swelling. "How you doing, darlin'?" Zach asked.

"I'm good, Zach. You?" Her eyes roamed him appreciatively, but before long returned to Maverick. They'd been messing around on and off for years. Zach suspected Carli was half in love with Mav and secretly hoped she'd one day become his ol' lady.

Never gonna happen.

But it wasn't surprising. Mav drew chicks like flies to honey. Something about his hair, or so he liked to brag. It was shaved to stubble on the sides and in back but long on top. He often slicked it back or sometimes even wore it in a man bun. What had he called it? An undercut or some shit. Regardless, he was convinced it was hair porn for the ladies.

Mav would give up his bike before he'd take on a woman long-term. Not that he didn't like women. Mav liked them too much to ever pick just one. That and a shit upbringing being passed from one foster home to another had built a deep-seated distrust of women. But he didn't need to trust them to fuck them.

"Beat it," Maverick said to her.

Her expression fell, but she left. In the end, she was just a club girl. Not anyone's ol' lady, so she did as she was told. Mav didn't mean to be a dick to her, but if he gave her an inch, she'd be writing his name with hearts and flowers. Cold hard truth of it was she was there to fuck, nothing more. Best not to blur the lines.

"Bad news?" Maverick asked after Carli was out of earshot.

Zach clinked the neck of his bottle against Mav's then downed half of it in one long gulp. "The worst."

"Fuck." Named Road Captain about a month ago, Maverick was new to board meetings, but no less invested than the guys who'd been in charge for years. The club was his life, as it was for most of them.

Mav was tall and strong but lean as a whip. And he modified his body as often as others changed their socks. Who knew what he'd do when he ran out of skin to ink. Maybe move on to piercings, though Zach's best friend claimed he was leaving the holes at eyebrow, tongue, nipples, and some kind of metal in his cock. Made Zach's balls shrivel imagining someone aiming at his junk with a needle.

"Any idea how Copper's gonna want to handle it?" Mav returned his pool cue to the rack.

"Not sure. But I'm guessing some kind of show of force will be necessary to get the message across. Let's move. You know Prez will flip his shit if we're late."

Zach

Just then, Copper poked his head out of the meeting room. "Why the fuck am I in here by myself? I get any more alone time and I'm gonna whip my dick out and start beating off."

"Told ya," Zach mumbled as Mav chuckled.

They filed into the meeting room along with the rest of the board members. Copper sat in his usual spot at the round table with his VP, Viper, at his right-hand side. Viper had a good fifteen plus years on Copper, but never wanted the president's patch. Instead, he was the best fucking VP around. Gave everything he had to the club and kept Copper in check. He'd been around, seen it all, and knew how to advise his leader. In great shape for a man in his late fifties, Viper had a long, graying beard and even longer hair. Mav often compared him to a young Willie Nelson.

Along with Zach and Maverick, Rocket, the Sergeant at Arms was present. He was a mean motherfucker who didn't speak much but seemed to notice any and everything that happened around him. His powers of observation were almost creepy. Rocket could get inside a man's head and see things buried deep.

Jigsaw, the club's treasurer, was last to arrive. Named for a nasty crisscross of scars on his left cheek that looked like puzzle pieces, he was the smartest fucker Zach knew. Much of his past was a mystery, but rumor had it he was some kind of NASA scientist in a previous life. Before his wife and child were killed in the attack that left him scarred.

"All right," Copper said as soon as Jig's ass hit the seat. "Let's not waste time with bullshit agenda items. We all know why we're here. Zach, tell me why there are motherfuckers pushing H through my town."

All eyes turned to Zach and he cleared his throat. "Gray Dragons are—"

"Godfuckingdamnit!" Copper slammed his meaty fist down on the table, rattling the wood and tipping a full glass. Amber liquid splashed across the table and onto the floor, but no one made a move to clean it up. One of the girls would be tasked with the chore after the meeting. "Fucking Shark," he said of the Gray Dragon's current president.

Zach nodded. "It ain't good, Prez. I spoke with one of Shark's girls, or former girls, before I went to see Bill yesterday. She's been hiding out from him. Finally wised up and left his ass. Only took a few broken bones, weekly beatings, and being passed around like a bad cold for her to get smart. I gave her some cash to disappear for a while."

Copper nodded and dragged a hand through his hair. "Good work." If there was one thing the man didn't stand for, it was mistreatment of women. "Fucking disgusting."

"Anyway, he's upping his game, looking for more territory. Townsend is a great place to sell. Lots of tourists coming through. Constant new business. He's also, uh…" This was the part Zach really dreaded telling Copper. "He also bought up a few debts owed to us."

Jigsaw's mouth turned down at that. As treasurer, he took the club's finances—particularly money owed from lending—very seriously. "The fuck you mean?"

Zach stared at the puddle still expanding across the table. "Remember Bill Durant? Borrowed ten large and owes over twenty now?"

Jigsaw nodded, his charcoal eyes hardening with displeasure. He knew what was coming.

"Got a call from him earlier saying he had the money and was ready to pay. There was no fucking way. I was just there last night and he was sniveling and pissing himself over it. Said he needed more time, a few weeks. Then this morning he's got it? Didn't take too many threats for the pussy to spill. Dragons gave him the cash. He's got two months to pay them back with only five percent interest."

"They've got enough expendable cash to be loaning it out with such shit return?" Mav asked, clicking his tongue ring against his teeth.

"Looks like it."

"Fuck," Jig said.

"What's the point?" Viper chimed in. "They're loaning out money with a long grace period and shit interest. They ain't gonna get rich doing that. It's bad business."

Jig shook his head and leaned forward, resting his elbows on the table. "Making money isn't the point. Stealing our business is. Loan sharking is where we make fifty percent of our income. Word gets out they're offering low interest and long payback periods, they'll hijack all our business before you can scratch your nuts. It will cripple our bottom line and allow them to move in easily. Once they've gotten our customers, they can raise the rates and start pulling in what we were."

"They the ones who fucked up our girls?" Copper asked.

Rocket hadn't spoken yet, but that was pretty par for the course. Didn't mean he wasn't fully engaged. Nothing escaped his attention. He was just a quiet fucker, so it was a surprise when he said, "Fucking pieces of shit. Who else would it be?"

With a shrug, Zach leaned forward on his elbows. "Gut feeling says it's them. But I don't have proof yet. Carli's been the most helpful and she said they all wore ski masks. No one spoke. Just jumped them as they were leaving. We've beefed up security at the strip club."

Silence descended on the table. Copper ran a hand across his bottom lip, something he did when he was deep in thought. Made him a shit poker player, but a good president. He never acted rashly. Never made decisions based on emotion. He was rational, logical, and steady.

Except when it came to one gorgeous waitress and her adorable kiddo. Then he was a damn fool. Shell had been in love with Copper since she was old enough to notice he was a man. Probably even before. They had a complicated, twisted history with one constant. Copper refused to admit any feelings or attraction toward her. He had sixteen years on her and used it as a giant stick to keep beating her back. Poor kid was bound to reach her limit and latch on to someone else at some point, and then all hell would break loose, because whether he was willing to admit it or not, Copper had it bad for the girl.

Thoughts of Shell and the diner steered his mind toward thoughts of Toni. And that was nothing but trouble. He had no use for a woman taking up space in his head. Not now, when shit was coming to a head with the Dragons.

"Here's what I want," Copper said, after what had to have been five minutes of silence. "Grab their dealers, see if you can get any info out of 'em. Rough 'em up a little. Not enough to warrant any hospital visits, but enough they won't be able to fuck any of those nasty gang bitches for a while."

Zach leaned back in his chair. As enforcer, that task would fall to him.

Copper met his gaze. "We need to send a message to Shark. We're on to him, and he can't fuck around in our territory. Actually, let's take it one step further. We've been lax about letting them through our turf because we've never had any beef. So, you see any of those banger assholes in our town, you bring 'em in. Zach will take care of 'em."

Copper stared straight at Zach who nodded in response to the unasked question. He understood. He agreed. He was ready. His mind was in the game. And he'd stay that way.

"We take a step back and impose strict territory rules. We stay off their turf, they aren't welcome in ours. I don't give a shit what you see them doing, eating pizza, mowing their grandma's lawn, having coffee at the fucking diner. You see 'em wearing their colors, they get a visit with Zach. Everyone on board?"

The men grunted their approval as Zach's brain whirled with possibilities. His life was about to get hectic as shit. Being seen around town was nothing new for the Gray Dragons. "We gonna let them know they're not welcome, or are we just going to start snatching them off the street?"

"I'll be letting them know." Copper's lips twitched. Crazy fuckin' Prez was enjoying this shit. "It's only fair to give them a heads up. All right. Let's get the fuck out of here. Bar's calling my name."

The men filed out thumping Zach on the shoulder as they left. They all knew he was up to the task and could handle it as enforcer. But, holding the title didn't mean he went looking for shitheads to pound on. Sure, he got enjoyment out of scaring little boys like Bill, but doling out punishment that could start a war between clubs? Not exactly something to look forward to.

"You good?" Mav asked, once they were the only two remaining at the table.

"Yep."

"Heard your sexy new neighbor lifted the ban on our kind at the diner."

An image of Toni and her mouthwatering curves floated through Zach's mind. "She sure did."

"Well, I gotta be out of town the next two days for Copper, but what do you say we get ourselves some fuckin' pancakes Sunday morning?"

Zach smiled. He'd be busy as hell himself the next few days. Early mornings, late nights. Probably meant he wouldn't lay eyes on Toni again. "Sounds perfect to me."

Watching Toni's ass flit around the diner would be the perfect way to turn what was bound to be a shitty weekend into something to look forward to.

CHAPTER SEVEN

Toni thought she understood busy, as far as the typical rush of the diner. Hungry townsfolk and visitors poured through the doors, keeping the tables full and the staff hopping. Everyone wanted to chat with her, and she was blown away by the number of patrons who had stories from when she was a child running loose in the diner.

Their memories never failed to bring a smile to her face. As she'd grown older and her relationship with her parents declined, it became difficult to recall any happiness from her younger days. Hearing the stories helped her to remember there were times of definite happiness in her childhood. It helped heal some of the wounds inflicted by her parents' rejection.

The mornings were so hectic, by the time they closed at one each afternoon, she was exhausted and dreading the supply ordering and bookkeeping awaiting her.

Then Saturday rolled around, and Toni learned a new definition of the word busy. The servers were practically sprinting between tables to keep up with the demands for coffee top-offs, extra butter, and checks. A long line out the door all morning led to a constant stream of orders, and lingering customers kept the diner open hours past its typical closing time. By the time they'd chased the final diners out the doors, cleaned the restaurant, and the staff headed for home, they were almost three hours past typical closing time.

Zach

"Holy crap," Toni said to Michelle as she flexed her feet in her sensible but ugly work shoes. The arches ached something fierce. "How the hell do you do this every week?" They were lounging in a booth, both too bushed to move.

Michelle chuckled and reached for a glass of water she'd been working on for a while. She looked weary and younger than her twenty-three years, dressed in skinny jeans and the diner's signature T-shirt. "First off, I stay hydrated. Second, I have no choice. You'll build up a tolerance for it."

A pang of sympathy hit Toni's heart. Of course, Michelle had no choice. She was a young single mother. Worst part of it was Toni got to go sit in her office for a few hours before going home to a quiet, peaceful house. Michelle spent three hours at home with a rambunctious toddler then moved on to her second job, cleaning offices in the evenings. No wonder the poor woman looked one stiff breeze from blowing over all the time.

"You working tonight?" she asked Michelle, after groaning at the pleasure of a good stretch to her calves.

"No!" A lightness came over Michelle that Toni hadn't seen yet. She smiled, revealing a straight set of shiny white teeth and then sighed in pleasure. "And, to make the day even better, my parents commandeered Beth for the evening. I'm a free woman for the next fifteen hours."

"Oooh! Any big plans?" Toni raised her arms over her head, lengthening the knotted muscles in her back. A hot bath and some solid couch time was just what the doctor ordered.

The laugh that came from Michelle was more of a scoff than a humorous sound. "I have no freakin' idea. I don't even want to tell you how long it's been since I've had more than two straight hours to myself."

After dropping her arms, Toni leaned against the back of the plush booth. "Do you want to hang out? I don't really have any girlfriends, and I haven't actually done anything fun since I've been here." Unless she counted sitting on her porch with a forbidden man. "Neither of us are up for a crazy night out, I'm sure, so why don't we just have some drinks at my house and watch a chick flick?"

"Yes! That sounds amazing. Most of my girlfriends have moved away over the last few years and then with Beth, I never get a chance to have any fun." A panicked look cross her face. "Not that being with Beth isn't fun, but—"

Toni held up a hand. "Please, no judgment. I think you're absolutely amazing for raising a daughter on your own while juggling two jobs. There's no way I'd begrudge you a night away."

"Will your boyfriend mind? That guy I saw you with at the funeral and a few other times. Tall, thin, always in a suit."

"Uh, he went back to Chicago." Toni hadn't introduced him to anyone at the diner, so she didn't really think her employees had even noticed his presence.

"Oh, you must miss him."

The momentary silence was thick, awkward. "I kinda broke up with him, so…"

Michelle's hand flew to her mouth in a poor attempt to stifle a gasp. "And I just stuffed my whole foot right in my mouth, didn't I? I'm so sorry. Are you doing okay?"

"I am. Very okay. Not upset at all, actually, which I suppose means I should have done it a long time ago." Toni straightened and winced when her back protested.

"Well then, goodbye and good riddance. I've learned that it's best to shed the baggage before it becomes too heavy." Shadows crossed Shell's face. "Trust me. Some baggage can be so heavy it's impossible to carry."

Toni knew about that kind of baggage. Maybe she and Shell would be kindred spirits. Have a lot in common.

With a shake of her head, Shell lost the gloom and smiled. "Girls night sounds perfect." Bouncing on her feet as though the idea of a chick flick and some booze was akin to an all-expense paid vacation to Hawaii. "Okay, let me run home and change so I don't smell like French toast and I'll meet you at your house."

Zach

"Perfect." Toni couldn't help the happy feeling warming her. A new friend in Tennessee.

A business, a house, a hot male neighbor, *and* a new friend. If she wasn't careful, she'd have a full, satisfying life in Tennessee without even meaning to.

The thought wasn't as uncomfortable as it had been just a few days ago.

When Toni arrived home, she shed her diner T-shirt and jeans, leaving them in a pile on her bedroom floor. The shower beckoned her and, hopefully, it would infuse her with enough energy to stay awake until Michelle got there. After showering the day off, she dressed in yoga pants and a Chicago Bulls T-shirt. Not much of a sports fan herself, Uncle Mark had dragged her to a game last winter and in the spirit of the game, she'd purchased a shirt for a team she didn't care about.

An hour later, a rap at the door announced Michelle's arrival.

"Come on in. It's open," Toni called out from the kitchen.

"You have any tequila?" Michelle asked as she appeared in the entrance to the kitchen. "I brought some margarita mix. Figured this was as good a time as any for a few margaritas."

"Oooh yes! They're my fav. Good thinking, Michelle. And I do have tequila. Always."

Michelle giggled and placed the mix on the counter. She'd also changed but wore capri leggings and an oversized tank. Her curly hair hung down her back in damp spirals. "One thing to get out of the way," she said. "No more calling me Michelle. My friends call me Shell, and I think we've officially graduated to friends."

Friends. It was nice. "We have. So, Shell it is. You mind rifling through my refrigerator? I've got some salsa in there. Can't have margaritas without chips and salsa."

"Sooo," she said as she stuck her head in the fridge, her voice full of mischief. "You didn't tell me you lived next door to Zach."

Midway through twisting the tray of ice cubes, Toni jolted and fumbled the tray. Slippery squares of ice scattered across the counter and slid to the floor, shooting throughout the kitchen.

Instead of apologizing for startling her, her new friend burst out laughing. So hard and so loud she snorted and slapped a hand over her mouth.

Heat rushed to Toni's face as she scrambled to rescue the ice before more plunged off the edge of the counter.

"I was going to ask what you thought of him next, but I think I've already got my answer," Michelle said, when she finally stopped giggling.

"What? Oh, that's just me being clumsy. Happens all the time." Toni dumped the ice in the blender and stared everywhere but at Shell. The excuse sounded lame, even to her own ears.

More laughter ensued. "You're a terrible liar. Come on, dish, girl."

With a sigh, Toni turned and leaned against the counter with the blender at her back. "There isn't anything to tell. I only just met him a few days ago. He introduced himself, we chatted. He's nice. That's it." She turned and pushed *blend* on the machine. Loud whirring from the motor drowned out whatever Shell was going to say next. The momentary reprieve gave Toni a second to compose herself.

Mention of Zach's name shouldn't send her into such a bumbling tailspin. She barely knew the guy. No, barely would imply she knew something about him. And she knew absolutely nothing. Maybe she'd known a few things about the boy he was years ago, but nothing about the man he was now. Nothing beyond the fact that he claimed to be attracted to her. And claimed he'd be acting on it in a week. Less than a week.

Just four more days.

Not that she was counting. No way. No how.

A shiver of anticipation raced down her spine. Not good. He was a mistake Toni wouldn't be making. Just physical attraction.

Zach

Chemicals and pheromones. And she didn't make any decisions based on those. Not anymore.

She chose her partners based on merit. Strength of character. Discipline. Mutual future goals. The downside was her last two relationships were devoid of the passion she craved, but it didn't matter. Passion faded anyway, right? Compatibility wasn't based on fireworks and lust. It was mental, not physical.

Punching the off button, Toni reached in the cabinet over her head for two margarita glasses. After pouring the frosty liquid into the glasses, she turned and was greeted by a smirking Shell.

"He's pretty potent, isn't he? All those muscles? And he's so good looking, he's almost pretty." Shell fanned herself. "There isn't a woman out there who could be immune to that."

Suddenly, she recalled Shell's uneasy reaction to news that the bikers would be allowed in the diner. Since that day, at least a handful of the leather-wearing men were in the diner every shift she worked. They asked for her section every single time. And called her Shell. Hadn't Zach mentioned she brought them food on occasion?

She was more than just a waitress they liked. She was a friend. Maybe even more. Oh God, could she possibly have a thing for Zach? Did they have a history?

"Oh. No!" Shell said. She waved her hands in front of her in a *stop* motion. "No, no, no, no, no. It's not like that, at all. I promise."

"Not like what?" Toni frowned. She hadn't even said anything.

"Your face. You looked crushed. I'm sorry if I implied I had a thing for Zach. I am one hundred percent immune to the charm that is Zach. Well," she winked. "Maybe ninety-three percent. He is hot as hell. But immune enough to be not interested at all. Not interested." She shuddered. Actually shuddered, as though the thought of being with the sexiest man Toni had ever laid eyes on was repulsive. "I see him, just about all of them, like brothers."

Oh. Well, that wasn't what she'd expected. "Here." Toni handed Shell the two glasses. Carry these, and I'll get the snacks. Couch is through there," she said, pointing to the den. "So, you know a lot of the Hell's Handlers well then?"

Instead of answering, Shell sipped her drink. Her eyes closed and she tilted her head back, letting out a little moan of pleasure. "Oh man, that's good. I need more of these in my life."

Toni chuckled. Befriending Shell was a breeze.

"I've known them my whole life. My dad was in the club until he was killed when I was a teen. It's a family more than anything else, so my mom and I were taken care of by the club members even after he died."

"You said just about all of them." Toni lowered herself to the couch and propped her feet on a giant square ottoman before sipping her drink. Shell was right. More margaritas were necessary in her life as well.

"What?" Confusion had Shell's eyebrows drawing down and her lips curling in.

"You said you saw just about all of them as brothers. That means there's someone you don't see as a brother." It was Toni's turn to smirk. "Come on, talk to Mama."

She thought she'd get a smile, maybe a laugh out of Shell, but instead the other woman lost some of her light. "Copper," she said with a heavy sigh. "Not like it's a secret. Pretty much everyone in town knows I've been pining away for him since I was a kid."

"Copper, seriously? The giant one with the beard and the eyes that look like they could fry you on the spot? He kinda scares the snot out of me."

A sad smile tilted Shell's lips. "He's not one to cross, that's for sure. But that's just one side of him." There was a wistful quality to her voice, as though she was recalling a memory she wished to return to.

"He know how you feel?"

Zach

"Oh yeah, he knows. Well, at least he knows how I felt before I moved away years ago. I was young and stupid and made it painfully obvious. I'm more discrete now."

Hmm. Interesting. Copper, the biker who showed up at the diner more than any of the others. Always sitting in Shell's section. Always watching her like a hawk but with a fierce frown.

"He says I'm too young. He'd never touch me." She stared at her drink, a far off look in her eyes. "But it wouldn't even matter if he dropped to his knees and professed his love to me tomorrow," she said in a small voice. "Too much has happened. Things he doesn't know about. Things from my past that make it impossible for me to ever be with him. Geez, listen to me. Three sips and I'm spilling my guts."

"No, it's okay. I get it. About the past. I did some things, and had some things done to me, that changed who I am. Especially when it comes to men. Things that occurred years ago but I'm still dealing with and paying for." Toni shrugged.

"I started working at the diner because of the no biker rule." Shell giggled. "Thought it would be a good way to keep myself away from Copper. At least there would be a few hours in the day where I wouldn't have to see him. Despite his refusal to be with me, he's always taken it upon himself to be my shadow. Protector, as he calls it." She chuckled and rubbed her eyes, exhaustion bleeding into her features. Exhaustion Toni now knew wasn't from physical fatigue alone, but from heavy emotional scars. "It's all so fucked up," she whispered almost to herself.

Desire to ease her new friend's pain hit Toni hard. Along with guilt. "God, Shell. I'm so sorry. I had no idea lifting that ban would cause you trouble."

Shell swallowed a healthy gulp of her drink, then took a deep breath. "Please, don't feel bad. I'm at the clubhouse all the time. Hell, one of the ol' ladies is my steady babysitter. I can't avoid them. And I don't really want to. They're my family. Sometimes it's just hard to pretend I don't feel what I do when I'm around them. So I got a job where I wouldn't have to be around them." With a wave of her hand she brushed it off. "You want to talk about your past shit? Because I really don't want to think about mine anymore."

"Hell no." Toni didn't talk about the mistakes of her past with anyone. Not even with Mark, who was privy to more than anyone. "Movie time?"

"Absolutely."

Toni leaned back on the couch and turned on the television. Three hours and one *Sex and The City* movie later, Shell begged off and headed home. Toni remained on the couch for a while. Thinking about all the decisions lingering out in space, waiting for her to act.

Keep the diner? Sell the diner?

Return to Chicago? Stay in Tennessee?

Live in the house? Unload the house?

Avoid the biker? Sleep with the biker?

And if her gaze drifted to the window where Zach's dark house was on display every few seconds, no one had to know about it. Nor did anyone have to know she was still on the couch watching when the headlights and rumble of a bike pulled in at well past midnight.

But what she'd really be keeping to herself was the intense feeling of relief that flooded her when only one rider hopped off the bike.

It didn't mean Zach hadn't been with a woman.

But it did mean there wouldn't be one sleeping in his bed and wouldn't be one waking with him in the morning.

Those were dangerous thoughts.

It was all dangerous. Staying in the house. Breaking up with Chris. Spending so many hours in the diner. Because with each passing day, she felt the options being selected without any real thought or planning on her part.

Keep the diner.

Zach

Stay in Tennessee.
Live in the house.
Sleep with the biker.

CHAPTER EIGHT

Zach's stomach growled so loud, Maverick was razzing him before he'd even gotten off his bike. "Fuck you," he grumbled. "I've been wanting to eat here my whole life, but the fucking Jennings' had log-size sticks up their asses. Bad enough they'd scurry from their cars to their house every time my pops walked around with his cut on. Like he was just going to go apeshit and attack. You know how many times they called the cops on him for bullshit? Engine too loud. Thinking he was smoking pot every time he lit a fuckin' cigarette." Zach shook his head. "Bunch of uppity assholes. Toni's lucky to have gotten away from them."

Maverick arched a pierced eyebrow. "Toni, huh? You two kids getting all chummy?"

"What, because I know her name?" Mav was baiting him, and like a moron Zach was falling straight for it. That's what four nights in a row of fewer than five hours sleep would do to a man. Made him lose his edge. Also made him hungry as fuck for a giant, energizing breakfast.

"So—" And there it came. The taunt Zach shouldn't fall for "—what you're saying is that I'm free to let all this loose on the lady?" Mav ran his hands over his whipcord lean body, stopping at his crotch where he gave his junk a squeeze.

Zach

And like the sucker he was that morning, Zach took the bait. "If I catch you so much as flicking a gaze in the direction of her tits there won't be anything left down there for you to fondle."

Maverick whistled. "Wooow," he said as they walked toward the diner's entrance. "You know—"

"Shut the fuck up," Zach muttered, pulling the door open and shooting Maverick a look he hoped would be interpreted as an I'll-kill-you-if-you-keep-running-your-trap glare.

Of course, Mav being Mav, he only laughed. "Well, hey there, baby doll," he said to Shell who walked by balancing a very full tray of steaming plates. Poor girl couldn't weigh more than a buck five soaking wet, and she worked herself to the bone for that kiddo of hers. Club always tried to help but she refused any so-called charity.

"Hey, Maverick," Shell said, accepting the kiss he pressed to her cheek. He lingered just long enough to have her giggling the laugh only Mav could wrangle from women. "Oh, Zach, you're here too!" She grinned. "Go sit on over there in my section, you guys. It's so busy this morning, I'll try my best to serve you, but I might have to send Toni over to give me a hand." Her eyes sparkled and her lips turned up in a too-innocent way. What was the little rascal up to?

"Will do, Shell," Zach said, smacking her cheek with his own kiss. She chuckled and swatted his shoulder. Kind of amazing she could do all that and manage to keep the plates from tumbling. Now that the biker ban was lifted, they could at least eat at the diner and leave overly generous tips to help her out. If she saw straight through it, who cared? She couldn't call it charity if it was direct payment for a job well done.

"Man, it smells so good," Mav said, rubbing his hands together in anticipation after they'd seated themselves in the booth.

A few of their brothers were there as well and Zach couldn't help but chuckle. If Toni wasn't careful, the place would become a biker den before she knew it. That's what happened when you served big hungry men delicious food. They kept coming 'round.

"Good morning, I'm Toni and I'm helping Shell this morn— oh!" Toni's mouth formed a perfect circle and her gorgeous eyes were wide with astonishment. "Zach. You're here."

He grinned at her statement of the obvious. "I'm here. And I'm hungry." He let his gaze roam over her. Hungry for way more than breakfast. Forget the damn menu, Toni looked good enough to eat in a short denim skirt that showed off her smooth, tanned legs. On top, she wore the diner's signature teal T-shirt and her hair was pulled high on her head in a ponytail. Since her hair wasn't longer than her shoulders, strands that didn't quite make it in the rubber band hung down in back. And, if he wasn't mistaken, there was a dusting of flour across her left breast.

What were the chances that she would slap his face if he reached out and brushed it off for her?

Pretty damn high.

Her eyes narrowed at him, as though she could sense his dirty thoughts, but a pretty pink flush stole across her cheeks. That flush had nothing to do with the heat of the kitchen and everything to do with the heat of Zach's stare. She may deny it until she turned blue, but she wanted him just as much as he wanted her. Now, how to bust down her walls?

A throat cleared. "You gonna hand over those menus, darlin' or you want me to read them with my mind?" Maverick did his own perusal of Toni, pausing his gaze on her tits before he turned his smug grin on Zach.

Swallowing down the urge to rip the bar right out of Maverick's eyebrow, he turned his attention back to Toni. Mav was harmless. Well not really, but despite his horny bastard status, he'd never poach on a brother's turf. The taunting was all in good fun. Fun for Mav, anyway.

Not that Toni was Zach's turf. But she would be. For a short while.

"Oh yes! Sorry. I, uh, I was just…"

Zach

Maverick laughed. "No need to explain. My man Zach here can turn even the most eloquent of women into a blabbering mess."

Toni raised an eyebrow at him. Wonderful. Now she'd think he was as much of a dog as Maverick. Not that it really mattered what she thought of his character. As long as the teasing didn't impair his chances for five weeks of no-strings sex.

She snickered. "I'm sure he does. Here's your menus. Coffee?" she asked, after placing a laminated menu in front of each of them. They both nodded. "Be right back."

Zach wanted to watch her ass as she walked away, but he also wanted to keep Maverick from staring at the same ass, so he kept his focus on his friend and asked. "What looks good?"

"Oh man." Mav groaned. "Think they'd look at me funny if I ordered one of everything?"

"I don't think your girlish figure could handle it."

"Fuck you. Not my fault I ain't built like the Hulk. What do you think cinnamon roll waffles are?" Face blocked by the tall menu, Maverick groaned again. "Scratch that. I don't care what it is as long as I can get enough bacon to clog each and every one of my arteries."

With a snicker, Zach glanced over his own menu. "I know I like cinnamon rolls. And I know I like waffles. Besides that, I don't have a clue what they are. You'll have to ask Toni."

"Ask Toni what?" She reappeared with a coffee pot and filled their glasses. "Sugar and creamer," she said, indicating a small bowl filled with coffee fixin's. "Now, what did you want to ask me?"

Zach opened his mouth, but Maverick beat him to the punch. "Two things," he said. "First, what are cinnamon roll waffles, and second, how the hell do you manage to make a diner T-shirt look so sexy?"

"Uh, well..." Her eyes cut to Zach, as though gauging his reaction to his brother's blatant flirting. To put her at ease, he rolled his eyes. Nothing in the world would change who

Maverick was. And neither Zach nor anyone from their club would have it any other way. He was the best of all of them in good times and could flip the switch to coldest and deadliest when necessary.

Pleasure surged in Zach when Toni decided to go along with the crazy. If she was going to be his fuck buddy for a month, she'd need to be able to handle his brothers. And they were an armful.

"It's my gift really. Looking like this in a diner shirt." With a giggle that was more of a snort, she struck a pose. "And my little gift to my customers."

Mav burst out laughing and winked at Toni. "Damn, Zach, I like this one. You chose wisely."

The smile slid right off Toni's face, and Zach could have killed his friend in that moment. Damn idiot was going to destroy his chances with one stupid comment. He cleared his throat. "The waffles?"

"Oh, right." She brightened again. "Well, they're cinnamon roll dough but instead of baking them in the oven, they are pressed in the waffle iron. And they're served with a cream cheese, cavity-inducing glaze. One of Ernesto's new creations, and they are to die for. Well worth the six pounds you'll gain eating just one."

"Sold." Mav held his menu out to Toni. "With a side of all the bacon in the joint."

"Make it two," Zach said. That sounded so damn good, saliva pooled in his mouth in anticipation.

"You won't be sorry. The second you get it in your mouth—" Her eyes widened as though she suddenly realized the implication of her words. "I mean, it's delicious, or, um…"

Maverick didn't even pretend to disguise his laughter and Zach let out a snicker or two as well.

"Oh, shut up. You know what I mean, you jerks." With a huff, Toni snatched the menus, spun on her heel, and stomped away.

Zach

This time Zach let himself watch the twitch and sway of her curvy ass as she stomped.

"You better watch yourself, brother," Mav said before taking a sip of his black coffee. "Oh man, that's damn good java."

"Watch myself how?" Hot liquid filled his mouth and he wanted to moan. Good java was an understatement. This was caffeine of the gods.

"With that little filly over there. She's the kinda woman you go after looking for a good time and before you know it you're buying a long chain for her to hitch to her very heavy ball."

Zach scoffed. "No worries. She's leaving in five weeks. I'm not looking for any shackles. Unless it's to tie her to my bed."

Now it was Maverick's turn to laugh. "We'll see."

Mav could think what he wanted, but Zach had one focus in his life at that moment. And that was his club. Fucking was fucking, but the club was his world.

They chatted about nothing but pointless bullshit while waiting for their meal. Thinking about anything but the Gray Dragons and the way they were fucking up his life was exactly what Zach needed. He'd spent the better part of the past three days putting processes in place to drive the heroin out of his town. And he'd spent some time with a few Gray Dragon members as well.

Zach had left them walking, but a bit more colorful and with a good fewer ounces of blood than they'd shown up with. Nothing that wouldn't heal in a week or so, but Zach had to make sure they knew their presence wasn't welcome in Double H territory.

"Here you go, gentlemen," Shell said as she set a heaping plate of food down in front of each of them.

"Whoa, you guys don't fuck around, do you?" Mav asked as he snatched up his fork and knife, licking his chops like a hungry bear.

Shell laughed. "No, Toni said she wants each person here to leave with pants unbuttoned."

Christ. Was every comment destined to be an innuendo that day? Zach would do just about anything to get his pants unbuttoned around Toni. But she'd sent Shell over with their food. A message? A dismissal? Who the fuck knew? Though growing pickier and pickier about who he spent his naked time with, Zach never had a problem attracting a woman when he wanted one. They pretty much dove head first into his bed, losing all clothes on the way.

Apparently, he wasn't doing an adequate job at hiding his disappointment. "Don't worry, big guy," Shell said. "Toni's not blowing you off. She got a phone call from that guy she dumped. I left her in the kitchen rolling her eyes so far back in her head, they probably made a full revolution."

Well, she hadn't given him the brush off. That was a step in the right direction, but the ex calling pissed him off. For a moment, he thought about busting into the kitchen and taking care of that phone call for her, but a stern look and a wag of a finger from Shell kept him in his place.

"Eat," she said. "Stay in your seat. Do not cause trouble for my new friend and maybe I'll see what I can do to help you get in good with her. Okay?"

Mav snorted and Zach bit his lip to keep the foul curse inside.

He didn't jump through hoops for a woman. If Toni didn't want him, who cared?

"Oh. My. Fucking. God." Maverick moaned like he was in the throes of an orgasm and placed his fork and knife on either side of his plate. His eyelids dropped closed and he let his head fall backward. "Keep talking. I just need a moment."

"You are such a dork." Shell swatted him with her order pad, but she was smiling. It was nice to see. Both before and after she left Townsend for the few years she was gone, she'd had a haunted look to her. Everyone in town attributed it to her unrequited love for Copper, but Zach was never fully convinced that's all it was. After moving back home six months ago, she'd gradually come into herself and now resembled the happy girl he'd grown up knowing. Some ghost still haunted her, but it was in the background now. Maybe someday she'd bring it to the club.

And then they'd take care of it.

Because no matter how screwed up Copper was when it came to his feelings for Shell, he'd slay any dragon that came her way. No matter how hot the fire they breathed.

"Try it, Zach. If I'm going to die, make sure it's right after I've eaten these waffles. No." He shook his head and picked up his utensils once again. "Make sure I've fucked that new chick whose been hanging around the club this week, then had these waffles. Then, I could go with no regrets."

"Shell's right. You are a dork. A perverted one, but a huge dork." The smell of cinnamon and sugar was so strong, Zach could practically taste the deliciousness without anything ever hitting his tongue. After cutting a huge chunk, he stuffed it into his mouth and froze.

Maverick was right. It was the kind of tasty that would make you not give a shit that death was right around the corner. "This is the best thing I've ever eaten," he said around the mouthful.

"Right?" Mav smiled and both men dug into their breakfasts as though it was the last they'd ever get. When there wasn't so much as a drop of glaze left on either plate, Zach leaned against the back of the booth. "Think they'd care if I took a nap right here?"

Toni chose that moment to stroll on over, looking just as scrumptious as the food. "Nope, don't mind. But we do charge by the hour for snoozing. It was good, I take it?" she asked, her beautiful bright green gaze shifting between Zach and Maverick.

Instead of answering, Maverick pushed out of the booth, slid one arm around Toni's waist and cupped the back of her head with his other hand. "Marry me," he said a fraction of a second before he dipped her, Hollywood style. Toni let out a squeak of surprise as Zach's ex-best friend planted his lips right on hers.

Even though it was Mav. And even though it was all in good fun. And even though it meant jack shit. And even though she smacked his shoulder. And even though the entire purpose was to be a jokester and get under Zach's skin, he grew angrier with each of the seven seconds that passed where Maverick was kissing Toni.

If it had gone on any longer, Zach would have been in danger of risking his patch, because he was a heartbeat away from ripping Mav's limbs from his body. The asshole must have sensed how close he was to death—not that he would have really cared after eating the waffles—but he wised up and righted Toni.

When she had her wits about her, Maverick released her and sat back down in front of his empty plate.

"Um," she said then laughed, bringing her hand up to her kiss swollen lips. "Guess you liked 'em." Her face was flushed and her ponytail a bit mussed. After cutting her gaze to Zach she laughed again. This time long and loud.

The sound was amazing, full of joy, hilarity, and even surprise. Mav may be a scoundrel, but he'd made her laugh for real after what Zach knew was a royally shitty few weeks for her.

Mav joined in her laughter then gave a half assed apology for the loss of control, blaming the fact that all the blood in his body was zooming toward his stomach leaving none for his brain.

A not uncommon problem for Mav except the blood was usually a little lower than his abdominal region. Zach remained quiet, just enjoying Toni's interaction with his brother. Enjoying it maybe a little too much. Because a woman who got on great with your friends? A woman who could roll with the punches, handle a rough and randy biker without batting an eye, and give as good as she got? Well that was the kind of woman who became an ol' lady. Not a short-term fuck buddy.

And there was only one thing Zach was interested in. Who the hell needed an ol' lady nagging, complaining, and distracting him from what was important?

Zach

"Everything okay?" Toni asked after Maverick scooted out of the booth and ambled toward the door. "You got kinda quiet after your friend, uh, kissed me." Pink stole across her cheeks.

Zach leaned in close enough to smell the citrusy scent of whatever crap she used in her hair. "Baby," he whispered against her ear, "if you thought that was a kiss, I can't wait to see how you react when I show you what I bring to the table."

With that parting shot, he tossed a generous stack of bills on the table, strolled out of the diner and mounted his bike. Unable to help himself, he glanced back at the building before riding off.

Toni stood in the window, fanning herself with a menu.

Mission accomplished.

She wanted him just as much as he wanted her. Now it was just a matter of getting her to admit it.

CHAPTER NINE

"Do you know what you're keeping me from?" Zach asked about two point two seconds before his balled fist collided with the ugliest mug he'd ever seen.

With a groan, the banger crumpled to the ground.

Pussy.

He glared up at Zach, blood trickling from his lip, and raised his middle finger.

Christ, this ugly fucker didn't have two brains cells rattling around in his empty skull.

He had a crooked nose. Not like broke-it-once-in-his-life crooked. But the kind of crooked that indicated someone smashed the hell out of his face a time or two. And his front teeth were missing. Guess pushing smack didn't rake in enough cash to visit a fucking dentist. Plus, Zach was pretty sure his right eye was glass instead of flesh.

Poor fucker. Bones was his name.

He already looked like he'd been hitched to the back of a truck and dragged for miles. The beating Zach was in the midst of delivering sure wouldn't do him any favors.

Zach smiled. That's what happened when you crossed into Handler's territory.

Still smiling the smile of a man who enjoyed his work, Zach gripped the Gray Dragon's hair and yanked him to a kneeling position. "I asked you a question, asshole. Do you have any idea what I could be doing right now if I didn't have to deal with your fugly ass in my town?" As he spoke, he placed his booted heel on the guy's calf and pressed down.

Hurt like a sonofabitch. Zach knew that from first-hand experience.

Bones mashed his teeth together and screamed through them. "No," he ground out. That one good eye bulged as though it would pop right out of his head. Wouldn't that suck for old Bones?

"I'll tell you," Zach said easing back on the pressure. "You see, there's this hot little number I know. And every evening, around this time, she sits out on her porch." He leaned forward and pushed against the man's calf again. The hiss of pain was music to his ears. "Now when I say hot, I mean H-O-T. Tits, ass, face, the whole package. And I was planning on getting all up in that tonight. Driving up on my bike—chicks love that shit. Gets 'em going. So, you see, you're keeping me from getting my dick taken care of."

"S-sorry," Bones said. His face was growing redder with each passing second.

The chance of his dick actually getting taken care of by Toni was probably around twenty-five percent. What was more likely to happen was a roll of her pretty eyes. It didn't make any sense. She was attracted to him. The way her breathing hitched and her gaze lingered on him was all he needed to see to know she wanted him. So why play hard to get? Why not give into a mutually satisfying few weeks? What was the hold up? Zach was determined to discover what lay beyond her walls.

But first…

"Don't you think I deserve to have my dick tended to, Bones?"

"Y-yes. Oh fuck," he whispered as Zach tightened his grip until a few of Bones's short greasy hairs burst free of his scalp.

Now for the fun part. Zach leaned down so he was eye to eye with his new friend. "So why the fuck are you selling heroin in my town and making me miss time with my girl?"

Slight exaggeration. Okay, bold faced lie.

My girl.

Sounded kind of nice.

Too nice.

Nice in a way that Zach was not interested in. Nice in a flowery, matching slippers kind of way.

"I'm j-just following orders," he said between pants.

"Just a good little gang soldier, huh?" He released both his hold on Bones's hair and the press of his boot.

Bones's relief was instantaneous. With a loud gasp, he sagged to the ground on all fours.

"All right," Zach said, running a hand through his hair as he paced in front of Bones. "You're the fourth Gray Dragon piece of shit that I've *chatted* with this week. Either you're all too afraid of Shark to bring our messages back or too stupid. Which is it?"

Jigsaw had called about a half hour ago with the tip. Someone saw Bones dealing behind an abandoned shoe store on the edge of town. Guy was smart enough not to wear his colors, but it didn't even matter. All Gray Dragons had a bright red dragon tattoo on their left hand. Never made any fucking sense to Zach, but it was a dead giveaway when trying to identify one of the bastards.

So, he'd dropped what he was doing—working on the class schedules for the gym he managed—and hightailed it to the shoe store.

Sure enough, Bones.

"Fuck you."

Guy was getting a little mouthy in the absence of acute pain. Zach sighed. Why couldn't it just be easy? Why couldn't this little shit just open his mouth and rat out his gang?

Not that Zach didn't respect the loyalty. He, himself, would die before turning on the club. But that wasn't usually the case with these gang members. They were young, stupid, and selfish. Each and every one would crack with the right motivation.

And fear for their life was typically right on the money.

"Guess we're going to do this the hard way." He drew his sidearm from the small of his back at the same time he shoved Bones to his back with a kick. There wasn't time to grab Louie after Jigsaw's call, so a gun was the only weapon available to him.

Before Bones knew what had hit him, Zach was kneeling with one knee on Bones's chest and his pistol jammed against Bones's kneecap. "You the one who roughed up our girls?"

"Fuck you."

"Does Shark know what happened to the other three guys I roughed up?"

"Fuck you."

Zach cocked the gun and returned it to the skin below Bones's shorts.

"How many loans has he purchased from our clients?"

"Fuck you." Despite the bold words, a line of sweat broke out across Bones's forehead.

"So the really hard way, then?" Zach pulled out his phone and scrolled through his contacts. "Hey, Viper, gonna need a cleanup crew, ASAP." After getting confirmation from Viper that three prospects would be there in under ten minutes, Zach returned the gun to Bones knee.

"Okay, last chance. You the one who roughed up our girls?"

Sweat was running in rivulets down Bones's red face now. "You're not going to shoot me in broad daylight. Fuck you."

Zach pulled the trigger sending lead straight through Bones's knee. The howl of pain was epic. A high-pitched squeal worthy of a slasher movie. "Shit, man, you scream like a scared high school girl. Do I have your attention now?" He held the gun against Bones's chest.

"Oh shit. Oh fuck. What the fuck did you do to me? I'm gonna lose my fucking leg?" Bones writhed on the ground and was actually sniveling.

"Bring it down a notch or two there, drama queen. If you shut up and answer my questions, you'll be at a hospital in under twenty minutes. You won't lose your damn leg. So...from the top?"

Then the floodgates opened and Bones forgot all about loyalty to Shark and the gang. "Yes. I was the one who had orders to go after the girls when the strip club closed. Shark knows you're coming after the guys you find here. He doesn't give a shit." Pausing to breathe, Bones tried to shift and ended up flopping to his back and groaning.

"Keep going. What's the end goal here? Money?"

Eyes closed and face ashen, Bones shook his head. "No. Drive you guys out. Create chaos in town by dealing H. Weaken you financially with the loans. Move in and push you out."

Shit. Shark's balls were getting too big for his brain if he thought he could drive the Handlers out of Townsend. His numbers were impressive, but if all of them were blubbering little boys like Bones, he didn't stand a chance. Still, if a war ensued, lives would be lost on both sides. Arrests would be made. It would be a costly fucking mess.

The rumble of a motorcycle alerted him to the cavalry's arrival. While he waited for the prospects to find him, he leaned closer to Bones. "Tell Shark he's wasting his time. He could come at us with a hundred of you shit-for-brains little boys and he'd still lose. He can take every fucking penny we have and we'll still gut him and your entire gang. Stay the fuck out of Townsend."

With that, a van and two bikes pulled to a stop about twenty feet from Zach. Confident Bones wasn't going anywhere, Zach moved to meet the prospects.

"Hey," Screwball said. He was Zach's favorite, despite his name, which was given to him because he was always screwing around. The guy was the master of practical jokes. Always had the brothers cracking up. Unless they were the ones at the butt of the joke. Then they wanted to kill him.

He kept his antics to parties and down time. At twenty-three, the dark haired, former Marine was eager for the patch and did every fucking thing asked.

"Hey," Zach bumped his fist against Screw's. "Take this sack of shit and dump him outside the ER in their county. Sorry about the mess." He pointed to the blood puddle expanding across the asphalt.

"No worries. Bleach ought to take care of it. Hey, LJ," he called to the prospect emerging from the van. "You and Fox wanna load him up? I'll get started on clean up."

"On it." LJ, short for Little Jack, who was not little in the least, hopped in the driver's seat and backed the van close to Bones who was ashen and whose chest was rising and falling in a shallow but rapid pattern.

"Need me to stick around?" Zach only asked because he knew they'd say no. No prospect worth his salt would make a patched member help with the shit detail. They'd appear lazy. Unwilling to pull their weight. Not brother material. Because if they weren't willing to take on a menial job, how could they be trusted when shit got real?

"Nah, we got this. You did the hard part." Screw stuck his head in the back of the van and pulled out a bucket and a gallon of bleach.

Zach snorted. "I had the fun part."

"Can't argue with that." Screw barked out a laugh. "We need to be gentle with this guy or is it okay for him to get a bump or two on the way?"

"Treat him however you'd like. If he'd been more willing to talk, you could be at the bar drinking instead of cleaning his DNA off the ground. Told him I'd get him to a hospital. As long as he can speak well enough to give Shark my well wishes, I don't care what condition he arrives in."

Prospects had to be able to have a little fun sometimes.

"Sounds good. See you tonight at the lodge?" There was a big club bonfire that evening. Viper's ol' lady was turning twenty-five for about the thirtieth time.

"I'll be there." And if the stars aligned, he'd be able to talk Toni into coming with him.

He left Bones in the prospects' capable, though not tender, hands.

With each mile that brought him closer to home, Zach's excitement grew. Toni would still be out on her wraparound porch, wineglass in hand, enjoying the sunset. It had become her ritual. And while Zach had been too busy to pop over in the last week, he'd found some excuse to run to his house or past his house almost every evening.

Just for a glimpse of her. The woman who turned his head. The woman who accepted him and his brothers by allowing them in her family business without knowing a damn thing about them.

After making the twenty-minute trip, he slowed and turned into his long driveway. The house he'd grown up in was set about a hundred feet back from the road. Toni's was even farther, another fifteen or so feet, so though they were next door neighbors, the houses weren't side-by-side. His bedroom, however, lined up with a window in Toni's living room.

Any excitement he'd been feeling died out when he realized she wasn't in her usual spot. She wasn't outside at all. Damn shame. The air was warm and the sky clear. Good day for sunset gazing.

"You've gotta be shitting me," Zach muttered. Toni may not be outside, but she was in the house, visible through the window. And she had a visitor. A suit-wearing, douche bag of a man who wasn't worth a smile from Toni.

Under her reserved exterior, Toni burned hot. Zach could sense it. For some reason, she was denying that part of herself, to him at least, but that didn't mean it wasn't there. And it didn't mean it could be ignored forever. A man like the suit wouldn't know what the hell to do with a woman like Toni. Wouldn't know how to coax out the passion and fire she'd buried under a layer of seriousness.

Zach did.

Zach knew just how to tease a response out of Toni that would shatter her defenses and have her screaming his name.

And that's exactly what he planned to do.

She just had to agree to let him touch her.

CHAPTER TEN

He'd actually done it.

Chris had shown up on her doorstep like he'd promised, both when he'd left and when he'd called a few days ago while she was working. While she was waiting on Zach's table, to be exact.

Damn him.

"Chris," she said, holding the door open and blocking the doorway. Half convinced it was going to be Zach paying an unexpected visit with a lame excuse like he needed some sugar, but really wanted to flirt, she'd flung the door open with far too much enthusiasm.

Zach had been on her mind each and every day. More specifically, his mouth had been on her mind. After he'd issued that challenge about kissing her, it was all she could do to keep her wits about her. And her vibrator in its drawer.

Yeah, she'd failed at that one.

"What are you doing here?" She kept her body in the doorway.

A frown marred Chris's otherwise perfect face. He was handsome, she had to give him that. But in a refined, snobbish, moneyed kind of way. Not like Zach, who was…well, Zach was straight up hot. Rugged. Muscled. A little dangerous. The kind of man who would know exactly what to do with a woman. Whether that was to throw her down on the bed, or slam her against the wall…

Zach

And she was fantasizing about Zach again. Why?

Whatever the reason, her body reacted to her wayward thoughts and she had to resist the urge to stick her head in the freezer.

"I told you I was coming. Remember? I told you we had some space and it was time to discuss our relationship and future. Hit the reset button. Any of this ringing a bell?" Chris stepped closer, as though he expected her to move back and let him into the house.

She didn't. He wasn't welcome.

"And I told you, as I told you before you left here, that it wasn't a break. It was a break up. I specifically asked you not to come." This was the last thing she wanted to deal with. He was making her miss the sunset. "We broke up, Chris. I'm sorry if you're hurt or upset, but my decision is final. There isn't anything for us to discuss."

He scoffed and had the gall to remove her arm from the door frame so he could push his way inside. "We didn't break up, honey. You were upset about your parents and it made you emotional. Irrational. Not to mention the unwanted interruption by your thug neighbor. Now that you've had some time to get your head on straight, we can talk about it like adults."

The snort that left her made his frown deepen. He was now standing in her living room, of course, wearing a perfectly pressed suit that seemed to defy the fact that he'd been on a plane only a short time ago. With no other choice but to deal with him, she released the door and let the screen slam shut. But she didn't have to be happy about it.

Toni jammed her hands on her hips. "That's rich coming from someone who not only wasn't invited but isn't wanted. And Zach may have interrupted us, but I'd already told you we were through and I repeated it to you on the phone the other day. So you can't blame Zach for your actions."

Chris advanced on her, and even though he wasn't an intimidating figure, the hair on the back of Toni's neck stood on end. Something about the look in his eyes screamed of desperation. Desperate people were unpredictable. "Seems like you and *Zach* got pretty friendly. You fucking him now?"

She gasped. "What? Geez, Chris. No, I'm not *fucking* him. Or anyone, for that matter. But you know what? If I wanted to fuck the whole damn MC, it wouldn't be any of your business."

Where on earth was this coming from? Wasn't Chris the one who always said swearing was the mark of an uneducated person? Not that she agreed with the comment, since she could swear like a sailor when riled and quite enjoyed it, but to hear him ask if she was *fucking* someone was so unlike him. The unease she'd felt seconds before morphed into anger as she stood on her toes in an attempt to get in his face.

Instead of firing another insulting question at her, he threw his head back and laughed as though she'd told the funniest joke in the world. "That'd be just like a whore like you, wouldn't it?"

"Excuse me?" The unease was back in full force. Unease and nausea as his comment hit a little too close to home. Could he know? Was is possible he knew about the mistakes of her past?

"Look at you," he flung a hand in her direction. "What the hell are you wearing? You look like a slut."

Gazing down at herself, Toni fought for control of her tongue. And her fists. Ramming one into his arrogant mouth would feel great. "I'm wearing a halter top and cutoffs. I'm alone in my home and it's hot out. What would you have me wear, thermals?" She took a deep breath and blew it out slowly. Hitting the jerk wouldn't solve anything.

But boy, would it be satisfying.

"It gets hot in Chicago. You never dressed like that. Like you were for sale."

For sale? Red clouded her vision. "Oh my God. Who are you? The clothing police? Do you even hear yourself?" She marched away and stared out the window. The sky was a gorgeous picture of pinks, purples, and oranges swirling as though an

Zach

artist's brush had created them. As had become custom, the sight brought an inner peace.

Something flickered in the corner of her field of vision. A squirrel or other small creature on Zach's property drew her attention to his house. He had the habit of arriving home for a few minutes in the evenings when she was out on the porch. Probably going from his job at the gym to the clubhouse. He'd throw her a wave, run in his house, and be back on the bike before she fully had the chance to appreciate the view.

Would he do that tonight? Would he wonder why she wasn't in her spot on the porch? Would he notice Chris's car? She almost laughed out loud at the idea of Chris seeing the women that hung around the MC. If he thought she was a slut, his prude ass would drop dead right then and there.

"You know what I hear?" he asked after a few moments. "I hear you. Or I remember hearing you. 'Fuck me harder, Chris. I want more, Chris.'" A look of disgust twisted his features as he spoke, mimicking her in a breathless tone.

How. Dare. He.

How dare he take what was supposed to be intimate, pleasurable, and special between them and turn it into something shameful. How dare he mock her desires. Sure, she liked sex. Liked it a little dirtier, a little rawer, a little rougher than he did. Hell, she just seemed to like it in general more than Mr. Missionary and Mr. Once-a-week did. He thought she was too much for him? If he only knew how much of her sexual self she suppressed when she was with him. How much she hid. How she squashed her own desires.

None of that really had anything to do with him. It was her own self-imposed restraint due to her past, but still. Nothing she asked of him, and nothing they shared, even bordered on kinky. It was as vanilla as it came.

If she was smart, she'd ask him to leave. Tell him the conversation was over and show him the door. But she was getting tired of always trying to do what was right. Always trying to pay penance for the way she'd lived her life as a teen. Instead of sticking with the character she'd created for herself, she said, "I'm sorry if my actually trying to find some enjoyment in having sex with you and your one boring position makes me a whore."

Chris bent forward until his nose was millimeters away from hers. "You know what? My career is important. I'm a corporate attorney, for fuck's sake. I can't take you to meet clients, or to company functions like this. You're an embarrassment, and I wouldn't be caught dead with you on my arm." His tone was low, threatening, but she wasn't scared.

Fury is what she felt.

"So why the hell are you here?" she asked, throwing her hands up and taking three steps back. "Why would you claim we haven't broken up if I'm such an embarrassment? If I'm such a whore. If you can't stand to be seen with me."

"Because I have no choice." He spun and paced away from her, dropping to sit on her couch.

"No choice? This conversation is getting really tired, Chris. You have three seconds to explain yourself before I kick you out. Which is three seconds more than you deserve, considering the way you just spoke to me."

He sagged like a balloon that just had its air let out. All the anger and ugliness he'd carried into her house disappeared and what remained was a defeated man. "They passed me by," he said, in a voice so low she had to move closer to hear more. "Your uncle passed me by again for junior partner."

A sheen of tears glistened in his eyes.

Mark never really discussed business with her. He kept his opinions about Chris's work performance to himself. He was big on separating business from personal and thought running into Toni at firm functions and client wine-and-dines was enough line crossing. They didn't need to talk about it afterward. She appreciated the distance, never wanting her relationship with Mark to cause Chris issues at the office.

Zach

As far Toni knew, her uncle never had any gripes about Chris's work performance. But would he have mentioned if he did? Probably not. Though he let it be known he didn't think Chris was the right man for Toni. Maybe that had something to do with poor performance at work and he'd never wanted to voice the concern.

With a sigh, she relaxed her posture and tried to be sympathetic to Chris's troubles. "I'm sorry about that, Chris." And she was. She understood spewing vile words under immense pressure. Words that would be regretted when the dust settled. But no amount of job strain gave him a pass for calling her a whore. Still, she'd try to deescalate the argument.

"I know you've been working yourself to the bone to make junior partner. And I can't imagine how disappointed you feel, but if you came here hoping I'd have some insight into Uncle Mark's thinking, you wasted your time. We don't talk about work, especially your part in the firm. You know that."

"Do you have any idea the pressure I'm under to make partner?"

Toni frowned and lowered herself to the couch next to him. "No, Chris. I honestly don't. You've never really discussed it with me."

"My father is displeased. He's threatening to cut me off." Chris dropped his head to his hands. "Everything's a mess."

None of this really made sense to her, but then she'd been on her own for a while. Independent and taking care of herself for years. "Chris, regardless of whether or not you made partner, you have a good career. You make good money. What does it matter if your father cuts you off at this point? You'll survive just fine."

Chris's father was a jackass on a good day. He had money coming out his ears. Old money and plenty of status and prestige. He was a retired attorney himself and had worked on multiple newsworthy cases that rocketed his career to the big leagues.

"You just don't understand." Chris straightened. "It's not about money. It's about connections, status, power."

He was right. She just didn't get it.

"Well, Chris. I really am sorry things didn't work out this time around, but that doesn't mean you'll never make partner. And I think you know we aren't right for each other."

"It doesn't matter if we aren't right for each other. We are going to be together." There was a hardness to his voice that hadn't been there moments ago, and the tinge of desperation was back.

"What?" She shook her head and screwed up her face. It was like he'd lost his sense in the past week.

"We are not done with each other. You will come home and we will continue to date. You'll dress better. Classy again. You'll accompany me when I need it. You'll act like a lady. And you'll put in a good word with Mark. More than that. You'll get him to make me a junior partner. That queer would do anything for you, wouldn't he?"

Toni clenched her teeth so hard they squeaked. She'd never experienced anger like she was feeling in that moment. White-hot fury. If there was one thing she wouldn't stand for, it was a homophobic attitude toward her uncle and his husband. Two of the most loving, supportive, and all around incredible people she'd ever met. Anyone would be lucky to have half as wonderful a relationship as they did.

With as much calm as she could muster, she stretched her hand toward the door. "It's time for you to leave now, Chris."

"No, Toni. You aren't the one calling the shots here. I hold all the cards." This wasn't the man she knew. Wasn't the man she'd shared meals with, spent her weekends with, shared her goals and dreams with. This was a frantic man who'd do anything to get what he wanted. He'd lost the ability to be reasonable.

"What freaking cards, Chris? Ooo, what are you going to do? Tell everyone your monogamous girlfriend is a whore because she likes to be fucked? News flash, you'd have to admit that you couldn't give a woman an orgasm with a roadmap and a set of instructions!" She was screaming and she didn't even care.

A rap on the door made her spin and dropped her jaw. Zach's bulky form filled the space on the other side of the screen. The jerk wasn't even pretending he hadn't been eavesdropping on the conversation. A giant smirk was plastered across his face.

Great. Just great.

What had she just screamed? Something about liking sex and Chris failing to satisfy her. All true, but mortifying.

Something like a combination of a growl and a whimper came from Chris. Like he was both warning off and intimidated by Zach at the same time. The intimidation she got, Zach would probably annihilate Chris with one half-powered punch.

But the warning? Did all men have to engage in pissing contests?

"What do you want, Zach?" she asked in a bright voice, as though false cheer could somehow erase the humiliation of what he'd overheard.

The smug grin only grew. Zach braced his arms on either side of the door frame and stared at her through the screen. Damn man. He had to know what he was doing, showing of the long, firm bulge of his biceps and stretching his shirt across his fitness model shoulders.

"You weren't in our spot. I came to see if you needed my help." His gaze flicked to Chris before dismissing him and returning to Toni. "I'm glad I did because, from the sound of it, you really *need* my help."

Our spot? Might as well wave a red flag in front of an angry bull. Ugh. Why did a grin so smug she'd want to slap it off anyone else look like a promise of sex and sin on Zach?

It didn't make a difference what Zach looked like, or how hot a night or two he was offering. Toni was looking for substance. Meaning. Connection beyond physical. She'd missed the boat with Chris, but at least that was an honest try. Getting tangled with Zach would be a backslide.

A delicious and mind-blowing backslide, but a regression, nonetheless.

"Thanks for the concern, but I'm good. Got all I need waiting for me in my nightstand."

A shocked gasp burst from Chris, but Zach's lips twitched in amusement. It would take a lot more than the threat of passing him over for a vibrator to get under his skin.

"I'm all for adding some battery-operated devices to the mix," Zach said.

"If you're done making vulgar propositions to my girlfriend, you can just scurry on home to your bike and your little leather orgy. I can take care of her myself." Leave it to Chris to be all mouthy with a closed door and a woman standing between him and Zach.

She clenched her teeth. How dare Chris talk about her like she wasn't standing right there. She didn't need Zach to help her in any way. Time to shut this shit down herself.

Giving Zach her back, she faced Chris. "Take care of me? Please. You take care of no one but yourself. I went through a pack of batteries a week with you. Get. Out. Now." She stepped to the side.

"Let me get the door for you, buddy," Zach said as he opened the screen and stepped to the side.

Chris stalked forward and stopped in front of her. Leaning forward he spoke next to her ear with a promise only for her. "This isn't over. Think about what I said."

"I don't need to think about anything, Chris. It's beyond over." She jerked her head back, very aware of Zach observing the entire exchange.

Chris righted and gave up whispering. "We can do things the easy way or the hard way, Toni. Your choice." He walked through the open door, knocking into Zach's shoulder in the process. If she wasn't so fed up with men at the moment, she'd have laughed. The shove didn't even budge Zach, but Chris bounced back as though he'd run into a rubber statue.

Zach

When she heard the screen door close, Toni dropped her head and massaged her temples.

"What the hell did he mean by that easy way or hard way shit?" Zach asked.

Without opening her eyes, she asked, "What are you still doing here, Zach?"

"Told you. You weren't on the porch. I saw that asshat through the window. Thought you could use some backup." She heard the heavy tread of his boots approaching, then he gripped her wrists and pulled her hands from her aching head. "Let me do that." Strong fingers replaced hers, rubbing gentle circles on the sides of her head.

Tension relief was immediate. As was arousal. Warmth spread from his talented fingers down her shoulders and to her nipples, drawing them tight. Her sex heated too. Anticipation. Desire.

Damn him.

"As you can see, I'm fine. Annoyed, but fine. You can go."

"Come with me." His magic hands moved to her neck where he dug those long fingers into the tense muscles. Toni bit back a groan. Letting him know how unbelievably wonderful his touch felt would only grow his already too-healthy ego.

"Where? To your bedroom for fifteen minutes of fun before you move on to some biker bunny who'll hop along after you with her tits and ass hanging out?" Her fear of being intimate with Zach had way more to do with herself than her worry about other women. But that was a personal tidbit she didn't share with anyone.

His hands fell away and her eyes popped open just in time to witness him throw his head back and burst out laughing.

Even his throat is sexy.

"First of all, babe," he said, after the hilarity ended. "Fifteen minutes? No wonder you're taking out stock in batteries. It would take all night just to scratch the surface of what I want to do to you."

She swallowed. Hard. All night? She hadn't had all night in a very, very long time. Before it all went bad.

"But I'll settle for a bonfire and some light flirting."

"Huh?" She blinked.

He smiled. Throwing her off her game seemed to amuse him to no end. "Our VP's ol' lady's birthday is tonight. Club is throwing her a party complete with a bonfire. I want you to come with me."

"Ol' lady, huh?"

"That's what we call—"

She waved him away and took a step back. The closeness, the manly smell of sweat and nature was weakening her resistance. "Yeah, yeah, I know. I've seen Sons of Anarchy."

Zach snorted and rolled his eyes. "I'm no Jax Teller, sweetheart."

"Never said you were." They stared at each other for a few heartbeats. If things were different. If she didn't already know how choosing the wrong man, letting hormones and pheromones overrule her brain could destroy her life, she'd jump him right then and there.

"Come with me." He stepped closer to her.

"A wild biker party, huh?"

He smirked. "Not too wild. Ol' ladies will be there. Viper's ol' lady is pretty…well, let's just say she's pretty uninhibited, so it's probably middle of the road as far as our parties can get. Probably a step above family barbeque and a step below naked frat party."

That got her laughing. Going would be such a mistake. But it would also distract her from her annoyance at Chris. And she'd meet some new people. Have some fun. Maybe Shell would even be there.

"Come with me," he said, running his hands up her arms until he cupped her shoulders.

She couldn't help it, she shivered and her gaze cut to those tanned hands where they rested against her lighter skin. They were strong, roughened, and felt heavenly coasting over her. "I don't think it's a good idea."

"No funny business, I promise."

She tilted her head. "Just some light flirting, huh?"

The playful grin was back. "That's right. Scout's honor."

Toni snorted. "Right." *Say no. Say no.* "Okay."

Now his grin was one of victory. "You ever been on a bike?"

She shook her head and bit her bottom lip to keep from telling him how much the thought of it excited her.

"You'll love it. Not that I want anything to cover those sexy stems of yours, ever, but you'd better throw on some jeans. Riding in shorts isn't fun, especially the first time."

"Okay."

"And make 'em tight. If we're gonna have a look-but-don't-touch rule for that ass, I want to at least have the best visual possible."

Toni chuckled and rolled her eyes as she turned toward her room. The crack of Zach's palm across her ass made her yelp and glare at him, mostly to hide the hot flare of desire that rose from her core.

Being the scoundrel that he was, he raised his hands in a pose of surrender and laughed. "Just the one, promise."

Light flirting, yeah right. Maybe by his definition. But by anyone else's, it was bound to be a night of extreme temptation.

Toni was strong. She'd been resisting temptation for years.

But temptation in the form of motorcycle-riding, tattoo-sporting, muscle-wielding Zach was a whole new level of torture.

She had a feeling his light flirting only offer was just the spider luring the fly to its web. It had been exactly one week since he issued his decree after all.

He was coming for her.

CHAPTER ELEVEN

"Thumbs up or thumbs down?" Zach asked Toni as she struggled her way off the bike. For the first time since he patched in, Zach was tempted to blow off a Handler's function for a woman. Dangerous thoughts. Women never, *never*, came before the club. At least not for him. But the feel of her feminine softness cushioned against him as they cruised through the back roads of Tennessee was enough to make the most pious of saints sin without regret.

She took two stumbling steps, then faced him. Still astride the bike, Zach grinned. There was no doubt in his mind she'd enjoyed her first motorcycle ride.

And that she was aroused.

Her skin had a rosy glow that was more than just wind burn and her eyes shone glassy and bright. She tucked her lower lip between her teeth in a manner so seductive Zach nearly went back on his word. It wouldn't take much. He could grab her and lift her over him until she was straddling both him and the bike. She'd love it, and he'd have her out of her mind and begging for his cock in seconds.

Surprisingly enough, he'd never fucked on his bike. Something to keep in the forefront of his mind once he and Toni started up. And they would start up. It was just a matter of time. And that certainty was the only thing keeping him in check.

"It was fun," she said, a little breathless.

"Just fun?" He cocked an eyebrow.

"Okay, it was amazing. I could get addicted to the feeling of freedom. And I've never enjoyed the scenery nearly as much from a car. I hope you'll take me for another ride soon. Better?"

Much better. But she failed to mention the way her heated pussy rested against his ass. No man gave a shit about scenery when he had two full tits hugged up tight against his back. "Sweetheart, I'll give you a ride any damn time you want."

The air between and around them felt thick and charged with the promise of sex. The kind of sex men lost their minds over. They stared at each other for a beat before Toni turned and broke the connection.

Always fighting what she felt. Always denying herself the pleasure he offered. Someday soon, he'd smash down those walls.

"So," she said after clearing her throat. "Anything I need to know before we go in there?"

"Well…" Zach hefted a leg over his bike then steered Toni toward the Double H bar, which was closed to all but invited guests for the evening. The club did that every now and again when they wanted the freedom to let the members act a fool without outsiders being privy to it.

"The virgin sacrifices are usually first—that's why we have the bonfire. Then they are followed by the live sex show, and if you're lucky, you might get picked to participate." He waggled his eyebrows and laughed as she slapped his arm.

"Oh, you're hilarious. But I'm serious. I've never been to a biker bar. I have no idea what to expect."

He slung an arm across her bare shoulders and propelled her past the long row of bikes in the parking lot outside the bar. "It will be loud, rowdy, smoky. I was fucking with you about the live sex show, but you'll probably see a thing or two that makes your beautiful face blush."

"Sounds like a grown-up frat party."

Zach laughed. "Maybe. In a way. But much more badass."

"Gotcha."

As they approached the door, Zach couldn't help but lean in and inhale her fresh scent. Citrus again. Bright, refreshing, a shining spot in his dark world.

He brushed his nose just under her right ear. Toni stiffened, but not before a tiny tremor coursed through her. "W-what are you doing?"

"You smell fucking fantastic," he murmured against her ear. "Has my dick hard as steel." They'd stopped moving and stood about fifteen feet away from the entrance.

"Zach," she whispered. "You promised."

"I know. Just light flirting." He drew back. Damn, she looked so good he couldn't think of anything besides getting her naked. "Did I mention how hot you look? What is this thing?" He fingered the strap of her top, unable to resist the allure of her silken skin.

"It's called a cold shoulder top."

It was white and flowy with large cutouts that left her shoulders uncovered. Zach liked it. Most women they would encounter throughout the night flaunted significantly more skin. Left very little to the imagination. The thing Toni wore dipped low in the front and back, showing some skin, but it didn't cling to her body. It left a man dying to get a peek at what lay beneath the fabric.

Shit, there wouldn't be a soft cock in the house once his brothers got a look at her in that shirt and the tight black jeans with heeled black boots. Funny thing was, she probably wore the blouse thinking it wouldn't be overtly sexy.

She was dead wrong.

"And are your shoulders cold?" he asked, stroking the soft skin one last time.

"No," she whispered. "Nothing is cold right now." She held herself stiff, but her eyes showed the internal struggle. The strong desire to let herself take what Zach offered fighting against whatever demons held her back.

Zach

Suddenly, Zach had the intense need to know what those demons were. To not just get past her defenses, but to learn why they were in place. What had happened to make her hold back sexually? Why did she settle for a relationship with a man who didn't spend all his time rocking her world? And why did she fight so damn hard against a man who was more than capable of making her every fantasy come to life?

Never before had he given a shit what made a woman tick. It didn't matter when sex was all he wanted from them. But he and Toni had struck up some kind of friendship along with the attraction and that had him wanting to discover all her secrets. It was unnerving, but he supposed he could deal with it, being friends with someone he fucked. But it couldn't go any further than that. He didn't need or want the distraction and responsibility of a committed relationship.

"If it isn't my favorite diner lady and some asshole." Maverick's voice cut through the spell that seemed to have woven itself around Zach and Toni.

She jumped and stepped back, making Zach's hand fall to his side. "Fuck off." He slapped Mav on the back in greeting.

"Hey, beautiful." Mav made like he was going to kiss Toni, and this time Zach was ready for him. He grabbed the collar of his friend's cut and yanked him back. Mav's mouth on Toni was something that was never going to happen again.

"Lips to yourself, dickwad."

Both Maverick and Toni laughed while Mav held his hands up in surrender. "I was just gonna peck her cheek, man. I know when I'm beat."

The girl standing next to Mav frowned and stared at the ground. Poor thing probably thought she was working toward something with him. Little did she know she was just another set of tits in a long, long line.

Toni cleared her throat. "Hi, I'm Toni." She held a hand out to Mav's date and shot a shitty look at Mav. Zach swallowed his laughter. He definitely needed to bring her around more often.

She'd knock Mav off his pedestal and it would be wonderful to witness.

"Missy," Mav's date said.

"Sorry, doll," Mav broke in, circling his arm around her waist. "That's Toni and this is Zach. My best friend and enforcer for the club. And he's an asshole."

The flare of Toni's eyes at the word *enforcer* wasn't lost on Zach. He'd failed to mention that tidbit. Hopefully it wouldn't scare her off. He wasn't violent by nature and would die before laying his hands on a woman in anger, but that didn't matter to some. Just the thought of being with a man who beat others for a living turned some women off. Turned some others way the fuck on, but Toni probably wasn't one of those women.

"Well, are you gentlemen gonna take us in and show us a good time or what?" Toni asked. She linked her arm with Zach's and started to tug him toward the door. It was the first time she'd initiated any contact, and while Zach knew it was more for Missy's benefit than some overwhelming desire to get her hands on him, he'd take it.

"Yes, ma'am," he said, pulling her close and dropping a kiss on her shoulder.

She shot him an evil glare. "Behave."

He laughed and held the door for her. "Ladies first." Joking around and teasing a woman was a new experience for him. And one he found himself trying to replicate often. Making Toni laugh was quickly becoming a highlight of his day.

After letting both woman pass, Zach slipped through the door, cutting off Maverick.

"Asshole," Mav muttered wrapping an arm around Zach's neck in a chokehold. "Now that I know you're such a jealous beast, I may just put my lips on your woman every chance I get. It's fun to watch you lose your shit."

With practiced ease, Zach broke the hold and turned the tables on Mav, wrenching his arm behind his back and crowding him against the wall.

Zach

"Okay, uncle, uncle," Mav yelled around his laughter.

Zach released him and slapped him on the side of his head. "It will serve you well to remember how easily I can kick your ass, brother." He walked to where Toni was waiting next to Missy, shaking her head with a smile on her face.

"Sorry 'bout that, sweetheart. Had some business to take care of."

"Boys will be boys, huh, Missy?" Toni asked, but Missy was no longer paying attention. Instead, she was fawning over Mav, who had the slightest red mark on his cheek from where he'd been held against the wall.

Never one to pass up the opportunity to have a woman's hands all over him, Mav ate that shit up. He winced when Missy pressed her very long neon blue nails to his face.

"He's really something, isn't he?" Toni asked.

"Sure is. Come on. I need a drink." He linked their fingers and pulled her toward the crowded bar. The place wasn't anything fancy. A large wooden bar spanned the entire length of the back wall and there was a dance floor and a number of tables and chairs throughout the room. Aside from some Harley memorabilia adorning the walls, the décor wasn't anything to write home about.

People didn't come there for the atmosphere. They came for the good booze and to find someone to fuck.

"What's your poison?" he asked Toni when they drew up to the bar.

"Does that happen all the time?"

"What?"

"There were tons of people here and they all scattered to make room for you at the bar."

She'd taken her hair down before they left and he brushed the strands off her shoulder. For some reason, he really liked seeing those shoulders bare. That little hint of skin. A sample. A tease.

"It's a sign of respect. As enforcer, I'm on the club's executive board." The club worked because of the importance of respect and loyalty. Otherwise, a group of twenty or so dominant, slightly violent men used to getting their way would implode. Respect, loyalty, and the fact that they had a strong leader kept them together.

"Huh," she said. "I'll have a vodka and club."

Zach chuckled. "Such a girl."

"Hey!" Toni bumped him with her shoulder. "I think that's something you're supposed to like about me."

He raked his gaze over her, lingering on her tits and ass. Bad idea. Now his dick was hard all over again. Seemed to be a constant thing where she was concerned. "Oh believe me, baby, I like it."

"Zach." The protest was weakened by the heated look on her face.

After ordering their drinks, Zach guided them back outside, to a large clearing behind the clubhouse where a roaring bonfire at least a story high blazed away.

They drank and mingled for about an hour. Toni had met many of the men at the diner and she seemed to hit it off with the women as well. Sure, a few of the Honeys shot her death glares, but that was par for the course when one of the guys brought around a woman they were serious about.

Shit. His mind was running away with itself. Zach was not serious about a woman. Any woman. Even Toni. This was purely a sex-driven mission. Once he got her into bed, they'd stoke their own fire until it burned out as it always did.

That was more than enough for Zach.

After Zach introduced her to the woman of the hour, Viper's wife Jacy, Copper caught his eye and summoned him with a chin lift. He had yet to fill his prez in on the clusterfuck with Bones. Most likely, Copper wouldn't be thrilled that Zach shot out the guy's knee, but he'd understand. As long as there wasn't any blowback on the club, Copper gave Zach a long leash as far as his role of enforcer.

Zach

"You okay if I leave you for a few while I talk to Copper, sweetheart?" he whispered in Toni's ear. Try as she might, she wasn't able to disguise the hitch in her breathing when his lips brushed the shell of her ear.

"Take your time." She wouldn't meet his gaze. More evidence that she felt what he did but was battling it for all she was worth. "I'm fine," she said.

And she was fine. Completely at ease in his world. Which was surprising. She wasn't fazed by the loud pounding music. A fight that broke out between two idiots barely made her radar. Even the poorly hidden fucking they witnessed only twenty feet away hadn't set her on edge. In fact, Zach caught her watching out of the corner of her eye more than once. He'd also noticed the prominent points of her nipples visible through her top.

"Won't be long," he said letting his need bleed through his voice. He dropped a kiss on her naked shoulder and pretended he didn't notice the way she tensed or the scowl she shot him.

No one came to a biker party for the first time and didn't have some sort of surprised reaction. Even if they liked it. There was still a level of shock.

Not for Toni.

Which meant she was either the best damn actress he'd ever seen.

Or this wasn't really her first biker party.

CHAPTER TWELVE

It was official. Toni loved hanging out with the guys in the MC and their women. Most of the women, anyway. The ones shooting daggers at her with their heavily made up eyes she could do without, but the ol' ladies were fantastic.

After Zach wandered off, the guys had her laughing until her sides ached. Stories of stupid stunts Zach pulled as a prospect could have kept her entertained for hours.

All around, it was a great night.

Which was bad. Poke your eye with a mascara wand bad.

Everyone she met treated her as if she was Zach's woman. As though they were a new couple and the guys gave their approval of the match. Keeping space between her and Zach was growing impossible in both the mental and physical sense. A lot of that had to do with Zach's inability to keep his hands off her. Especially her open shoulders.

With Zach occupied, she tried to use the time to collect herself and steel her spine. He was her ultimate temptation. He was chocolate, wine, shoe shopping, and cheese all wrapped in one orgasm-promising package. The hardest test of her strength. Zach was everything she wanted in a man physically, and as it turned out, he had so many other qualities she admired. Loyalty, strength, responsibility, respect.

He lived in a world that drew her. A little dark, a little dangerous, a little out of control. Damn her libido for finding that such a draw. But it didn't matter how attracted to him or his life she was. Toni knew first-hand how rotten it could all turn, and she'd vowed to stay far away from the realm of gangs for the rest of her life. And while they called it a club, it still paralleled gang life.

Yet, here she was. Drinking, and laughing, and generally having a rocking time.

"Toni! I had no idea you'd be here." Shell practically bounced over to where Toni stood by the fire talking to Maverick, his date, and a scary dude named Rocket who'd said all of two words.

"Shell!" She threw her arms around her friend and nearly took them both to the ground.

"Whoa, girl, had a few drinks, have we?" Shell's uninhibited laughter was always nice to hear. She had so much responsibility on her slender shoulders.

"Yes! I was just going to have one drink, but Maverick gave me this," Toni held up her red cup full of something heinous Maverick poured from a flask he kept in his pocket.

"Oh, Mav." Shell shook her head at the shitty grin on his face. "Sorry, honey, he makes that crap in his garage. It'll give you one hell of a hangover. Good news is it will also burn all the hair off your body so you won't have to shave for a few days." She laughed and waved her hands in a keep-away motion when Toni offered her a sip of the cup. "No way in hell. I've made that mistake before. Took me days to recover."

Toni shrugged and took a sip. "Hmm. It's starting to taste better."

"That means you've hit the sweet spot," Mav said before lowering his lips to Missy's neck. His date seemed to have gotten over whatever issue she'd had at the beginning of the night and was now practically humping his leg. Toni gave it five minutes before they found a dark corner to go at it.

"Shut up, Mav. Get out of here, your *date* looks like she needs some attention." Shell made a shooing motion with her hand

and somehow managed to make the word *date* sound like a disease.

Completely unoffended, Maverick threw back his head and laughed. "I think you might be right, Shell. We'll be over there." He pointed to the side of the building. "Shield your eyes, ladies. You especially, Toni. Don't want you to feel like Zach can't live up."

"What the fuck are you running your mouth about now?" Zach wrapped his arm around Toni from behind, cupping the ball of her shoulder in his warm, rough hand. He pulled her flush against him, his forearm banded across her chest.

Damn him. The press of his insanely toned body so snug against her was more intoxicating than Maverick's mystery booze.

A minute. Just one minute she'd allow herself to soak in the warm male vitality flowing from him. Then she'd push him away.

"Everything okay?" she asked.

The conversation between him and his president had been fraught with frowns, shaking heads, and clenched jaws.

"You worried about me, sweetheart?"

"What? No. Of course not. Just making conversation."

Zach laughed, and Shell snorted. "As much as I'd love to stay and see this play out, I've gotta run," she said.

"What?" Toni asked. "You just got here." She'd been looking forward to spending more time with Shell.

"I know. But I had to work my second job, and my sitter could only give me an extra hour tonight. We'll hang out soon, okay?"

Toni nodded and accepted a kiss on the cheek from Shell. She laid one on Zach as well before making her way toward the parking lot.

"She works too damn hard," Zach said sounding disgusted. "Fucking Copper. He needs to pull his head out of his ass and start something up with that woman. Then she wouldn't have to work herself to exhaustion."

Zach

Toni searched the crowd until she found the Handlers' president. Not surprisingly, his focus was one hundred percent on Shell as she walked out of the party. Toni couldn't decipher the expression on his face, but whatever his thoughts, they were deep. He looked tormented. Like a man who wanted something with every fiber of his being but knew it would never be his.

"Wanna head inside? It's getting chilly out here." Zach unwound his arm from her shoulders and grasped her hand, tugging her toward the clubhouse before she'd answered.

The night air might have been cold, but be it the alcohol, the warmth of the fire, or heat from the man beside her, Toni wasn't chilled in the least. The more time she spent with Zach's hand in hers or his body against her, the hotter she grew. If something didn't give soon, she might just combust.

"Let me ask you something," she said to distract both of them from the growing need. "How come you don't have a nickname?"

"Huh?" Zach stopped walking and faced her, still holding her hand.

"Yeah, you know…Maverick, Viper, Rocket, *Jigsaw*. Those clearly are nicknames. And you're just called Zach."

He cocked his head and snickered. "Zach is my road name, babe. Well, not really a road name, but a nickname given to me when I was in middle school. The club didn't bother to change it."

"Wait? Really? I always thought Zach was your real name." She searched the back recesses of her mind but couldn't come up with anything. "Well, you're a few years older than I am so we'd never really talked. And it's not like our parents were friends. I'm sure I knew at one point, but I don't remember now. Eek, that sounds horrible." Her face heated. What a selfish bitch he must think she was.

He laughed and tugged her near, slipping his arm around her waist. "My name is Jason."

Once again, the feel of him so close threatened to overtake her senses. Especially when she felt a stiff bulge bump her lower abdomen.

Ignore his hard cock. Ignore his hard, large cock.

"I, um…" She swallowed. "Why, Zach?"

He rolled his eyes and slid his hand from the base of her spine to the very top, where her blouse dipped and left her upper back bare. "My cousin gave me the name when I was about eleven." He traced his callused fingertips along the neck of her shirt making little goosebumps rise all over her back. She wanted to rip the thing off and beg him to touch her everywhere, but somehow, she found the strength to resist.

"H-how come?"

His gaze was intense on her face, absorbing her every reaction. She was pretty sure he could see straight through her mask to the needy woman hiding underneath.

"Because he said I looked like Zack Morris from *Saved by the Bell*."

And the spell was broken. "Oh, my God." Toni slapped a hand over her mouth in a vain attempt to muffle her laughter. It was so true. He looked exactly like an older and extra buff Zack Morris.

He scowled and gave her hair a gentle tug when her laughter only grew. "I loved it when I was a kid because all the chicks dug him." He winked. "When I got older, I fucking hated it. Being named after a freaking pretty boy teen? Fuckin' joke. Copper tried to help me out by spelling it with an H instead of a K. Then he tried to pretend the name came from some other Zach. But that never worked. Everyone in town already knew."

"I-I'm sor-sorry." She could barely speak she was laughing so hard. "It's not funny. It's really not. If it makes you feel any better, I had a big crush on him growing up." Trying to make the hilarity stop, she worked to turn the laugh into a cough. "I'll stop now."

And then she snorted. Her eyes flew wide and heat rushed to her face.

How mortifying.

Now it was Zach's turn to laugh, but his amusement turned lustful after a moment. His clear blue eyes darkened and he tightened his hold on her hair, tipping her head back until their mouths were mere inches apart. Against her stomach, his hardness seemed to grow. Something she wouldn't have thought possible seconds ago.

"Zach," she whispered. Her body was screaming at him to close the distance and claim her mouth while her mind fought for control and the strength to stop him.

Fought and lost.

He leaned in at the same time he drew her closer with the hand on her head. Fractions of a second before their mouths met, Toni's stomach flipped. And then he was on her. His large hand cupped the back of her head, holding her where he wanted while his mouth slanted over hers.

Warm, firm, insistent lips pressed against her, leaving hers no choice but to open to him. Somewhere in the distance a woman moaned in pleasure. Maverick's date no doubt about to be fucked against the outside of the building.

She should be horrified. Turned off. Disgusted.

Anything but turned on.

But apparently, she was some kind of perverted voyeur, because the knowledge that another couple was getting their rocks off just feet away ramped up her desire. Moaning into Zach's mouth, Toni grabbed fistfuls of the back of his shirt and hugged him close.

There was no mistaking his desire for her nestled against her stomach. As though she no longer had any control over her actions, she rubbed against his erection.

Restraint lost, Zach growled and the kiss turned ravenous. His free hand dropped to her ass, squeezing her cheek and trapping her as he ground his dick into her stomach. The feel of those strong fingers so close to her sex flooded her panties.

Her head spun with the combination of alcohol and Zach, a mind-altering pairing. It had been so long since she felt such strong desire. Since a man's hands on her body made her lose her senses.

And that's exactly what was happening. Because if she had any working brain cells left, she'd put an end to it before it went any farther.

He sank his teeth into her bottom lip and tugged it outward. As good as his hand on her ass and his mouth on hers felt, she needed more. She needed relief from the building pressure in her lower abdomen.

A shrill whistle sounded right before someone screamed. "Hey, Zach, don't be so fucking selfish. Why don't you let one of us have a go at her?"

It was as though someone doused her with a bucket of ice. Every sexy thought, erotic feeling, and need she'd been experiencing shut off in an instant as the comment knocked her back seven years. Memories she'd long buried assaulted her. Male grunts of satisfaction, laughter, and voices egging each other on. Multiple sets of hands on her. Humiliation. Helplessness.

Her stomach flipped again, this time turning sour.

Shit.

Shit.

She'd just done exactly what she'd vowed she'd never do again. She'd thought with her pussy instead of her mind. Gave in to lust and physical craving instead of holding out for more. And she'd done it with a man whose world too closely resembled that of her past.

"Let me go," she said as she wriggled in Zach's hold. She didn't sound strong. Her voice wavered and her legs shook from residual pleasure chemicals, unfulfilled desire, and unwanted memories.

Zach

Zach released her immediately, but it was too late. The blood rushing through her veins switched from lustful to furious.

"Step the fuck back, Zach." She threw up her hands and shoved him away. "You promised. Light and flirty was what you said."

"Ton—"

"No!" When he reached for her she stepped back. Her heart pounded so fast her head spun. "You talked me into coming. You said you wouldn't do this and I trusted you. Guess you're just another man who's a fucking liar. Stay the hell away from me, Zach."

After dropping that bomb, she fled toward the parking lot with Zach calling after her. It didn't matter how sorry he was, or what his excuse was. It didn't matter that the noise level of the party dropped to nonexistent as the club members stared after her.

She needed space. Needed to get away. To breathe.

"Of course," she muttered when she reached the parking lot. No car. Hands on her hips she scanned the lot. Shell was just disappearing into the driver's side of her crappy sedan.

"Shell!" she called, wobbling through the parking lot on three-inch heels.

A head of blonde curls popped back out. "Toni? What's wrong?"

By the time she reached the car she was panting and nauseated. "Please take me home."

Shell studied her for about five seconds before she said, "Of course, hon. Hop in."

"Thank you." Toni slipped in the passenger's seat and rested her head against the seat back.

"Wanna talk about it?" Shell asked.

"No."

"Okay. But you should know, he looks pissed."

Toni's eyes popped open. Visible in the side mirror, Zach stood, legs spread and hands on his hips near the entrance to the bar. The scowl on his face would have scared paint off the wall.

Pissed may have been too tame a word. Irate was more like it. This wasn't over. He wanted her. He wouldn't just let it die. She could feel it in her bones.

She just wasn't sure what to do about it.

CHAPTER THIRTEEN

"So, you aren't able to start until the middle of September?" Toni asked the woman sitting on the opposite side of her desk. Jazmine Walker was her name. She came with restaurant management experience, a sunny personality, and claimed to fall in love with Toni's diner on the spot.

"That's right. I'm locked into something until just after Labor Day. Then I'll be moving here from Arizona."

Toni's heart sank. She needed someone to begin August twentieth. School resumed the Tuesday after Labor Day and she planned to return to Chicago before the end of August so she had time to get back into guidance counselor mode. That meant her replacement would have to be trained starting around mid-August.

Not possible for Jazmine, who happened to be the best of the six people she'd interviewed that week. Still no manager and no buyer for the diner. Her commercial realtor had brought a developer by who was interested in the diner, only to inform Toni he planned to gut the building and turn it into a Starbucks.

Over Toni's dead body.

She realized she may have been having some inflated separation anxiety when it came to the restaurant. It shouldn't matter what the new owners planned to do. Once Toni left, she wouldn't be coming back. There wouldn't be anything left for her in Townsend. But with each passing day, she admittedly grew a little more attached to the diner, her staff, the mountains, and the townspeople.

But not to a sexy biker. No, she refused to allow herself to grow attached to him.

With a heavy sigh, she closed the notebook she'd written the answers to her questions in. "I'll be honest with you, Jazmine." She propped her elbows on the desk and rested her chin on her folded hands. "I want you to manage the diner. I think you'd be absolutely perfect for the position. But I need someone to start earlier, and I'm not sure how permanent the position even is, since I'm selling it."

Jazmine wrung her hands in her lap and nodded. "The second part is fine. I'm kind of going into nomad mode and just plan to stay as long as I'm needed. But unfortunately, my start date is not flexible, so while I'm sad to lose the opportunity, I completely understand if you have to pass me by."

Maybe Shell would be willing to run things for a few weeks. Just until Jazmine could get there. Shell didn't want the job for the long term—Toni had actually offered it to her before interviewing anyone—but maybe she'd be willing for a short time.

"I'd like to think about it for a bit, see if I can figure a few things out. Would that work for you?"

Jazmine's face lit up. She was a few years older than Toni, closing in on thirty, and had dark brown hair in the cutest pixie cut. "That would definitely work for me." She rose and extended her hand. "Thank you so much for your time, Toni. I look forward to hearing from you."

Toni shook her hand and started to stand.

"Don't get up. I can show myself out."

"Sounds good. Have a safe trip back to Arizona."

After the door to her office closed behind Jazmine, Toni slouched in her chair and sighed. The diner would be closing in the next hour, and it would be safe for her to leave the office she'd admittedly been hiding in for the past three days.

Zach

Hiding like the chicken shit she was.

Hiding because Zach had eaten at the diner each of those days.

And Toni was avoiding him with a capital A. Still a mess of mixed emotions, embarrassment, desire, anger, shame, she'd done everything in her power to escape a run in with Zach. Peeking out her windows before she left the house to make sure he wasn't outside. Skipping her nightly sunset. Cowering in her office from the moment he entered the diner until she was sure the coast was clear.

What the hell was wrong with her?

She wasn't a coward.

She was a grown woman. A business owner and home owner. A responsible and respected member of the community. Why the hell was she hiding? Because she regretted one kiss? Because it brought her back to a time she'd rather never think about again?

Pathetic.

Her past was just that, *her* past. It was a part of her and, somehow, she had to be able to think about it without freaking out again.

Disgusted with her spinelessness, Toni stomped to the door of her office. After a fortifying breath and a quick mental pep talk, she emerged and headed behind the counter.

Much of the crowd had cleared, leaving behind three booths full of muscled bikers. Shell stood behind the counter restocking juice glasses while sneaking longing looks at Copper. Toni joined her and picked up a rag, wiping down the spot in front of her.

A few minutes passed in silence before Shell turned to her. "And here we are pretending to work while stealing glances at men we shouldn't want or can't have. Not very feminist of us."

"Tell me about it." Toni harrumphed. "At least you haven't been hiding in your office like a child for days."

"I noticed your face hasn't been around much."

"Yeah. To be honest, I'm surprised he's left me alone this long. I figured he'd have found me and chewed me out by now. I think I really pissed him off."

Shell's gaze shifted from Copper to Zach and back again. "I don't think he's mad. Maybe at himself. He's asked me how you were doing a few times. Seemed genuinely concerned. Not angry."

Mad at himself.

Probably not as mad as she was at herself. Despite her reaction at the party, she wasn't really upset with him at all. All of the anger was directed at herself. For being too weak to stick to her guns. For allowing herself to fall under the spell of another sexy man.

"Don't look now, but I think we've been spotted." Shell jerked her chin in the direction of Zach's table. "I'll give you two a minute." She squeezed Toni's hand. "Talk to him. He's not a bad guy."

"Hey," Zach said, coming to a stop on the other side of the counter.

"Hi." Suddenly, she felt beyond foolish for the way she'd been dodging him. "I'm sorry."

He frowned. "Thought I was the one who fucked up here."

"No." Toni shook her head. "Well maybe a little. But it's more my own stuff."

He looked good in low slung jeans, a muscle shirt, and his club leathers. Arm porn was a real thing and Zach had it going on in spades. Also, chest porn and ab porn. Even hair porn.

"I've got something for you. Maybe once you see it we can go back to the way things were. Where I shamelessly flirt with you and try to entice you into my bed and you shut me down on all fronts."

Toni chuckled. What a waste of three days. Had she not been such a coward, they could have moved past the screw-up and continued their friendship. A friendship she'd really missed. "Guess that depends what it is."

Zach

"Here." He pulled his phone from his pocket and unlocked the screen. "Scroll forward." After he handed over the phone he rested his forearms on the counter and watched her.

On the screen was a gorgeous sunset. Streaks of color surrounding a giant orange orb sinking behind a row of trees.

Trees she recognized.

Trees that were in the direct line of sight of her porch.

She scrolled to the next picture only to find another beautiful sunset. Then another. "What is this?" she asked, her voice hoarse.

"You missed three sunsets because of me." He shrugged and gave her a smile that was almost bashful. "I know how much you like them, so I made sure to come home and capture them each evening."

Her throat thickened and tears sprang to her eyes. Why? Why did the one man she had to resist happen to be the sweetest outlaw to ever live? "Thank you," she croaked.

"It was nothing." He winked. "I do it for all the ladies."

With a chuckle she handed him back his phone. It wasn't nothing. It was a whole lot to her.

"I'm hoping you'll be out there to see it in person tonight."

"I think I will."

"Good." He rapped his scarred knuckles on the countertop. "Maybe I'll see you there." He leaned forward and dropped his voice to a whisper. "And while I still fully plan to show you everything you were missing with the suit, I promise I will not touch you again until you beg me to."

Oh God. That meant he'd be working on making her beg.

Devious man.

"Zach." The horror in Jigsaw's tone had Zach's brow furrowing before he turned toward the booth where his club brothers were finishing their meals.

"What's wrong?"

Jigsaw didn't answer. Just motioned for Zach to join them. Worry was clear across his features. Zach turned back to her and nodded before speed walking to the booth. After thirty seconds of murmured conversation, Zach's face morphed into one of devastation while Copper's hardened to stone cold fury.

Three booths worth of bikers flew out the door and mounted their bikes. The roar of ten bikes firing up simultaneously was deafening. Worry coursed through her and she wanted to smack herself. She was already in too deep if she was worrying about the man. What the hell was she thinking, befriending an outlaw?

Shell rushed out of the kitchen. "What's going on?" she asked, wide-eyed.

Toni shook her head. "I don't know. But I don't think it's good."

With a muttered curse, Shell gripped her hand and squeezed tight. Something was very wrong. She could feel it in her gut. Toni clutched Shell's hand like a lifeline as the two women watched a trail of bikes tear out of the parking lot, each fretting over a man they shouldn't want or couldn't have.

CHAPTER FOURTEEN

Zach, Copper, and Rocket burst through the double doors leading to the bustling Emergency Department of the University of Tennessee Medical Center. Copper had sent the rest of the members back to the clubhouse to lock it down until the threat was identified and neutralized. Ol' ladies, club girls, everyone would be holed up at the clubhouse until further notice.

Each second of the forty-five-minute ride to the hospital felt like slow torture. Like Zach was being dragged along the blacktop behind Copper's bike instead of riding hot on his prez's heels.

UTMC wasn't the closest hospital. No, that would be Blount Memorial Hospital, so the fact that Little Jack had been airlifted to UTMC could only mean one thing; he was in a bad fuckin' way. LJ was a beast of man who worked out in Zach's gym daily. Hell, the prospect even coached two boxers who were quickly making names for themselves.

Whatever had taken him down was big and bad. And it would be the beginning of the shitstorm from hell for whoever attacked him.

"Looking for Jack Ulrich, darlin'," Copper said to the gaping receptionist. "He was brought in by chopper over an hour ago." He flashed her a dazzling grin that didn't meet his stormy eyes.

"Um, sure. Let me just, ah…" The middle-aged receptionist's fingers trembled as she fumbled them over her keyboard, having to backspace at least three times before entering the name correctly.

Somehow, Copper managed to remain calm and cool, still flashing her that I'm-not-as-dangerous-as-I-look smile. Which was true. He wasn't as dangerous as he looked.

He was ten times more dangerous.

As the seconds ticked by, Zach blew out a breath and stared at the ceiling. Anything to distract himself from the urge to vault over the desk and shake the woman until she moved faster. One of the many reasons Copper was the solid leader he was, while Zach never stood a chance at the position. Copper could be having his toenails yanked out and no one would know it by his facial expression.

"Room eight, it's down the hall on the le—"

The three of them stormed down the hall boots pounding on the white tile floor. "Here," Zach said, skidding to a stop outside a room with an *eight* placard sticking out from the door frame. He shouldered the door open and came to a dead stop.

"Fuck me hard," Rocket swore under his breath.

Zach couldn't have said it better himself. The supine man dwarfing the small hospital bed barely resembled the prospect Zach had seen almost every day for the past nine months. His right arm was propped on pillows and wrapped in what appeared to be miles of ace bandages. On the same side, his leg was splinted and elevated.

Then there was his face. The face Shell had once described as a *baby face* was varying shades of purple with one eye swollen so bad it looked like a near black bubble. Across his hairline, a jagged wound that had been stitched was visible against the light brown hair.

And those were the injuries they could see on first glance. Zach had no doubt under his hospital gown his torso would be a mess of painful bruising and probably broken ribs.

Copper walked to the head of the bed and gripped LJ's uninjured hand. "Hey, brother, can you hear me?"

Zach

Zach moved to his other side, near his head. He needed to hear everything that was said. The motherfuckers who did this had no idea the hell they were about to have rain down on them.

"I'm sorry, Prez," LJ whispered through lips so swollen they didn't move when he spoke.

Both Zach and Copper leaned closer. "You did good, prospect. Viper told us they didn't get the money."

LJ had been on a run for Zach, collecting an almost eighty grand repayment owed by one of the very few clients who always paid on time. When Viper called Copper to let him know what happened, he'd mentioned all the money was still at the scene. Something must have spooked whoever went after LJ enough to make them flee without the cash.

"Not after—" LJ shook his head. "Water," he rasped out.

"Here, man." Zach snatched a paper cup off the bedside table and held the straw to LJ's abused lips while Copper raised the head of his bed. It took a few tries for him to capture the straw, but after he finally caught it, he swallowed greedily.

"Thanks," LJ said, his voice a smidge stronger. "They weren't after the money." He closed his puffy eye and shook his head. "Mav." His voice choked up and Zach wouldn't have believed it was possible, but LJ sounded near tears.

Copper frowned. "What about Mav?"

"I'm sorry. I fought like hell, but there were four of them. And they had crowbars. I didn't stand a chance." He sounded tortured, riddled with guilt and a tear leaked out the corner of one distended eye.

"What about Mav?" Copper asked, steel in his tone this time.

"They took him."

Ice slid through Zach's veins as the horror of that statement registered. "Mav was with you?" He was supposed to be on a job, installing a system of security cameras for an eccentric millionaire who owned a house high in the mountains where cell reception was hard to come by. It was the only reason Zach hadn't tried to contact him.

"What the fuck do you mean they took him?" Copper growled.

"He got done early. Saw me riding and tagged along. Dragons —oh fuck." He inhaled a sharp breath and cringed. "Sorry. Five fuckin' cracked ribs." After a cough and another grimace, he continued. "Three of them grabbed Mav. Tossed him in a van. Other four teamed up on me."

"You sure it was the Gray Dragons?"

He nodded and his "yes" was full of agony. "Stupid fucking red tattoo on their hands."

"You had anything for pain?" Copper asked.

"Nah," LJ said. "Wanted to talk to you first."

"You did good, LJ." Copper pushed the nurse button on the side of LJ's bed. "We'll have them bring you something." When Copper raised his head, his gaze bore into Zach's.

Zach imagined the murderous fury in Copper's eyes matched his own. "Go," Copper said. "Take Rocket. I want you at the clubhouse at eight tonight."

Zach nodded and placed a hand on LJ's shoulder before making for the door. Rocket was ending a phone call he'd made as soon as LJ mentioned the Dragons. "Let's go," Zach said.

The two men marched down the hall on a deadly mission. "What do we know about where they might take him?"

"Nothing," Rocket said in his typical limited chatter.

"Shit. You've had eyes on their headquarters, haven't you?"

Rocket nodded.

"What have you been seeing?" In times like this, talking to Rocket could frustrate a man to violence.

"Nothin'. Ain't been around much." Rocket shook his head.

Shit. Mav had mentioned the same thing yesterday. That something wonky was going on with the Dragons. They'd all but abandoned their headquarters. No one coming or going for days.

What the hell was going on?

The club messed up. Hell, Zach messed up. It was his job to protect his club from outside threats. They'd gotten complacent, left the Gray Dragons alone without any fear of the Handlers. In his defense, there had never been any indication, until recently, that the Dragons might be looking to up their game.

Christ, he'd sent LJ to make the pickup in his place so he could go flirt with Toni at the diner. *Fuck!* Where the hell were his priorities? Pussy was pussy and while fun, should never be a priority over his brothers. Look what happened when he took his eye off the game. One of his brothers was beaten unconscious and another kidnapped.

He needed to stay away from Toni. She was fucking with his head and his concentration.

The club's mistake had been not flexing their muscles when Shark took over the gang a year ago. Rumors had been circulating about the man for ages. Sick shit he did to his girls. Even sicker shit he did to guys looking to leave the gang. Still, they hadn't seen him for the predator he was turning out to be.

Big fucking mistake.

Because apparently, he was a shark in more than just name.

And now Mav was his prisoner.

"Shit!" Zach yelled when he reached the bikes. "Fuck!" He slammed his fists down on the trunk of a car parked next to him. Pain shot up his forearms and he welcomed the sharp jolt. Again and again, he pounded them into the denting metal. The shrill piercing of a car alarm blared through the quiet parking lot.

"Zach!" Rocket's voice didn't pull him from his rage. "Knock it the fuck off, brother." A muscled arm banded across his chest and yanked him away from his punching bag. "You ain't gonna be able to do shit for Mav if you're locked up for the night."

Hearing the long string of words from his typically silent friend was enough to snap Zach out of it and made him see past the rage clouding his vision. Rocket kept an arm around him and dragged Zach back ten feet.

Zach held out his hands. "I'm cool," he said. "I'm cool." He'd fake it, anyway, because inside he was anything but.

With a jerky nod, Rocket released him. "How do you want to play this?"

Zach propped his hands on his head and stared at the hospital building. "I can't just sit around and wait until Shark contacts us with whatever the fuck he wants in exchange for Mav."

"You sure he wants something?"

It was a chilling question. "I hope so." If Shark didn't want anything, if he took Mav simply because he wanted to, then Mav was in the worst kind of shit. Shark would torture him then kill him. Just to fuck with the Handlers. Just because he could.

Zach wasn't willing to give up on his friend like that, so they'd operate under the assumption that Shark wanted something and was willing to snatch Mav for ransom.

Throwing his leg over his bike and dropping his sunglasses down over his eyes, Zach said, "Let's hit the streets. Start talking to people. Someone's bound to know where the fuck they might have taken Mav besides their headquarters." After receiving a nod of agreement from Rocket, he revved the engine and shot out of the lot.

On the way back, he'd call Viper and have him hand out jobs. They needed all hands on deck to scour the dregs of Tennessee in search of information.

Mav would be tortured. There were no two ways around it. Somehow, Zach would have to wrap his mind around that conclusion and come to terms with it or he'd be useless to his club. Even though he wasn't the biggest fucker in the club, Mav was strong, mentally and physically. He also had a smart mouth and would probably make things worse for himself by giving his captors lip.

But he'd survive.

And Zach would do whatever the fuck it took to get him out of there.

Zach

Six hours later, Zach and the rest of the Hell's Handlers had spoken to every lowlife, criminal, junkie, and general asshole in a fifty-mile radius.

And they were no further along than they'd been when the day started.

All they heard was that the Dragons hadn't been using their headquarters for the past week. But they'd already known that. No one had any clue if the gang owned any other property, and that fact had Zach's gut screaming. Someone knew something. Of that he was sure, but they'd yet to find motivation big enough to get someone to rat on Shark.

Zach had even brought Louie out a few times. If a few well-placed whacks with a solid wood bat wasn't enough to loosen some tongues, Shark's threats must be severe. They'd get information out of somebody at some point; it was just a matter of picking the weakest link and finding out exactly what would make them cave.

Probably just what Shark did.

A sobering thought, but one Zach didn't have time to dwell on, because every second wasted was another second Mav was suffering.

"So we've got jack shit?" Copper slammed a bottle of Johnnie Walker down before bracing his hands on the table. He loomed over the group, looking ready to tear the clubhouse apart with his bare hands. A feeling Zach was familiar with.

The question was for Zach, but suddenly he found himself unable to answer. Fear for Mav, fury over his ineffectiveness, and guilt for not keeping the club and his friends safe clogged his throat. He shook his head, unable to meet Copper's gaze.

It was at that moment, Zach's phone chirped in his pocket. Under normal circumstances, Copper would castrate any man who whipped out his phone during a meeting. Instead, he met Zach's gaze and nodded.

A lead brick settled in Zach's stomach as he drew out the phone. It was from Shark. He knew it without even looking, as sure as he knew he wanted to fuck Toni. Christ, it seemed like years ago he'd been angling to get in her pants. In reality a few short hours had shifted all his priorities. What he wouldn't give to have her rejection be his biggest setback again.

Swallowing down the ice-cold dread, Zach unlocked his phone to find an image of his best friend staring back at him. He couldn't help the wildly inappropriate snort of laughter that flew from him.

Mav was in bad shape as predicted. Two black eyes. Blood running from both his nose and mouth. Wrists and ankles tied to a chair. He was slumped over, as if it was too painful or required too much energy to sit straight.

But in typical Mav fashion, he had a big fuck you for the assholes who held him. A smirk as big as the Smoky Mountains themselves was on his face. Each fist was curled except for two middle fingers. They pointed toward the ground, since his forearms were bound to the chair and he couldn't twist his arms for a proper gesture, but he still got the point across. And the best part was, the lackey of Shark's that sent the photo hadn't noticed. Otherwise, they'd never have sent it.

It was Maverick's clever way of letting Zach know that while he was down, he was not out.

Nothing accompanied the photo. No ransom requests. No demands. Nothing. More and more this was looking like nothing more than a power play. Shark letting the Handlers know he could get at them whenever he wanted and there wasn't a damn thing they could do about it.

Zach held the photo up for Copper to see.

His president's face hardened and he bowed his head for a moment before saying, "Fuck."

The weight of that word crashed down upon Zach like a sledgehammer. Copper was never without an idea. Never without confidence. Never defeated. He tried to inhale, but it felt as if a heavy rubber band had wound itself around his chest.

Zach

With each passing second, it grew tighter and tighter until he couldn't breathe.

Zach shoved back from the table and stumbled out of the meeting room. As he lurched past the bar, two of the Honeys tried to get his attention. He wasn't even tempted, but normally he'd at least have said hello and let them down easy. Now, he just didn't give a shit.

"Get the fuck out of my way," he barked at Becky, who dropped her jaw and scurried behind the bar.

He didn't care who he pissed off. All he knew was he needed out of the clubhouse. He needed oxygen.

Shoving through the door, he stumbled out into the quiet night. A cool breeze washed over him, loosening the grip of the rubber band and allowing him to draw in a breath.

"Fuck!" he yelled when he had enough air.

The panic that had been rushing through his system transformed into an anger so great he could think of nothing but wreaking havoc on whatever was near.

Balling his fists, he rammed them into the nearest tree again and again with no regard to the damage he was causing himself. The skin over his knuckles split and tore, but he welcomed the pain. It was nothing compared to what was in store for Maverick, and the sting only fueled his anger and need for blood.

When all his energy was spent, he was sweating and gasping for breath. He propped himself against the defeated tree and tried to get his head straight.

He had no idea how long he stood there before Copper walked up, liquor in hand.

"Better?" Copper asked, holding the bottle out.

Zach accepted the bottle and tipped it to his lips. After a good eight second guzzle, he handed it back to his prez. Blood ran in streams from his hands, coasting over the bottle and dripping to the grassy ground.

Copper wouldn't give a shit. If there was ever a man not afraid of a little blood, it was Copper.

"Better."

"I'm gonna say this one fucking time, Zach, so listen the fuck up." Copper took a long drink. "I didn't appoint you enforcer because I thought you'd be able to anticipate every problem that would come our way. I didn't give you the position because I thought you would somehow know shit the rest of us didn't." He passed off the bottle then lit a cigarette. "I made you enforcer because this club is in your blood and you will rain holy hell down on anyone who fucks with it."

That was the damn truth.

"So stop beating the fuck out of my trees and yourself because of some misplaced guilt. Save your fury for Shark."

After another long drink, Zach tried to return the bottle, but Copper waved it away. "Finish it," he said. The orange tip of his cigarette glowed as he returned it to his mouth.

"You know, Cop, Shell was at the diner when we tore out of there this morning."

Copper grunted. "Feels like years ago."

Zach swallowed the last eighth of the bottle in two large gulps. "She's gonna be worried. Probably heard something about Mav by now. You should swing on by. Might want to warn her to be vigilant."

"Yeah," Copper said as he flicked ash off the end of his cigarette. He spoke as though it was no big deal. As though he wasn't in love with the woman he refused to take. And as though it didn't break her heart to be in the same room as him. "Both she and Toni are gonna be wondering why we had prospects tail them home."

"She's gonna get on your ass if you show up smelling like a tobacco factory."

The cigarette was midway to Copper's mouth. "What are you my mother now, Zach?" He tossed the thing to the grass and ground it under his size thirteen heel before walking halfway

Zach

back inside. "Have Jig give you a ride home. You drank half that bottle."

"I'll have Jig drive me around and search a little longer."

Copper nodded. "Make sure you get some rest at some point, brother. You're no good to Mav if you can't function."

Alone again, Zach stared up at the starry sky. Heading home was the best thing. He was fried, half drunk, and not thinking clearly. He could hit it hard again in the morning. But he couldn't do it. Not with Mav out there enduring fuck knew what. He'd give it another hour or two.

For a moment, he let himself wonder what it would be like to have a woman in his life for more than sex. Might be kind of nice after the day he'd had. To go home to a warm, soft woman he could lose himself in. A woman who'd let him use her body to drown out the horrors of the day.

Toni's face came to mind. And Toni's body came to mind.

It was then he recalled telling Toni he'd meet her on her porch to watch the sunset.

Shit. She was going to be pissed he bailed on her. Not that anything about the day was normal, but she wouldn't appreciate it.

Still, he couldn't help but indulge in the fantasy of having her waiting at home warm, wet, and his for the taking.

CHAPTER FIFTEEN

Drinking a cup of coffee at midnight was always a foolish idea, but Toni was exhausted to the point of blurry vision. And she needed not to be.

No matter what time he rolled in, she planned to be awake when Zach returned home. Something had transpired earlier in the day, something that scared the fuck out of a tough group of men who were usually the ones scaring the fuck out of others.

When Zach had been a no show around the time the sun was setting her concern turned to full-on worry. Even though she didn't have any right to inquire about Zach's business, she'd called Shell in the hopes of at least learning if he was okay.

All her friend had been able to do was ratchet the worry up another notch with her own anxiety. Both of them had bikers follow them home from the diner. Then, Copper had called Shell and told her to stay put with Beth until she heard from him again. The call had been hours ago.

So that left Toni sitting outside in the rocking chair for three hours with her mug of coffee, in a slightly stalkerish manner. The porch lights were off in the hopes that Zach wouldn't notice her watching out for him. She just needed to know when he arrived home and that he was safe.

And every one of those one hundred and eighty-four minutes was spent trying to think about anything other than why she cared so much. Cared to the point she couldn't stop her knee

Zach

from bouncing and her stomach from churning with apprehension.

Twenty minutes and a fresh cup of coffee later, headlights popped up in the distance. A caravan of two single lights followed by a double traveled down the road toward her. Two bikes and a car. Toni straightened as they drew near and slowed.

One of the bikes turned into Zach's driveway while an SUV and the other motorcycle rode the extra few feet to her property. Before her mind had a chance to process what was happening, she shot to her feet and started down the walkway toward the vehicles.

A man climbed off the bike and removed his helmet. As he came into clearer view, Toni's steps faltered. She'd assumed it would be Zach. But it wasn't. It was the really severe, unsmiling man who hadn't spoken but two words to her when Zach introduced them at the bonfire. Rocket, if she recalled correctly.

"Is Zach okay?" she asked. No point in social pleasantries. She wanted one thing from the man in front of her and it was to learn about Zach.

"In the car." Rocket jerked a thumb in the direction of the car.

Zach sat in the passenger seat, staring out the window with a vacant expression.

"That didn't answer my question." The temperature had dropped over the past few hours, and Toni now regretted the denim shorts and thin T-shirt that read *Sunny with a Chance of Wine*. She crossed her arms over her chest feeling somewhat naked under Rocket's assessing gaze.

Instead of talking, he focused on observing and seemed to see so much.

"Shit day," he said.

Guess that was all she was gonna get out of Rocket. Whoever was in the driver's seat spoke to Zach and he blinked as if just realizing the car was no longer in motion. With a nod for the driver, he opened the door and climbed out, stumbling before he got his footing.

"Is he drunk?" she asked without taking her eyes off the man whose blue eyes were devoid of their usual verve for life.

"Nah, not really. Just exhausted. He needs to sleep. He won't hurt you."

"What? No. I wasn't worried about that. I know he won't. I'm just concerned for him."

As Zach closed the distance between them, Toni gasped and rushed forward. "What the hell happened to your hands?" She lifted one large hand and stared in horror at the ravaged knuckles. The skin resembled meat fresh out of a grinder.

"Picked the wrong opponent." His voice was so flat, so dead, a prickle of fear coasted up her spine. This was a man in pain. Suffering. "Way too tall and hard for me to beat."

Her face screwed up and she looked to Rocket. What on earth was Zach talking about?

"Tree," was all he said.

A tree? Zach had attacked a tree? In all the time she spent with him, she'd never seen him lose his cool. Sure, he was the enforcer for an MC, so she was well aware he had a capacity for violence, but she always imagined it was meticulous, calculated. Pounding a tree until he decimated his knuckles was an act based purely on out of control emotion.

Whatever happened that day had devastated him. He needed care, softness, and she could give that to him. She could put her reservations about men like him on hold for one night to care for him.

"Come on inside," she said.

He stared at her for a moment, then nodded and trudged toward the house.

With a heavy heart, Toni gave Rocket a sad smile. "Thanks for bringing him here."

He scratched at the dark stubble covering his square jaw. "Take good care of my boy. Be gentle with him."

His message seemed to have a deeper meaning than just being gentle as she doctored his wounds, but she wasn't in the mood

Zach

to decipher riddles. As it was, those were more words than he'd strung together in the two times she'd met him.

"Will do."

Without further discussion, he returned to his bike and followed the car down the drive. The second biker must have been returning Zach's bike because he deposited the motorcycle in Zach's garage then took his place in the passenger's seat of the car. Probably not the easiest to ride a motorcycle with hands that were falling apart.

Face expressionless, he waited for her on the porch. "Didn't want to bleed all over your door," he said raising his bloody right hand as though she'd forgotten.

"No worries. I'll get the door." When she reached the top of the three steps leading to the house, she grabbed her recently poured mug of coffee. The porcelain was still warm to the touch, so the coffee would be as well.

"Here," she said taking extra care with him as she placed the cup in his hand. "Drink it. It will help sober you the rest of the way up. Hope you like it sweet."

She opened the door and moved to let him pass. Once he was in her home, she wrapped an arm around his waist and guided him to the bathroom. "Sit." She pointed to the closed toilet lid.

Listening to her for once, he sat. "Ugh, shit." He spat a sip of coffee back into the mug. "That's fuckin' sweet."

Her lips quirked. "I warned you. Drink it anyway."

He grunted then sipped again, swallowing this time.

While he choked down the coffee, Toni rummaged through the cabinet under her bathroom sink for first aid supplies. There wasn't much, but at least she found some antibiotic cream and bandages. She also grabbed a wash cloth and an empty basin.

Zach's gaze never strayed from her, heating her skin with its intensity. So many thoughts swirled through her head. The situation was so far out of her normal, she had no idea how to proceed. Did she ask him what happened? Should she play it off and act as normal as possible? How the hell was someone supposed to know what to do when a sexy outlaw biker ended up in their bathroom injured and distraught in the middle of the night? Why was there no precedent for that?

Oh, because things like that never happened.

After she'd filled the basin with warm, soapy water, she placed it on the countertop next to the sink. Taking the wet cloth, she moved over to Zach. Without her asking, he widened his legs and let her move in close.

The second she stepped between his spread thighs, she realized her mistake. He may have been injured, and his head may have been fucked up at the moment, but he was no less potent. In fact, his slightly vulnerable state only drew her more. Playing on every caring, nurturing, feminine instinct she possessed.

And then there was the heat; his body radiated it. And the scent; woodsy, fresh, masculine. And of course, the arms; muscled, inked, and so close they could wrap around her with ease. But worst of all was the fact that his head was now breast-height. If he wanted, all he had to do was lean forward and capture her aching nipple in his mouth. Her thin T-shirt and even thinner lace bra did nothing to hide the effect he was having on her.

She could ignore the pull to him. The pheromones. The chemistry. The need. Hell, she'd been ignoring those things for years. This was no different.

Except it was. Everything about this was different because he wasn't trying to get in her pants. He wasn't flirting, joking, flashing her that panty-melting grin. He was just himself. Completely open and at her mercy.

Straightening her spine, she did her best to pretend she wasn't more turned on in that moment than she'd ever been with Chris or even her boyfriend before him. She lifted one of Zach's ragged hands and inspected it from all angles. Geez, it was a mess. "I don't want to hurt you."

Zach

He shrugged. "It's inevitable. And it needs to be cleaned. Don't worry about it."

She turned the hand over until the palm was facing up and began to scrub the dried blood off the intact skin. With just a few swipes, the wash cloth was red and needing to be rinsed. She submerged it and couldn't help but shudder as the water in the basin grew pink.

Despite the mangled knuckles, his hands felt as strong as they ever did. Once his palm was clean, Toni had the insane urge to lift the hand and hold his palm to her aching breast. Instead, she bent forward and pressed a kiss to the clean skin.

Zach's sharp inhale had her lifting her head until their gazes me. They stared at each other, the connection so strong she couldn't break it.

Finally, Zach cleared his throat, popping the bubble of intimacy. "Thanks for this," he said.

"It's nothing." She blinked, then resumed her task. When all of the unmarred skin on both hands was free of dried blood, she had no choice but to move to the wounds.

As gently as she possibly could, she pressed the wet cloth to the torn knuckles. A sharp hiss shot out of Zach's mouth and made her jump. "I'm sorry," she said pulling back. The thought of causing him further pain made her want to weep.

"It's fine. Just finish it." No longer detached, his voice held the pain he couldn't mask.

She got back to work and washed the cuts quickly. When she was satisfied both hands were clean, she dabbed on the antibiotic cream then wrapped the bandages around his battered knuckles. Thankfully, it was just the knuckles, the rest of his hands and fingers were intact.

"There," she said tossing an extra bandage in the sink. "I think that will hold."

"Thanks."

That would have been the perfect time to step back. To put some space between them and remind herself of the reasons she didn't jump into bed with bad boy bikers. Instead, she said, "If you want to talk abo—"

He gripped her hips in each of his wrapped hands, hauling her even closer as he dropped his head to her stomach.

For about thirty seconds, she stood statue still, frozen with shock. Toni's mouth opened and closed as she fought for words and her arms hovered in the air. Slowly, she lowered her arms until one hand was on Zach's head and the other dangled limply at her side. The golden strands of his hair were so soft, she couldn't help but sift her fingers through them.

He groaned and slid his hands from her hips, around back until he gripped her upper thighs. Or really, the lower curve of her ass. Under her shorts. Skin on skin.

And even though the bulky bandages prevented her from feeling the full effect of his hands on her, it was no less potent. No less stimulating.

Heat shot to her core, dampening her panties and making her knees wobble.

This was not good. Well it *felt* really good. But it was bad. So, so bad. Because she was about five seconds away from begging him to rip off her shorts and put an end to years of unsatisfying sex.

Then, it happened again. The flash of remembrance. Humiliation, loss of control, panic. All because she fell for the wrong man. Just as she was coming to her senses and was about to step out of his hold, Zach spoke.

"Maverick is missing."

It was as though someone slammed on the brake while going eighty miles an hour. The screech of skidding tires sounded in her brain, bringing all other thoughts to a halt. "Missing? What do you mean, missing?"

"They took him." His voice was tortured.

"Who took him?" Who in the world would be stupid enough to *take* an outlaw biker? How was that even possible? It wasn't like they could lure Maverick into the back of a van with the promise of candy.

Zach shook his head, rocking it back and forth across her stomach. He tightened his grip on her ass as though afraid she'd leave. While she waited for him to continue, she stroked through his hair, hopefully bringing some sort of comfort with her touch.

"An evil motherfucker. Beat the fuck out of one of our prospects and had a couple guys snatch Mav. We have no clue where he is." Zach choked on what sounded like a sob. "It's my job to protect the club and my brothers from outside threats. I fucking failed Mav."

"No." She tugged on his head until he lifted it and met her gaze. "No, baby, you did not fail him." *Shit.* Why did she call him that? His vulnerability was going to be her greatest downfall. "I'm guessing you spent the entire day working your ass off trying to find him?"

He nodded.

"That right there proves you didn't fail him. We may not have known each other long, but I know you well enough to know you'll do everything in your power to find him and bring him home. And you will find him. I have complete faith in you."

"But what will they do to him before I get there?"

The anguish in his voice nearly knocked her to her knees. If she could take it away, bandage it as she'd done his hands, she would in a heartbeat. A man as powerful and strong as Zach should never feel such anguish. But this was an internal wound, so there was nothing she could do.

Except…

As his gaze bore into hers, the temperature in the bathroom seemed to rise and the air thickened. He flexed his fingers against the backs of her thighs and she whimpered. Those hands would be her undoing. Strong, rough, capable; they could bring both pleasure and pain in equal measures.

"Zach," she whispered as he nuzzled the side of her cloth covered breast with his nose. "This is a b-bad idea."

He pressed an open-mouthed kiss to the valley between her breasts. The wet warmth of his mouth had her imagining how amazing it would feel just a couple of inches to the left. Or right.

She needed to stop him. Fist his hair harder and pull his mouth off her.

"Probably," he whispered, sliding one hand up to the back of her neck. "But I don't give a fuck." He applied pressure until she bent her head forward. Their mouths were a mere breath apart when he whispered, "I need you tonight, Toni."

I need you tonight.

Had there ever been a woman alive able to resist that plea? Need implied so much more than want. It told her that she was vital to him. That he couldn't make it through the night without her.

And so, as she stared into the depths of his ocean blue eyes, she had a choice to make. Take the safe road she'd been traveling on for years or jump into the abyss that promised pleasure but also had the ability to crush her into dust.

She inhaled, ignored the warning voice in her head, and... jumped.

CHAPTER SIXTEEN

"Fucking finally," Zach whispered, seconds before Toni's mouth met his. He wasn't kidding when he said he needed her. Needed to lose himself in something good to erase the filth of the day.

Maybe it was wrong to use her for his selfish needs, but he'd been dreaming about the feel and taste of her pussy for weeks. And she was finally offering herself up on a silver platter. No matter the fallout, he wasn't stupid enough to turn her away.

He dove right into the kiss, stroking his tongue into her mouth and giving her his best. She moaned and swayed so he yanked her down into his right leg. With her hand still gripping his hair, she shifted around as best as possible and awkwardly straddled him. When her sex landed against his iron-hard cock, they both groaned.

Even through her shorts, she was so hot she nearly burned him. He hooked an arm around her lower back and held her snug against him as he ground his erection into her. In response, she deepened the kiss and tightened her hold on his hair to the point of painful.

He knew it. She would be wild and wanton in bed. Maybe not at first. He might need to lure it out of her, but an uninhibited sexual woman was there just waiting to burst free. And he was more than man enough to turn her into a sex junkie. His sex junkie.

"More, baby?" he asked. If she said no now, he'd be in for a hell of a shitty night. And that was the last thing he wanted following the shitty day. No, he wanted to forget for a few hours. Until the morning when he had to descend right back into hell.

"More, yes. Everything," she said, flexing her hips over his length.

That was all he needed to hear. Zach stood, chuckling when Toni yelped and wrapped her legs around his waist, clinging for dear life. Like he would ever let her fall.

"I got you, baby," he said as he backed her against the wall. He kissed her again, until the need for more of her grew painful. If he didn't free his erection in the next ten seconds he'd be in danger of permanent damage. Though he hated to, he pulled his mouth away. "Slide down."

Toni uncurled her legs and let them drop to the floor. Zach's hands immediately went to the button on her denim shorts. "Fuck," he grumbled as the bandages got in the way of a quick clothing removal.

Even though it was at his expense, Toni's giggle was music to his ears. His head was so fucked, he was afraid he'd be too rough, or not be as attentive to her needs as he otherwise would be. Ladies first. Always his policy. Hearing her laugh let him know she was enjoying herself.

"Stop, stop, stop," she said, swatting his fumbling hands away. "I got this." With a smirk that could only be described as sinful, she popped the button on her shorts open. Then, she lowered the zipper, one torturous tooth at a time.

"Toni," Zach growled. "Playin' with fire, babe."

"Then burn me, Zach," she said as she reached the end of the zipper and shimmied the shorts down her smooth, tanned legs.

Zach groaned at the sight of her lower half clad in nothing but a lacy blue thong. His balls ached with the need for release. "Get my pants off."

Zach

She complied without hesitation, scrambling to get his jeans and boxer briefs off without any teasing this time. "Damnit," she muttered when his belt wouldn't cooperate.

"Aww, what's wrong? Thought you were all about going slow." Teasing her could easily become one of his favorite pastimes.

She stuck her tongue out, drawing a deep laugh from him. He snapped forward, catching her tongue between his teeth and making her squeak and giggle all at the same time.

Christ, this woman made him feel good constantly. Just moments ago, he couldn't have imagined even cracking a smile, now he was laughing. Something about her soothed all his ails. The moment her hands had entered his hair, he'd wanted to purr like a cat.

And now that she had his pants at his ankles and her soft hand around his cock, he couldn't play games any longer. His head dropped back, and he let out a long, low groan.

"Shit. As good as that little hand feels, babe, this show will be over before it gets started if you keep that up."

With a smile, she gave him a squeeze then let go, moving her hands to the string of her panties to remove the last barrier between them.

"Don't." He nudged her hand out of the way. "Leave them." He wanted them wet. Soaked through with the scent of her arousal. Those panties would be going home with him.

He glided one finger over the damp lace between her legs. Her intake of breath made him smile. "I'm dying to sink my fingers deep into this pussy and feel how wet you are. Feel you clench around them. I've jacked off a hundred times thinking of this pussy." He shook his head in disgust. "Fucking bandages."

"Next time." Her voice was breathless with need. "Right now, I just want you to fuck me. I don't need anything else."

"You just need my dick, huh?"

"God, yes. Give it to me, Zach."

Shit, her words were as hot as her pussy. He stared into her eyes, gauging her honesty. All he saw back was need. "Condom?"

"Drawer behind you."

He hated to take his attention off her even for a second, but he turned and rummaged through the drawer until he found a small box of condoms. "You're gonna have to do it."

"Aww gee, what a hardship," she said as she grabbed the foil packet from him. Placing it between her perfectly straight teeth, she ripped it open and had it over the head of his dick in seconds.

"Jesus fuck." he said as her nimble fingers rolled the latex down his length. How mortifying would it be to shoot into the condom before she even had it fully on him? The very second she had the rubber in place, he knocked her hands out of the way, hooked his arms under her thighs, and hoisted her up the wall.

He palmed her ass with his left hand and used the right to grab the string of her thong and yank it to the side. Then, with a grunt, he snapped his hips forward and entered in one harsh thrust.

"Oh," she cried out, clutching his shoulders, at the same time Zach whispered, "Fuck."

She was hot, she was tight, and she was so wet he pulled back with ease.

"Now, Zach, please don't wait. Fuck me."

He drove back into her over and over until she was gasping and moaning with every thrust. Her pussy was so tight, he wasn't going to last two minutes. It was so fucking selfish, especially considering how amazing she'd been to him since he arrived, but he couldn't stop himself from fucking her like it was his last fuck on earth.

All of the fear, frustration, and anger from the day faded away, replaced by the pleasure of possessing Toni's body. It went beyond the physical. She was like some kind of sexual witch, wrapping herself around his soul as well as his dick. He wasn't sure he'd ever be able to get enough of her.

After only a few short minutes, Zach's balls drew up tight and his gut tensed. He fused his mouth to hers, drinking her in as he pounded into her. Anything that wasn't Toni's pussy on his cock disappeared. He had no idea if she was close and would owe her a million times over if she wasn't, because he could no sooner stop himself from coming than he could stop his heart from beating.

With one last push, he settled deep inside her and let the climax claim him. As his body shook he was distantly aware of Toni crying out, then sagging against him.

"God damn," he said, some amount of time later when he could breathe again.

"Well said," Toni mumbled into his neck.

"I'm sorry."

"What for?" She sounded genuinely confused.

"That was all about me. I attacked you like some kind of beast."

She chuckled. "Seriously? Well, then, I'm not sure I'd survive it if it was about me, because that was one good orgasm. I think I like your beast."

Zach quirked an eyebrow. "Was it now?"

A red flush stole across her face as though she hadn't meant to be so forward and she shrugged.

He slowly pulled out of her, let her down to the ground and righted her panties. They were so wet they might as well have just come out of the washer.

Perfect.

"Come on," he said. "Let's sleep for a few hours. Then I'll treat you to what I should have done this first time."

She hesitated. Just a fraction of a second, but Zach noticed it. Had she been expecting a one off? He almost snorted out loud. If that was the case, little Miss Toni had another thing coming to her.

Because now that he'd had a taste of her, she wasn't getting away from him anytime soon. If that meant he had to keep her too fuck-drunk to think, then that's exactly what he'd do.

And he'd love every damn second of it.

CHAPTER SEVENTEEN

Toni's eyes fluttered open, then dropped closed again as sunshine flooded her room. She must have forgotten to close the blinds before turning in for the night.

With a sigh she burrowed deeper into the warm cocoon of blankets and body heat. The soft cotton of her favorite sheets against her naked body was soothing and pulled her back toward sleep.

Wait. Naked?

Her eyes popped open as an intense barrage of erotic memories came at her from all angles.

Oh shit.

Just hours ago, Zach had fucked her against her bathroom wall like he'd die if he didn't have her. She wasn't deluded enough to say she'd slept with Zach or even that they'd had sex. No. He'd fucked her, plain and simple.

And she'd loved it more than she'd loved anything in a very long time.

It was quick, dirty, raw, and gave her an orgasm that topped the charts.

Just how she liked it.

Argh, just thinking about it made her want to spread her legs and invite him back in.

But that wasn't possible for two reasons. One, because she refused to allow it again. She'd broken her rule and acted on lust instead of sticking to her search for a good partner. She hadn't been fucked like that in a long time. Since before it all went bad.

And now, she had the perfect example of why she didn't allow herself to indulge in those desires. There she was, lying in the bed bright and early, wet with desire from nothing but some memories. She'd enjoyed it too much. Too much to think rationally and choose a man that would participate in a healthy relationship. So she stayed away from the sexy, alpha, bad boys. No matter how good they gave it.

There was a second reason she wouldn't be hopping on Zach for a morning repeat ride. And that was because the side of the bed he'd slept on was empty.

He'd left.

And she told herself in her sternest inner voice that she wasn't remotely disappointed.

Liar, liar.

The sound of the toilet flushing came from Toni's master bathroom and every muscle in her body tensed. Holding her breath, she rolled over and peered at the strip of light under the bathroom door.

He was in there. Zach hadn't left.

Was it possible to feel both elation and dread at the exact same time?

Yes. It was.

The water turned on and Toni turned on her back then squeezed her eyes shut. It was simple. She'd pretend to be asleep. Zach was probably banking on her still being in dreamland anyway. This way he could grab his clothes and leave without any morning after awkwardness. Hell, he'd probably be grateful for the reprieve.

The plan might not be the most mature, but it would work.

The bathroom door opened and Zach's heavy tread sounded across her wood floor.

And then, it stopped.

Zach

She had the feeling he was standing at the foot of her bed, but since she couldn't see, she wasn't confident in his location.

Nothing happened for a few moments, and Toni's skin grew prickly with awareness.

What was he doing? Watching her? Dressing? No, it was too quiet for him to be putting his clothes on.

She fought hard to keep her breathing as deep and even as it would be in slumber, but not knowing exactly where he stood and the thought of him watching her had her body going crazy. The tiny hairs on her arms stood straight out from skin that felt overly sensitive. Her nipples tightened and her soaking wet sex clenched as though calling out to him.

Damn it.

Seconds ticked by and then his hand gripped the sheet next to her foot and drew it off her at a pace so slow she wanted to scream. The fabric coasted down her body, baring one inch at a time to the cool air and his hot gaze. Her upper chest was leisurely exposed. Then her nipples, her abdomen, hips, and finally the wet and achy spot between her legs.

"You know," he said in an amused voice. "I've got fifteen minutes until I have to leave for the clubhouse. Just enough time to make up for last night's missing foreplay. What do you say, baby, you going to stop pretending to be asleep and open those pretty legs so I can eat you before I have to leave?"

Holy shit the guy gave good dirty talk.

Her eyes flew open and she met his smoldering gaze. Wearing nothing but unfastened jeans, he stood at the foot of her bed with his naked torso a feast for her eyes. The definition of temptation.

And all Toni's very sound arguments from moments ago vaporized. God, she was weak. She could berate herself for hours later. For the whole afternoon if she wanted. For now, she'd be taking what he offered. "Well," she said, bending her knees and separating her legs, "I suppose I'd be a terrible hostess if I sent you away hungry."

His attention was one hundred percent focused on her dripping pussy, but his lips quirked at her remark. "I'd say you've been a pretty damn good hostess so far."

She smiled and held her breath as he crawled onto the bed and settled between her spread legs. "Damn, Toni. Look how wet this pussy is, and I haven't even touched you yet. Were you lying here thinking about my cock? Thinking about how it filled you up? Stretched you? Thinking about how you want more?" He tsked and ran a finger through her saturated folds. "That's greedy, baby."

Toni gasped. This man could own her body so easily. And maybe even her heart. She had to put a stop to it before she got sucked in and lost herself.

"You know what men do with a greedy pussy?" He swiped his tongue across the path his finger had just taken and this time Toni jolted and cried out.

Later. Later she would put a stop to it. After she came. "W-what?"

"We fuckin' own it, baby."

Oh God. Exactly what she was afraid of.

And then there was no more talking. He licked her again, this time a slow journey around her clit. And slow was the key word. He took his sweet time circling her clit. It was its own kind of torture, ramping her up and holding her steady in a state of frenzied need.

Her hands fisted the sheets and she squirmed, lifting her hips against his mouth. Anything to get him to move faster and put the pressure right on her clit. It didn't work. He kept at her in a unhurried manner. What happened to only having fifteen minutes until he had to leave?

"Zach." She moaned, then bit her lip. She'd always loved sex, but sometimes had a little bit of trouble really losing herself in the moment. All the therapy she'd had years ago taught her that was completely normal. It was probably also part of the reason she chose men like Chris. They were safer in her mind. Wouldn't make her lose control.

But she wanted to lose control, even if her subconscious was a little afraid of it. The previous night was the only time in her adult life she'd really let the moment consume her.

"What's wrong, babe? You need something different? More?" His voice was laced with amusement.

Damn him. He knew exactly what he was doing to her. And he was going to make her ask for it.

"All you gotta do is tell me what you want and I'll give it to you, beautiful. You have any idea how hot it is when a woman knows what she wants and demands it? It's hot as hell, Toni. Tell me what you want."

What woman could resist that? "More," she said, gripping the sheets for dear life.

"More what? Tell me."

She screwed her eyes shut and shook her head. "More on my clit. Harder. Right on it."

"Ahh," he said on a chuckle. "Like this?" He flattened his tongue and pressed it right against the swollen nub.

Sharp pleasure blasted through her on contact and her hips jerked hard, banging him in the face. "Yesss," she hissed.

"What else?" he asked before he blew on her, making her back arch.

"A finger." Shit, she could barely speak with him tonging her clit again and again.

"What about my finger? This?" He rimmed her entrance with the lightest of touches and she almost screamed at him.

"No! Fuck me with it."

"Ohhh. Now I get it. Finger fucking and lots of clit action. Your wish is my command, beautiful." Without any further teasing, he speared her with two fingers at the same time he flicked his tongue in a rapid clip over her clit.

Toni saw stars. Without thinking—because it was no longer possible—she released the sheets and grabbed his hair. She held his face against her and ground her hips against his mouth. All shame, all self-preservation ceased to exist. All that mattered was the extreme pleasure coursing through her coupled with the powerful orgasm that loomed just out of reach. Exactly what she both wanted and feared.

"Fuck yeah," he said. His voice was slightly muffled by her pussy. "I knew this version of Toni was in there. All you needed was a real man to draw her out."

Oh God. She should say something. Deny his claim. But it was the truth. She'd needed a man like Zach to fuck her right for so long.

When she did nothing but whimper in response, he wrapped his lips around her clit and sucked. He wasn't gentle. No, that went out the window when she grabbed him and tried to suffocate him with her pussy.

Toni's legs shook and her breath came in spurts. Zach curled his fingers inside her, rubbing exactly where she needed and she finally got release. The orgasm burst through her, making her scream his name as her body trembled.

It seemed to go on and on, the shaking, the pleasure streaming through her veins, the gentling of Zach's mouth. And when it finally subsided, she was a limp sack of bones on her bed.

She opened her eyes to find Zach braced on his hands, looming over her. He pressed a quick kiss that tasted of her to her lips then smiled. "Thanks for breakfast, beautiful. Think that was good enough to earn me a cup of coffee before I go?"

Toni couldn't keep the slap happy grin off her face if she tried. "I think that earned you the whole pot."

With a laugh that lit up his handsome face, Zach sat back on his heels. "I've only got time for a cup, but I'll take a rain check on the rest of the pot."

She stiffened. He was asking for more. As much as she wanted to say yes, it was time to pull the plug. "No, uh, that's fine. I'll just make a cup. I'm due at the restaurant soon anyway. That was, uh," she cleared her throat, "really great. I guess I'll see you around."

Zach's lips quirked. "See me around, huh?"

She shimmied until he was no longer straddling her and backed against the headboard, pulling the sheet up around her nakedness. "Yes. Thank you for, uh…" She motioned the bed.

"Thank you for eating your pussy until you screamed my name and almost crushed my head with your legs? Believe me, baby, the pleasure was almost as much mine as yours." He winked. "Almost."

Her face heated until she felt like she had a fever. He was going to make this difficult. Damn man. Looked like she was just going to have to be straight with him. "Look, Zach, it was great. Actually, there isn't even a word for how great it was, but it can't happen again. I'm not looking for this. I'm looking for—"

"A boring suit who wouldn't know how to fuck a woman if she came with an instruction video?"

Okay, maybe that was an accurate description of Chris, but it was still a low blow. "No," she said. Her feet hit the floor and she yanked the sheet out from under him with all her might. She must have looked like an idiot tugging on the thing until it sprang free and she stumbled back. Straightening her spine like she wasn't mortified, she wrapped the sheet around her chest and paced. "I don't want to turn this into something ugly. We had fun, let's just leave it at that. Okay?"

Zach stood as well and shook his head while he folded his arms over that damn chest. "No."

Her feet stopped moving and her mouth dropped open. "No?"

"No. I will not leave it at one night. I haven't begun to tap into what I've imagined doing to you. You're running scared."

"Um, I am not scared of anything." *Liar. Liar.* She was scared. Scared of choosing the wrong man. Scared of being hurt. Scared of losing control of herself. "I just don't want this with you. Are you trying to tell me you're looking for a serious relationship?

Gonna get a nine to five job? Put up a picket fence? Have the neighbors over for game night?"

Zach snorted. "Fuck no. But I don't see what one thing has to do with the other. You're here for a few more weeks. I'm here. We fuck like we're made for each other. Why not wear each other out for the next few weeks?"

Because she would become addicted to the pleasure. And she'd lose herself and the life she worked so hard to create. Worked so hard to fix. She'd lost so much because of her mistakes. Sometimes she could still hear her parents' disapproving voices in her head, telling her she was no longer welcome in their home. She'd sullied herself and they were through cleaning up her messes. "Because I don't want that. I'm not some fuck toy you can play with when you're in the mood."

Zach snorted and stalked toward her until he crowded her against the wall. "That's not what I meant and you know it. Besides, you weren't exactly complaining when I had my face buried in your pussy."

She closed her eyes. No, she hadn't complained. No woman in the world would complain about that. But a few orgasms didn't make everything all right. It was all the more reason to remain firm.

"Running scared. Like I said." He backed away from her and she tightened her hold on the sheet. "No worries. I'm a patient man." He continued walking backward toward her door. "Forget the coffee. I know a great diner that serves kick ass coffee. I'll swing by later on."

As he neared the door, he bent and scooped his shirt from the floor. After shrugging into it—Toni looked anywhere but at his sexy form bunching and stretching while he dressed—he picked up something else. With a grin so wicked it could have come from the devil himself, Zach held up the lacy panties she'd been wearing the night before. Her eyes widened as he brought them to his face and inhaled before stuffing them in his pocket.

Zach

"Catch ya later, babe." He winked, then the playful look disappeared from his face. "Oh, I'm gonna have a prospect tail you to and from the diner today. I'm not really worried, but you've been seen with me and with the shit going down with Mav, we can't be too cautious. Just go about your business and pay no attention to him."

Toni couldn't process the rapid change in him from lover to MC enforcer, so she just nodded.

And then he was gone.

Toni sagged against the wall. There was no use denying how amazing she felt after two Zach-given orgasms. But in the span of one night her life had gone from complicated to uber complicated. And now she had to have a biker follow her around?

What the hell had she gotten herself into?

CHAPTER EIGHTEEN

"Something's gotta fucking give," Zach said as he ran his hand through his hair for the tenth time in as many minutes.

Somehow, he managed to resist the urge to slam his fist down on the table top. A few hours ago, he'd removed the knuckle bandages for good and was managing pretty well. He was even able to ride without splitting the scabs, but his knuckles wouldn't handle another bashing like he'd given them the other night.

"It's like they've all just up and vanished," Viper said as he lit a cigarette and blew out a long stream of smoke.

Zach gave up the habit years ago and didn't miss it until times of high stress. And stress was at an all-time high with Mav still missing. The monster orgasm he'd had inside Toni had helped at the time, but he'd left her house hard and tense all over again two mornings ago and hadn't been gifted a moment of peace since.

"They didn't fucking disappear. They ain't Houdini or some shit. They just went to ground. They're laying low and we have no fucking idea where." Copper rubbed his chin. "What I'm stuck on is the why. Why grab Maverick? What are they gaining from holding him?"

Rocket grunted. "To fuck with us."

"Could it be that simple?" Zach added. "Just Shark getting his rocks off fucking with us?"

Zach

With a shake of his head, Copper tapped his index finger on the table. "But there's been no demand for any kind of ransom. I hate to say it, but I expected they'd either ask for something or we'd find a body by now."

Nausea rolled through Zach's stomach. He was tired. So fucking tired. For days, they'd been tapping all their contacts, exhausting all their resources, and calling in every favor they'd ever earned. No one knew shit. Or if they did, they weren't willing to run their mouths. And Zach, with a little help from Louie, had been very persuasive.

Each day, they'd received one texted picture of Maverick. And each day he'd had his ass beat a little more. He looked like shit, but not bad enough to be worrisome as far as his survival. Just enough to ensure he was miserable. How long would that last? At what point would Shark decide Mav's survival was no longer necessary?

"I have a theory." Jigsaw's glasses sat propped on the top of his head and an open laptop rested in front of him. A sure sign the clever bastard was thinking. Good for the Handlers, bad for the Dragons. For the first time since Mav was snatched, Zach felt a small seed of hope growing in his gut. Jig was the smartest motherfucker he knew. If anyone could figure this shit out, Jig could.

"Spit it out, Jig," Copper said.

"Think about what's been going on since Mav disappeared." He tapped the end of his pen on his computer. "We stopped collecting on debts. Rocket's construction projects are on hold. We closed the bar and the gym. Obviously, we've suspended Maverick's security gigs. Our women are nervous and being told to either stay home or we're tailing them everywhere. Basically, we're dead in the water. All business has been halted in favor of searching for Mav."

"He's crippled us," Zach said. Jesus, when had Shark become such a force?

"Exactly. He's frozen us in our tracks and completely knocked us on our asses. If we continue on this way for too much longer we'll lose clients, money, business. He's attacked us with hardly any effort on his part. And he'll steal our club right out from under us if this continues."

As he stood, Copper shoved his chair back so hard it slammed against the wall then clattered to the ground. "Fuck!" He kicked the downed chair, splintering off a leg. It shot across the room before landing with a loud clang.

No one cared. Even if they did, no one was stupid enough to tell Copper how to react.

"So, we need to go back to business as usual. That's what you're telling me?" Copper asked.

"I think so," Jig said. "Shark wants a piece of our pie. Actually, fuck that, he wants the whole damn thing. We need to show him he won't be getting it. At least not while we're still breathing."

Copper circled the table until he was behind Jig's chair. He clapped the treasurer on the back and said, "Nice work, Jig."

While the rest of the exec board discussed getting their operations up and running again, Zach let his mind wander to the implications of Jig's plan. No matter how he looked at it, he kept coming back to one sickening conclusion: Mav was fucked.

"Hold up," Zach said, resting his forearms on the table. "Not to shit all over this party, but getting back to normal is going to be like throwing a big fuck you to Shark, right?"

"That's right," Viper said rubbing his hands together in glee. "Gonna be sweet."

"But if he thinks his plan failed, what's to keep him from sending Mav back to us in chunks?"

"Fuck!" The expletive came from at least two of his brothers.

All eyes turned to Copper. It was shit like this that made Zach glad he wasn't the one on the throne. Rubbing his chin again, Copper trod to an empty, unbroken seat and dropped down. For a few moments, he stared at the ceiling and then his shoulders rose and fell with the heavy force of his sigh.

Zach

"This is a war and Dragons drew first blood. We have to present a strong front. We have to protect the club. I'll give it three days, but then we *have* to get shit running again. Both to stick it to Shark and because we can't take the financial hit. Over the next three days we search for Mav round the clock in shifts." He looked to Zach. "You make a schedule, Zach."

Zach nodded. "I'll get right on it."

"I don't care if we've talked to our contacts ten times already. Hit everyone up again. When the guys are on shift I want them looking in every hole and under every rock. When off shift, sleep. I need the men rested and sharp. If we haven't found him in three days, we'll reconvene before we open the businesses back up. Someone knows where the fuck Mav is, boys. Bring me that person and I promise you, they'll talk."

Zach almost shivered. It wasn't often Copper got his hands dirty these days, but when he did, the results were catastrophic.

Two hours later, assignments distributed, Zach was on his bike heading for home. He was on day shifts, so he had the night off. Even though he hadn't slept in almost forty hours, a restless energy zinged through him making thoughts of sleep impossible.

What he really wanted to do was bust down Toni's door, tackle her to the bed, and keep her there until she forgot everything but how to scream his name. But that wasn't going to happen. He needed to keep his focus on Mav and his club. Spending another night between Toni's silky thighs would only make his obsession with her grow. And he just couldn't split his time between a woman and his club.

Not now. Not with Mav's life on the line.

The club needed him. How would he ever look any of his brothers in the eye again if something happened to Mav because his head was in the clouds?

Or between Toni's legs?

* * *

The moment Toni's front door slammed shut behind her, she dropped her bag, kicked off her flip-flops, and unhooked her bra. She let the offending undergarment fall at her feet and then breathed out a sigh of relief. One of the perks of living alone was the lack of accountability to anyone. She could drop whatever she wanted at the front door and deal with it hours later if that's what she was in the mood for.

The past two days had been trying. Whatever was going on with the MC and Maverick's disappearance, it felt like there was a black cloud hovering over the entire town. Many of the Hell's Handlers had still been in the diner, but only for a quick bite or coffee before they went out to search for Maverick or home to crash.

Each man's body bore the stress of the situation. Baggy eyes, deep-set scowls, tense postures. Then there were the quick to enflame tempers. She'd stopped a fight that morning between some poor business man who'd been staring at his phone while walking and had plowed straight into Rocket. Hot coffee splashed all over Rocket's leather cut and you'd have thought the clumsy man had launched an all-out attack on the MC by Rocket's reaction.

When Rocket went for the terrified man's throat, Toni had dived between the two. A stern glare and gentle shove backed Rocket off. A free coffee refill from Shell had the businessman out of the diner and away from imminent death two minutes later. Toni had comped Rocket's breakfast despite his statements that it was unnecessary, and all ended well.

But it had been tense. As had the atmosphere in the diner for the entirety of those two days. Then there was the poor biker who trailed her everywhere she went. To make it easy on him, Toni brought him free food and coffee throughout the day and tried to limit her travels to the diner and home. She had this burning desire to do whatever she could to help and make life and more bearable for the Handlers. Even if it was something as simple as a smile and some coffee.

Zach

Worst part about the past two days had been the lack of Zach in her life. As much as she hated to admit it, she'd been searching for him in every face that walked into her diner. But he'd been absent. Working his ass off in the search for his best friend, if the chatter was correct.

Each evening she sat on her porch hoping he'd come home, but he hadn't. And when she heard his motorcycle pulling in at all hours of the night, she'd been so tempted to make her way to his house and check on him, but something held her back.

And now, at the end of the third day, she felt extremely guilty and childish. She'd basically thrown him out of her house instead of handling their encounter like an adult. So they'd had sex? Big deal.

Though it had been the best two sexual encounters of her life.

Okay, that was a big deal, but still, she shouldn't have freaked out. Adults had casual sex, even fuck-buddy relationships all the time without losing their shit. Maybe she could find a way to have a causal relationship without repeating past mistakes.

Her sex-starved body sure seemed to think it was possible. Just thoughts of Zach's hard physique, skilled hands, and talented tongue had her wet and needy. And then there was that cock...

Damn him and his incredible body.

Now that she'd had a sample of what the man had to offer, getting back in bed with him was all she could think about.

Mark's ringtone blared from her phone. She dug it out of her pocket and answered with a clipped, "Yeah?"

"Well, hello to you too, favorite niece of mine," came the amused reply.

Her lips quirked. "Sorry, Uncle Mark. Been a stressful few days."

"Well sweetie, you know what's the best form of stress relief, don't you?"

"Mark, I don't need to get laid, okay? I already—" Oops. Her brain must be foggier than she'd thought, because there is no way she would have admitted that in her right mind.

"Oh, my God, Andrew!" Mark yelled, making Toni wince as his voice pierced her eardrum through the phone. "Toni had sex!"

"Seriously? What are you fifteen?"

Laughter was her only answer. "Okay, tell me about your new man."

"I'm not telling you anything about, Zach. It's my private business. Okay?" So, she may have sounded like a huffy teenager, but really, what woman, at any age, wanted to discuss her sex life with her uncle?

"You know I have my ways of finding out. You might as well just tel—wait a second. Did you say Zach?"

Aw crap.

"Your next-door neighbor's name is Zach."

Really? Why the hell did Mark have to go and remember that?

"He's a fucking outlaw biker, Toni. Are you crazy? Do you have any idea how dangerous those guys can be?"

Are you trying to make the same mistake you made before?

He'd never say it, but the accusation hung heavily between them.

"It's nothing, Uncle Mark, seriously. Barely a blip on my radar." Oh, that lie was gonna come back to bite her. "Can we please talk about something else?"

"Shit, my work phone is ringing. Don't think that means we're done talking about this, missy."

Toni laughed. Mark always called her missy when he was trying to move into parent mode. Unfortunately for him, he never quite got the knack of parental lectures. "Whatever you say, Mark. Love you!"

He shouted, "You too!" into the phone, then disconnected. But that wouldn't be the end of it. He was as tenacious as they came.

Zach

Done with her call, Toni leaned against the door again and wished she could skip the walk to her room. She was just that tired.

A few minutes later, the growing rumble of motorcycle pipes chased away her exhaustion and had the ache in her feet shifting to an ache between her legs.

Zach.

It was the earliest he'd been home in days.

She could go to him. See how he was holding up under the strain of Maverick's disappearance. See if he'd rip her clothes off and take her in ten different ways before morning.

"Ugh. You're pathetic," she scolded herself.

Pushing off the door, she walked across her living room and stared out the window at Zach's dark house. After a few seconds, the light in Zach's bedroom flipped on, illuminating him where he stood.

Toni gasped and jumped away from the window.

Did he see her?

She rolled her eyes. Probably not, it was still dark in her house. Slowly, she tiptoed back in front of the glass and stared transfixed as he prowled around his bedroom. There was a restless energy to him, like a caged tiger denied its freedom. He seemed like he was close to losing his shit.

As she continued to watch, he stripped off his shirt and stalked to the doorway where a pull-up bar hung from the frame. Ten pull-ups in and Toni needed to wipe the drool from her mouth. He was hands-down the most gorgeous man she'd ever seen. The way his biceps and forearms balled up then released with each up and down movement was a perfect representation of male strength in its purest form.

She lost count of the number of pull-ups he completed, but after a few minutes, he dropped to the floor and started on push-ups. Jesus, if she didn't know better, she'd think he was doing it on purpose. Showing off the play of his muscles to drive her insane with lust.

About a hundred push-ups and a thousand sit-ups later, Zach seemed to have burned through some of the agitation he'd arrived home with.

He stood facing away from the window, stripping out of his shorts while Toni still stared at his perfect ass.

She should move. She *had* to move. Watching someone naked through their window wasn't okay. Not only did it top the creeper charts, it was technically illegal.

No matter how many signals her brain sent to her feet, they didn't move.

And then he turned.

Oh my God, he was hard.

Need slammed into her with the force of a tornado. Toni clenched her legs together, trying to ease the longing. Like that had a chance of working. After a night with Zach, nothing but his cock would do. Except maybe his fingers. Or, oh God, that tongue.

Her eyes widened and she gasped as he wrapped a large hand around his even larger erection.

"Holy shit," she muttered, grabbing the frame around her window to steady herself.

For a few moments, he stroked up and down his length, his body growing tauter with each caress. Toni couldn't have torn her gaze away if her house was on fire. He was just so captivating as he pleasured himself.

He released his dick and strode to his nightstand which was next to his bed and very close to the window. She had a perfect view.

Still naked and hard, he opened the drawer and pulled something out.

"What the hell?" Toni muttered. Then her jaw dropped and she gasped as an almost embarrassing amount of wetness gushed between her legs.

Her panties.

Zach

The ones he'd stolen after fucking her into oblivion with his mouth.

He lifted them to his nose and inhaled before fisting his cock again. This time, he rubbed her panties all over his shaft.

Toni couldn't help it, this was the hottest, filthiest thing she'd ever seen. She moved her hands to her shorts and unbuttoned the top button before diving on down to her clit. It wouldn't take long, watching his show had her so worked up she thought she might explode with just one touch.

When her fingers grazed her clit, she groaned. Zach's strokes grew faster, stronger.

Then he turned his head, looking straight out his own window.

And he gave Toni the most wicked grin possible.

Hand in her shorts, she froze.

Holy shit.

He knew she was watching.

CHAPTER NINETEEN

Zach couldn't say why, but the moment he walked into his bedroom, he could feel Toni's gaze on him as though it was a physical thing.

A light was on in her kitchen, making her outline faintly visible through the shadows where she hovered at the edge of her living room window. She probably thought she was all but invisible since the living room was dark, but that kitchen light provided just enough illumination to make out her basic shape.

He'd missed her like hell over the past few days, but they'd been so busy and full of shit he hadn't even had a moment to swing by the diner. Plus, he'd offered her casual. A few weeks of fun until she left. That meant he didn't need and shouldn't want to check in with her every five seconds. Especially when it was pulling him from his responsibilities.

But staring at him through his window while he worked out then jerked off? Yeah that would break the strongest guy's resolve.

Man, how he wished he could see her shocked and aroused expression when he turned his gaze on her.

The silky feel of her panties wrapped around his dick was a distant second to the sensation of her pussy squeezing the life out of him, but it was all he'd had for the past few nights. That was about to be over. Toni didn't know it, but he was done with her flimsy attempts at distance.

Zach

They'd wasted enough time already. She was his for the duration of her time in Tennessee.

His cock was so hard, it felt like it could snap right off. Time to move the show along.

He reached for his phone on top of the nightstand and called Toni.

"Hello?" Her breathless voice picked up on the third ring.

"If I'd have known you were a peeping Tom, I'd have done this weeks ago."

"I, uh, I was just, um…"

Even though it was too dark on her side, he could imagine her face turning an adorable shade of pink.

"Nothing to be embarrassed about, sweetheart. I understand it's hard to resist a peek at all this." He ran a hand down his naked torso and over the ridges of his six-pack.

Zach wasn't stupid, nor was he falsely modest. He knew his body attracted women. Hell, it was one of the reasons he worked so damn hard in the gym and didn't buy ice cream. But he'd never wanted one woman to enjoy the view as much as he did with Toni.

"How long have you known I was watching?"

"Since I took off my shirt."

She squeaked. "God, that's embarrassing."

Zach chuckled. "Turn your light on, baby. I want to see more than the outline of you."

After an audible swallow, the light in Toni's living room flashed on. She stood, wide-eyed in the window, phone at her ear and shorts open.

Fuck. Knowing she'd gotten so turned on watching him stroke his cock that she had to touch herself made him almost insane.

Zach squeezed the base of his cock with the silken panties. He wanted to play a little and draw this out, but he was on the verge of coming. "Does watching me fuck my hand make your pussy all needy, baby?"

"Yes," she whispered.

"Let me watch you." She switched the phone to her other hand and slowly slid her dominant hand inside her shorts. Suddenly, Zach had the violent need to see more. To watch her fingers playing with her clit and disappearing into her pussy.

"Drop your shorts and take off your top. I want to see your tits while I stroke myself."

The line fell silent and seconds ticked by. Zach was just about to speak again when Toni set her phone down on the windowsill. She crossed her arms at her waist, gripped her T-shirt, then drew it over her head.

Zach groaned. No bra. Her gorgeous tits were on full display. He hadn't thought it possible, but his dick swelled even more.

After shimmying out of her shorts, she picked the phone up and returned it to her ear. "What now?" Her voice had lost that shocked, breathy quality and taken on a sultry seductress tone.

This wasn't gonna take long.

"Put down the phone and put me on speaker. Then, one hand on your tit, one back on your pussy. Finger yourself."

A sly smile tipped her lips and she nodded. A second later she placed the phone on the window sill. Her right hand cupped her tit, lifting it before she pinched the nipple between her thumb and forefinger.

At the same time, she coasted her left hand over the slight swell of her belly and straight into her sex. A low moan filtered through the phone when she entered herself.

Shit, she was putting on her own show for him. He'd started out fully in control of the encounter, but felt it slipping away with each thrust of her finger in her pussy. Fuck, he wanted to feel that wetness for himself. To taste the proof of her arousal and hear her noises in person.

But he was going to see this through, because he absolutely loved drawing out the naughty, uninhibited side of Toni.

* * *

Zach

Toni's legs trembled and her breath came in choppy hitches. She loved to masturbate as much as the next person, but often needed a vibrator to get the job done.

Not tonight.

Zach had her so worked up just from his voice and the sight of him jerking off that a stiff breeze would have sent her careening off the cliff.

"Fuck, that's hot, baby," Zach said, his attention glued to the hand between her legs. He increased the speed of his strokes. "Feel good?" He sounded almost in pain.

"Y-yes," she managed.

"Feel as good as my cock? As my tongue?"

"God, no. Nothing feels that good."

Zach grunted. "More, baby. Play with your clit. I've got about sixty seconds left in me and I need you there too. Think about what it's going to be like next time. Think of how much bigger my fingers are than yours and how good it will feel when I get them inside you."

Toni released her breast and dropped her hand down, rubbing quick, firm circles over her clit. Her body flared in response to Zach's dirty talk. His mouth did it for her whether it was on her skin or just talking.

"When I'm done finger fucking that pretty pussy, I'll fuck you with my cock again. You want that, sweetheart? You want my cock back inside you? It hasn't spent nearly enough time in there yet. But we're gonna change that, aren't we? Tell me you want my cock, Toni." There was no playfulness to him. This was a command. This was Zach exerting dominance over their sex life.

And she fucking loved it.

"I want that." She plunged her fingers in and out at a furious clip until she couldn't stand it any longer. Pressing her thumb over her clit, the orgasm hit and nearly took her to her knees. "Oh my God, Zach," she cried as she came.

"That's my girl."

His girl.

She ignored the possessive statement in favor of watching him reach his own climax. His body jerked and twitched as he rubbed the panties over his dick like he was trying to make them one. It was only another ten seconds or so before he let out a violent curse and covered the tip of his dick with her panties as the orgasm ripped through him.

His shoulders hunched forward and his head dropped down. The muscles she loved flexed and relaxed over and over until finally quieting. When he reached for his phone, she did the same, turning off the speaker.

"I'm coming over," he said in a much more relaxed voice.

"Okay." She hadn't even pretended to put up an argument. Geez, she was so easy for him. It was pointless to deny him when she wanted him as much as he claimed to want her.

"And I'm staying until the morning."

"Okay."

"And you're going to come a few more times before the night is over."

She smiled. "What about you?"

"I'm hoping you'll let me come too."

Toni laughed at that. It was rare to spend time with a man who both blew her mind and made her laugh. "I'll think about it."

He stepped into his shorts. "Go get into bed, baby. Leave the door unlocked for me. I'll be there in ten minutes. I just want to chat with the prospect outside your house and send him home for the night since I'll be there."

It was even rarer to find a man who blew her mind, made her laugh, *and* cared about her safety. His concern made her a little warm and gooey inside.

"I'll be waiting."

He disconnected the call and Toni blew out a breath.

Did that really just happen? Did she really just stand butt naked in her window and finger herself to completion?

Zach

She shivered as a blast of air-conditioned air blew on her from the overhead vent. Yep, she had stood naked in the window. And she had climaxed. And she'd watched Zach do the same.

A huge smile hit her face. It had been the most fun she'd had in a while.

Her phone rang and butterflies flitted through her stomach. What other instructions did Zach have for her? "Yeeess?" she answered while still peeking through the window. "You better not be calling for a naked pic to get you through the next ten minutes." Toni laughed as she tried to make him out in his now darkened room.

She expected to see Zach, but he wasn't anywhere in sight. With a shrug, she started down the hallway toward the master bedroom.

"Zach?" she asked when silence greeted her.

"That didn't take long, did it?"

Toni's steps faltered and she bobbled the phone. "Chris? Why the hell are you calling me?"

Where seconds ago, strolling through her home naked felt sexy and freeing, she now felt the fierce need to be covered. Toni darted into her room and stuffed her arms into her robe. "I asked you a question," she said as she belted the robe.

Chris's huff of laughter infuriated her. "I was calling to see if you'd come to your senses and decided to return to me."

Seriously? Why couldn't he take the hint and leave her alone? Actually, there wasn't even a hint for him to grasp. She'd flat out told him to leave her alone the last time they spoke. When he issued that vague threat she'd all but forgotten about. Something with regards to doing things the easy or hard way.

What a drama queen.

"Chris, I'm going to say this one last time, then I'm hanging up, okay? We are over. And if there was any question about that, I think calling me a slut and telling me you only want me so you can advance your career sealed that coffin shut tight."

She was about to hit end when he spoke. "So you're fucking him, then? The biker?" Disgust dripped from every word.

"Don't see how my personal life is any of your business anymore, Chris. Are we done here?"

He snickered and she wanted to reach through the phone and strangle him. Normally, she wasn't prone to violent fantasies, but his laughter grated across her nerves like coarse sandpaper. He thought he was so superior. What a self-important jerk. How had she not seen that while they were dating?

"I wouldn't be so quick to dismiss me, Toni. I plan to make partner in your uncle's firm no matter what I have to do. I emailed you something I'd like you to take a look at. I'll call you again in a few days and we can discuss when you'll arrive back in Chicago."

"Of all the misguided, egotistical, arrogant shit I've ever heard—"

Her phone beeped three times.

"Chris?" She held it out and stared at the screen. He'd hung up. "Asshole," she muttered.

Her front door slammed.

"I'm here, beautiful. You better be naked with those sexy legs spread by the time I get to your room or your punishment will be severe."

Zach's voice made her smile. She placed the phone on her dresser. No way in hell would she let Chris ruin this night for her. Whatever garbage he'd sent her could wait. Forever, if she had her way.

As fast as possible, she slipped out of her robe and dashed to the bed. Flopping back on a pile of pillows, she managed to draw up her knees and widen her legs seconds before Zach appeared in the door.

Part of her had wanted to disobey his orders and find out exactly what he viewed as *punishment*. But that could wait for another time.

Zach

Another time. Toni stared at him as he walked into her room. It was time to give into the fact that this would be occurring again. No matter that she knew it shouldn't.

"Fuck me," he said, and her core clenched at the raw appreciation in his eyes. He stalked toward the bed like a predator ready to pounce. Tossing a strip of condoms on the foot of the bed he groaned. "You ready for this, baby?"

Toni winked. "Bring it on."

CHAPTER TWENTY

Zach was in her shower.

Because he'd slept in her bed.

Because they'd finally stopped making love—*having sex*—somewhere around three in the morning. And what was the point of him going home at that hour? Right? He had to be at the clubhouse by nine, and she'd planned to swing by the diner at the same time. That left precious few hours of sleep and it would have been pointless to send him home for what amounted to a long nap.

These were the excuses running through her mind as Toni watched the coffee drip into the pot. All very flimsy excuses when the reality of the situation was she hadn't wanted him to leave. He felt so wonderful spooned all around her after they'd finally collapsed, sated and sleepy.

She should be exhausted. The lack of sleep should have had her stumbling around like a zombie. Instead, her body hummed and zinged with anticipation of what was next. Must have had something to do with the number of times he'd made her come the previous night—and once when they first woke up.

With a huff, Toni strummed her nails on the countertop. She needed something to occupy her until the coffee percolated and Zach finished up in the shower. It was either that or hop in there with him and start the process all over again. Fun, but not the wisest choice if she wanted any chance of keeping some distance between them.

It was becoming harder, no pun intended, to be with him and remain detached. A sex-only thing wasn't going to work for her. Not when he was sweet, and funny, and seemed to genuinely care for her. And that sex? Well, it was off the charts. So much so that she found herself replaying it over and over, then fantasizing about what was to come.

And there in lie her biggest concern. She didn't have the greatest track record making sound decisions when her body was in charge.

The coffee maker beeped twice and Toni poured herself a steaming cup before settling at the kitchen table. Sometimes she doctored it up, but today was a black coffee kind of day. Nothing to dilute the caffeine. Maybe it would wake her mind up enough to clear it of its sexy cobwebs.

While she waited for Zach, she powered up her laptop and skimmed through neglected emails. It'd been at least three days since she'd even checked them. A few messages awaited from the school district she worked for. The reminder of that part of her life gave her an uneasy feeling. With each passing day, she felt the desire to return to her life and job in Chicago fading away. The time in Tennessee had been wonderful. She'd found a passion for running the diner and seemed to be performing well, if the steadily crowded tables were any indication.

Decisions had to be made, and soon, as the summer was moving full-steam ahead. But nothing had to be decided in that moment. She bypassed the work emails and then her eyes landed on a message from Chris.

Shit.

How could she have forgotten?

Lots of orgasms, that's how.

"What do you think you have that will make me come running back to you, jerk?" she asked aloud as she clicked open the email. It consisted of a short message and a video attachment. Unease slid through her. A video?

Toni,

The school district would love a copy of this. So would everyone in your shit town. You'll be sorry if you mention this to Mark. Shit like this goes viral in a heartbeat. Come home and convince Mark to make me a junior partner.

See you back in Chicago soon. You have three weeks to return home.

-Chris

Fear turned her blood to ice while she stared at the unopened attachment. Chris had something. Something big. Something that would bring her running back to Chicago. "Please don't let Mark have done something stupid or illegal," she whispered. She'd do damn near anything to protect her beloved uncle.

Her finger hovered on the trackpad, but she couldn't make it click the video.

"Just open it," she muttered then clicked. A video screen filled the monitor and Toni stared in horror at what played before her.

"No." She shook her head as her eyes flooded with tears. "No, no, no. This can't be happening." She tried to close it, but her hand was shaking so badly she couldn't control the cursor.

Unable to turn away from her nightmare, Toni's hand flew to her mouth, knocking her coffee mug to the floor in the process. The clatter made her jump so violently, she fell off the chair and onto the floor.

She kicked out at the chair and scrambled backward as though a million spiders were coming out of the laptop and gunning for her. When her back hit the cabinets below the sink, she burst into heaving sobs.

"Toni?" Concern laced Zach's voice as his footsteps moved down the hall. "I heard a loud bang. You okay?" He stopped dead in the entrance to the kitchen. "Fuck, baby what's wrong?"

Toni couldn't speak around the hysteria coursing through her. As Zach started to kneel beside her, her stomach lurched and she shot to her feet, shoving him out of her way. Managing to position herself over the sink just in time, she lost whatever little coffee she'd drank that morning.

Zach rubbed her back. "Shit, baby, what's wrong? Are you sick? Did, fuck, did I hurt you?"

Toni wiped her mouth and slid back down to the floor. She couldn't speak, couldn't process, couldn't even think. Terrible memories that she'd worked so hard to move past descended on her like a category five hurricane. She'd have to return to Chicago.

Chris would win. No one could be allowed see that video. She dropped her head to her knees and let the tears fall.

"Toni?" Zach's voice was starting to sound panicked. "What can I do for you, baby? Are you hurt? Do I need to call an ambulance? I think your phone is on the table."

He spun toward the table.

Toni's heart stopped. The video still played on the open laptop screen. He was going to see the very worst, most humiliating, and degrading moments of her life.

"No!" she cried crawling toward the table, but it was too late.

Zach's arms dangled at his sides and his face was an ashen mask of confused fury. "What is this?" he whispered before screaming, "What the fuck is this? Is that fucking Shark?"

Oh God. He knew Shark.

Were they friends?

No one knew. Her parents had been so mortified by her behavior they kicked her out and never spoke of it. Mark would never betray her trust by telling her secrets. The Gray Dragons gang operated in a different county. It had been rare for any of them to be seen in Townsend, so no one from her younger days even knew about her association with Shark.

This was the first time she'd returned home since Mark rescued her from herself. No one was ever supposed to know about this. Did the MC know? Had things changed so much in the years she'd been gone that the MC and Shark's gang were now connected?

"Fuck," he spat out, pacing away from the computer then returning and pointing at the screen. "This is the motherfucker who has Maverick. That piece of shit that has his hands all over you? He fucking kidnapped my brother."

Toni felt her world unraveling. The room started to spin out of control and bile climbed up her esophagus again. She sprang up, turned to the sink, and dry heaved since there was nothing left to lose.

Only there was. There was so much to lose now.

And one of those things was standing three feet away, witnessing her greatest sins.

How would Zach ever be able to look at her with anything but revulsion?

CHAPTER TWENTY-ONE

Anger was his first reaction. A deep, soul-staining anger. The kind of rage that made men do stupid things. Like commit murder. And if Shark was in the room, that's exactly what would have happened.

The image of Shark fucking Zach's woman would be branded onto his brain forever. And he'd thought getting the Hell's Handlers logo burned into his skin was painful. It was nothing compared to the agony of watching a woman he cared about being fucked by his enemy.

He was so close to the edge, so close to losing it, he missed what was going on behind him. Then, the sound of Toni retching broke through the red haze, and Zach realized something was very wrong. For her sake, he used every bit of self-control he possessed and pushed the fury aside. He needed answers and losing his temper wouldn't get them. At least, not without scaring the shit out of Toni.

Once he quieted the beast inside him, a few things became clear. First, was that the Toni in the video was a very young Toni. This was filmed years ago. Second, was that she looked drugged out of her mind. Glassy, unfocused eyes stared at nothing and she barely reacted to what was happening to and around her. And third, his Toni had her slender arms wrapped around her drawn up knees and was rocking back and forth on the floor. She was so freaked out by the video that there was no way that what had happened on it was something she'd been okay with.

He looked back over his shoulder. The video must have been on some kind of loop because it launched again. On the screen, Toni was naked and lying on a bed surrounded by three men. Shark was the only one Zach recognized, and he seemed to be running the show, but all three had the Dragons' signature tattoo on their left hands. And all three had their fucking hands on Toni.

They groped, pinched, fondled, and made lewd laughing comments throughout. Toni's eyes remained open, but she wasn't an active participant. And for Christ's sake, she couldn't have been older than seventeen.

Fuck.

For some sick reason Zach couldn't tear his gaze from the screen. Not even to go to Toni. She needed comforting and he needed answers, but it was as though he was trapped, weighed down by lead boots that wouldn't let him escape the horror show playing out before him.

When it became obvious Shark climaxed, Zach's fists curled and his nostrils flared. He was going to personally tear the man's dick off. And he'd revel in every second of Shark's suffering.

When Shark stepped away from Toni and some other fucker positioned himself between her legs, Zach hit his limit. With a roar, he slammed the laptop lid closed hard enough to crack the screen. Then he spun and froze at the sight of Toni.

His heart clenched as though a man's fist was squeezing the life out of it. His woman sat in a devastated ball on the floor, eyes closed, with silent tears streaming down her face.

And she *was* his woman. She may not be ready to hear that now, but she'd get there. He'd make sure of it.

"Baby," he said in a soft voice so as not to cause her any more upset. "Come on." Bending down, he scooped her up. She jumped, but settled quickly, tucking her head under his chin.

Zach

This was where she belonged. Right there in his arms where he could stand between her and the world.

That she didn't fight him carrying her through the house and outside to the front porch was telling. Toni wasn't a weak woman. She'd handled her parents' unexpected death without blinking an eye. She took over the diner and house, settled well into a new area, and managed a bunch of bikers without a second thought. To see her so broken fucked with his head and sealed Shark's fate. His raping buddies' as well.

When he sank down to a rocking chair with her on his lap, she tried to pull away, but he held her close and rubbed a hand up and down her back. "Shh, just relax, baby." All she wore was his T-shirt from the night before and he had nothing on but his jeans. The moment was quiet, intimate, peaceful, and after a few minutes she relaxed into him. It would have been a perfect way to spend the morning if they didn't have a tough conversation looming over them like a dark storm cloud.

They sat in silence for a while, Zach holding her and gliding the chair back and forth with his foot.

"Can you tell me?" he asked after a while. The need to know more clawed at him, overshadowing the brief peace they'd found.

Toni nodded against his chest. "You know who my parents were. Very conservative, closed-minded, prejudiced against everyone who wasn't exactly like them. Did you know they were terrified of your father?"

Zach huffed out a laugh. "I knew. They called the cops on him at least three or four times a year for stupid shit."

Toni traced her finger over the Handlers' emblem, scarred onto his forearm. "Yeah, they were convinced he was going to break in and rob us blind one night." She scoffed. "They were paranoid like that about the entire MC or anyone who looked like what my mom called a hoodlum. Anyway, their views led them to keeping me on a very tight leash. Once I hit middle school, I wasn't allowed to go to birthday parties, to the mall with friends, no after-school activities, definitely no dating. Basically, I wasn't allowed any normal teenage activities. Friends weren't even permitted at the house, and I could never go to their houses, either."

"Must have been tough." As she spoke, Zach snaked his hand under her T-shirt and stroked her soft hip. It seemed to have the desired effect as she stayed pliant and relaxed against him.

"Did this hurt?" She drew a circle around his scar with her index finger.

"Like a sonofabitch, babe," he said, giving her hip a gentle squeeze.

That got a small chuckle out of her. "Once I hit high school, I rebelled. Hard core. Sneaking out, smoking, drinking, having sex. I refused to have anything to do with the diner and I specifically chose a rough crowd that my parents despised. Looking back on it now, I see how stupid and disrespectful I was, but I was so angry at them all the time. And I was young and unequipped to make wise decisions."

"How did they respond?"

"Well, now, through the eyes of an adult I can see I was craving their attention, understanding, and acceptance. Basically, I just wanted them to love me, even if it meant yelling and punishments. At least I would have known they cared. I got none of that. They basically washed their hands of me. Stopped trying to discipline or parent me because they felt I was a lost cause."

"Shit."

"Yeah. When I was sixteen, pretty close to seventeen, I went to a Gray Dragon's party with some girl who'd dropped out of high school. That's where I met Eddie."

"Shark?"

Toni nodded and shifted, sitting straight and turning until she straddled him. "I want to be able to look at you while I finish this."

Zach

He tilted his head and nodded. "Okay." He'd never turn down a chance to have her draped over his body.

Her gaze was searching, like she was anticipating some specific reaction from him. Acceptance? Or maybe she expected him to react like her parents did and reject her. That would never happen. No none deserved to be judged by the mistakes of their youth. Hell, Zach had done his share of things he wasn't proud of and would rather forget. "Whatever it is you have to tell me, baby, just spit it out. It's not going to change the way I see you."

She gave him a sad smile and placed her hands on his chest. "You say that now, but you saw the video." A small shudder ran through her. "That wasn't even the worst of it."

Fuck, it was going to be near impossible to keep from reacting negatively, but he had no fucking choice. "Why don't you tell me the rest, sweetheart?" Keeping the anger hidden no matter what she told him would be imperative. She had to learn she could trust him with her secrets. With whatever shamed her.

"Eddie is about a year older than I am and he dazzled me from the first moment I met him. Handsome, a smooth talker, sexy. He was everything my parents hated in one male package. I fell hard and fast. At first, it was exciting. We went to wild parties every night. Four out of the five school days per week I was either hungover or absent. I didn't even make it halfway through my senior year before I dropped out. By then, I'd missed so many days the school had refused to graduate me. The angry teenage me sure as hell wasn't going to repeat a year."

Well, that explained why she wasn't fazed by the party at the clubhouse.

"Eddie wasn't the first guy I'd slept with by that point, but he was the most...adventurous." She sighed. "You sure you want to hear all this?"

Fuck no. "Yes." Zach sounded like he'd swallowed shards of glass. Hearing about any Toni had been with would be torture, but listening while she talked about sex with Shark was like having his toenails ripped out with a pair of rusty pliers.

"All right. At first, it was exciting and hot and if I'm being honest, I loved it. I found out that—this is so embarrassing." She looked up for a second then took a deep breath. "I discovered that I like sex. Really like it. Wild, rough, a little taboo, I was into it all."

This conversation was worse than having his skin peeled off, but he knew there was a reason she was revealing all of it. And it was probably going to get worse before it was over.

"So, at first, that's what it was. Partying and sex. I was drinking like a fish, doing drugs, the works. I hardly spent any time at home and I think my parents were relieved by that point. I'd caused so much trouble it was easier to pretend I didn't exist."

"I don't remember anything about this. I don't think my parents ever mentioned it."

She shrugged. "Well you were away by then. In the army, right?"

He scratched the morning stubble on his chin. "Yeah, I guess I wasn't home. So, what happened?"

"Eddie started to rise up the ranks in the gang. He was making a name for himself by being ruthless with anyone who crossed him. All he wanted was to move up higher on the food chain. He wanted to run the gang one day."

"He's in charge now."

She nodded. "I'm not surprised. It's where he was headed. Anyway, as he got more power, he got even crazier and wanted to share me with his friends. The guys who ran the gang at the time. It's part of their bylaws. If you want in the very tight knit and elite inner circle, you had to have a woman and had to share her. It's so fucked up. Back then, I was so stupid and thought I was in love. I went along with it for a while." Her eyes closed and tears leaked out. "I thought it wouldn't be so bad. That it would make him proud of me. Make him love me. For about six months I was nothing better than a drugged-out gang slut."

Zach

Zach wrapped his arms around her, as much for himself as to soothe her. She'd been carrying this around, beating herself up for years. "Shit, babe, that's not true. You were young. Underage for fuck's sake. And I saw that video. You were fuckin' zonked. There's no way you could have consented. It was rape, babe."

"You think that video was bad?" She hopped off his lap and paced the length of the porch. "I'd done it all before, Zach. And stone cold sober. I took the drugs willingly. I agreed to everything they wanted. I never said no or put up a fight. I was so screwed up and looking for any kind of attention. Even if I ended up completely losing myself in the process."

He stood. As much as he hated hearing about other men getting their hands on her, it was even worse to see her self-hatred over it. "It doesn't matter," he said, stopping her with his hands on her shoulders. "Baby, you were too young and fucked up from parents who didn't do right by you to handle making those kinds of decisions. It's nothing to be ashamed of. You were in a shit circumstance that led to even more shit. And you got out."

Wait. She *did* get out, didn't she?

The Dragons didn't just let people out. "How did you get away from them? They don't just let people walk away from the gang."

"By the end, my relationship with Eddie was no longer fun or sexy. The guys got rougher each time, none of it was ever about me. It was just a game to them; humiliating me, passing me around. Seeing who could be the biggest man. By that point I was too afraid to leave. I started using drugs more because it gave me an escape. My Uncle Mark came to visit. He's my mother's brother. He couldn't believe I wasn't living at home and my parents had no idea where I was. Somehow, he found me and literally carried me out of there. It was the night that video was made. I don't know how Chris got his hands on it. I didn't even know I'd been recorded."

Zach's head was spinning with a million questions. He gripped Toni's upper arms. "Wait, that video was from Chris? The suit?"

She nodded. "He said he'd send it to the school where I work and send it out on social media. He said it'd go viral in a matter of hours. I have three weeks to get back to Chicago before he posts it. He doesn't actually want to be with me. Just wants me to convince my uncle to advance his position at work. He's nothing but an opportunist, and a desperate one."

"Fuck. That fucking piece of shit." Zach spun away and raked his fingers through his hair. Could this situation be more fucked up? "Okay. We'll deal with him. No one else will ever see that video. I promise you. Now how did your uncle get you away? Because, baby, no one leaves the Dragons in one piece."

Toni looked startled. "I have no idea. I was pretty messed up back then, and it took me a long time and a lot of therapy to straighten myself out. I don't think I ever asked, or really even thought about it."

"We need to call him."

Toni grabbed his arm, panic in her eyes. "No! Chris said if I mentioned anything to Mark, he'd post the video immediately."

Zach snorted. "Fucking piece of shit isn't going to do anything. I'll talk to your uncle. Convince him to keep quiet and let me handle it. We got this, okay?"

"We?" she asked.

"Yeah, we."

For the first time since he'd walked out of that bathroom he was treated to a genuine smile from Toni. "Okay."

"Okay, I need to call Copper." As he pulled his phone out, Toni's hand landed on his arm.

"Wait. Did you say Shark was the one who took Maverick?"

Shit. He had blurted that. Club business wasn't for open discussion, but Toni had just bared her soul to him. He owed her something in return. Something to show the same level of trust. "Yes. And we've been spinning our wheels for days because we have no idea where to find him. Shark's definitely grown some teeth, because no one is talking no matter how much pressure we put on them. The gang's all but disappeared. No one's been at their headquarters since before Mav was taken. We've got fucking nothing."

Toni's eyes widened and her grip tightened until her nails pricked his forearm. Her mouth opened but no sound came out.

"What, baby?"

"I know where he might be," she whispered.

CHAPTER TWENTY-TWO

Over the past few weeks, Toni had spent a considerable amount of time in the presence of the MC members. Of course, that was in her diner where they were well fed, caffeinated, and happy. The one time she was on their turf, they were drunk, raucous, and looking for sex, but still happy.

Now, she was in their clubhouse once again, and the mood couldn't be further away from amusement and fun. She sat at a gigantic round table with no less than twenty tired, stressed, and pissed off bikers staring at her. Never in her life had she seen so many murderous scowls in one place.

The scowls weren't aimed at her, but they were still intimidating as hell.

Beside her, Zach squeezed her knee and whispered in her ear. "It's okay, baby. I promise. Everyone here is on your side. No one will hurt you or ever make you do anything you don't want to do."

She swallowed and nodded. If only his supportive words softened the bikers' expressions.

Copper cleared his throat and her attention shifted to him. How Shell could be attracted to him was a mystery to Toni. That wasn't entirely true. The physical attraction she got. He was hot in a growly, brooding kind of way. But he was also intense and crazy menacing, and that trumped the hotness in her mind.

Zach

"Thanks for coming here, Toni. I get that you had a rough morning and are dealing with some major shit. I'm sorry if this dredges up bad memories for you."

"That's all right," she croaked then cleared her throat. She wasn't some wilting flower. She could handle this. "It's fine. I'm just hoping I can help you find Maverick."

"So, Zach tells me you know a little about the Gray Dragons."

Zach curled an arm around her shoulders. "You don't have to give any details you're uncomfortable with, baby," he whispered in her ear.

She placed her hand on his thigh and squeezed in gratitude. Recounting the entire humiliating story of her shameful past would be traumatizing at best.

"You want me to tell them for you?"

Zach was being so sweet and supportive. Never would she have imagined a rough and gruff biker could handle her with such care. Like she was a fine china plate that had just cracked down the center. Ready to shatter at any point.

Giving him that impression was her mistake and it was time to put a stop to it. While she loved his attentiveness, she wasn't, in fact, going to shatter at any point. Zach wasn't to blame for thinking her weak. She'd lost her shit in her kitchen. But that was just the shock of watching herself being violated. And knowing Zach was a witness to it as well.

"I'm good," she whispered, then spoke to Copper. "I was with Shark for a little over a year. It was a long time ago, but I was his girlfriend. Or I guess you guys would have called me his ol' lady."

"No fucking way," Zach broke in. "An ol' lady is a term that denotes respect. Shark doesn't know the meaning of the word."

If she'd found him hard to resist before, this caring and protective side of Zach made it impossible to even think of walking away from him. Instead, she felt herself falling. So stupid considering she was dealing with the fallout of her last dysfunctional relationship.

"Whatever," she said shaking her head. "That doesn't matter. What matters is that I was really young and really stupid. Things went...bad and I had an uncle pull me out of a really terrible situation. I haven't seen or spoken to anyone from the Gray Dragons since I was eighteen."

Copper frowned and rubbed at his bearded chin. "How did you get out?"

"My uncle literally walked in, picked me up, and left with me. I was uh..." Her face flamed. "I was really high at the time and don't remember it. I woke up in my uncle's house about a day later. To be honest, I'm not sure how he found me. I think he had a PI tailing Shark."

Zach mentioned respect. None of these men were going to have an ounce of respect for her. They'd think she was nothing better than a junkie whore.

"Breathe, baby. You're doing great." Zach pressed a kiss to her temple and warmth filled her chest.

"There's no fucking way they just let you leave."

"Huh?"

Zach's hand landed on her thigh again. "I had the same thought. It was too easy."

"What do you mean?" She frowned and looked between Zach and Copper.

"There are two ways out of the gang. Death or a beat out," Zach said.

"A beat out?" Was that as horrible as it sounded?

"Yes." Copper said as though reading her mind. "They literally beat you bloody. If you survive it, you're out. But you keep your mouth shut about anything gang related when you leave or they'll kill you. And very few people are even granted a beat out. Most of the time you're in till you die."

A chill ran down her spine. Zach must have noticed her tremble because he pulled her from her chair onto his lap. Normally, she'd have shoved him away, but today she allowed herself the comfort of his body. Nothing about the day was normal. Tomorrow she could repent for her weakness.

"But I wasn't in the gang. I was just some whore they used."

Zach growled, but it was Rocket who spoke first. "No!" he said with so much vehemence, Toni gaped at him. "Don't wanna ever hear you describe yourself that way again, babe. You were a kid that was taken advantage of. They fucked with your head and your body. That's all on Shark. And he'll fuckin' pay for that. None of it's on you."

"Holy shit, was that the most you've ever spoken in your life?"

Laughter broke out around the table cutting the tension down a few notches.

"Women are treated to the same rules as the actual gang members," Copper said.

"So why did they let me leave?"

"I'm thinking money," Zach answered as he wrapped his arms around her and locked her against his chest.

Copper nodded. "Makes sense. Her uncle must have paid a pretty penny for her."

"What?" Someone was going to have to scoop her jaw off the floor at this point. "Paid for me. Like Shark sold me to my uncle?" In what was now becoming a familiar sensation, her stomach flipped. "This is mortifying. I-I'm going to be sick," she said.

Zach cupped her cheek and turned her to face him. "Hey," he said in a soothing tone. "It's just me here. No one else. Just focus on me." He pressed his lips to hers in a kiss that was so tender it brought tears to her eyes.

As Zach kissed her, in a room full of rowdy bikers, the world faded away. The past wasn't important any more. Old shame disappeared. All that mattered was the way he made her feel in that moment. Important, cherished, wanted...dare she say, loved.

It wasn't love. Couldn't be. But it sure worked to chase away the pain.

"Better?" he asked when he pulled back.

Her eyelids fluttered open and she sighed. "Better."

"I know it sounds bad, but your uncle did the right thing. He got you out of there without any further trauma. Who gives a shit about the money?"

She nodded. It wasn't about the money, though she felt guilty as hell that Mark had parted with his hard-earned cash for her. It was the principle of the matter. That some man, some vile piece of shit, thought he owned her and had the right to demand money for her freedom.

"You surprise me," she said.

Zach winked. "There's more where that came from, baby."

Toni laughed, which had to be his intent and, suddenly, a heavy weight lifted off her. Zach was right. This was over. Done. She'd survived and had been using her experience to try to help other misguided youth. Preferably before their situations got as bad as hers. How could she give that up? She might be coming to love life in Tennessee, but she had a passion for helping troubled teens she couldn't just ignore. Sometime soon she was going to have to make some serious life decisions.

She turned back to Copper. "Sorry about that."

Copper waved it away.

"Shark had a great grandfather that lived to be a hundred and six years old. He was a nasty, paranoid old bastard. Lived off the grid in a cabin in the woods. I think he was one of those guys prepared for anything from nuclear fallout to an alien invasion." She rolled her eyes and rubbed at an ache in her neck. "Anyway, the old guy loved his great grandson and left his cabin to Shark when he died."

Finally, Copper smiled. It was almost hard to see with the bushy beard. "That's the best news we've had in days, darlin'. Why don't you give the address to Jig over there, and we'll get a plan together to get Mav back."

Zach

"Well, uh, that's the thing. I don't know the address. I'm not sure it actually has an address. And it's been so many years, I can't remember exactly how to get there." When grumbling started around the table, she rushed on. "But I could find it. I'm sure of it. Take me with you, and I know it will come back to me as we drive."

"Over my dead fucking body." Zach stood so fast she nearly tumbled to the floor. "No fucking way, Copper. This is not happening."

"Uh, Zach, it might be the only way to get Maverick back," Toni pointed out. She *had* to help. It felt like destiny. Like giving a purpose to all the shit she went through in the past. So she could now use her knowledge to help these men who'd come to mean something to her over the past few weeks. Help them save Maverick.

"You are not getting within ten miles of fuckin' Shark. You hear me? This is not up for discussion. The answer is no fucking way."

"Excuse me? Not up for discussion? Um, you're damn right it's not up for discussion. You do not get a say in this, Zach. If I want to go do a naked rain dance on Shark's front stoop, I'll damn well do it."

The sound that came from Zach probably should have scared her, but she was done being scared. Now she was pissed. Pissed at what she'd gone through, pissed Maverick was missing, and even a little pissed at Zach's macho bullshit.

"There is no way in hell my woman is going anywhere near the man who abused her for over a year. If I have to tie you to my bed and fuck you stupid to keep you from going, then that's what I'll do."

Toni's jaw dropped while a couple of the guys chuckled. She wasn't his woman and he had absolutely no say over her actions. And if thoughts of him tying her to his bed and making good on his promise made her wet, that would just be her little secret.

Zach's lips quirked.

Damnit. The stupid man knew his effect on her.

"Fighters, to your corners," Copper said, his eyes dancing with laughter. Toni wouldn't have thought it possible, but the man actually looked amused. "I know you don't want to hear this, Zach, but Toni's right. We have a shot to get Mav back and we have to take it. We can keep your woman safe. I swear it on my life. Shark won't get within shouting distance of her."

Zach gripped the edge of the table so hard his neck corded and the muscles in his arms bunched until it looked like his shirt sleeves were going to split. He bowed his head and sighed. "Answer me one thing, Cop, what would you be saying if it were Shell we were talking about taking with us?"

Copper's face darkened in an instant and his fists curled.

Afraid he was going to take a swing at Zach, Toni jumped in. "Zach," she said, cupping the tense muscles at the back of his neck. He turned his head until his ice blue gaze bore into hers. "I can do this. I need to do this. To help. To put some purpose behind everything I went through in the past. Shark won't get near me. You guys will see to that. I trust you completely."

She tried to convey to Zach how important this was through her gaze. If she could take the errors of her past and turn them around to help Maverick, maybe she could put that part of her life to rest permanently.

"Fine," Zach said after a few minutes. Then he looked to Copper. "But she stays out of the building and as far as fucking possible from Shark. I don't want that motherfucker anywhere near her."

Copper nodded.

"And we take him back here. Alive. I want fifteen minutes alone with him."

Toni inhaled a sharp breath. This was a discussion she probably shouldn't be hearing. Club business and all that. It was also something she should protest. But she didn't. Who knew how many women Shark had abused through the years? She'd been too young, scared, stupid, and screwed up to do anything at the time, but she could help end it now. She could help ensure he never harmed another woman again.

Copper's gaze flicked to Toni then back to Zach. "You got it."

Toni glanced around the room at the determined faces of the Handlers. Each one would like a crack at Shark, but they'd leave it for Zach because they saw her as his woman.

It was a lot to process.

Zach cupped the back of her neck. "Why don't you head on out to the bar and relax while we plan. Shell should be there."

She nodded and Zach pulled her in for a quick firm kiss.

As she left the room, something that had been dancing at the edges of her mind fought its way to the forefront.

How the hell did Chris get his hands on a video file of Shark's?

CHAPTER TWENTY-THREE

It had been over a decade since Zach left the army, but some shit stayed with a man for life. Like the ability to silently creep through the forest with the butt of a rifle secured against his shoulder. Granted, jungle training took a back seat to desert drills, but there were quite a few places in the world where it came in handy, so it was still practiced.

Over and over.

For years.

Until it became as second nature as scratching his balls.

As a young enlisted soldier, it sucked. Now? As he tiptoed through the dense backwoods of Tennessee with an M16, yeah, he was damn grateful for muscle memory and all those drill sergeants who rode his ass over the years.

"'Bout a hundred feet up. Twelve o'clock." Rocket's eager voice came through his com unit. The former Marine loved this shit. Sometimes it surprised Zach he didn't join some swat team after he left the corps. Then he remembered Rocket's hatred for authority, which was the reason he'd left the Marine Corps in the first place. It was a testament to Copper's leadership that Rocket was willing to fall in line and obey orders.

The Handlers were spread out, making their way toward the Gray Dragon's compound. Six of the men had done at least one tour in the military and the other four were just crazy motherfuckers who'd jump at any chance to get in on some action.

About two hours ago, the sun had set, throwing a thick blanket of darkness over the entire area. The only reason any of the men could see was thanks to Rocket and some crazy ass connections.

After hours of planning, Rocket had placed a call to someone and within forty-five minutes, com units and night vision goggles were waiting for them at a warehouse outside of town. Didn't matter where they came from, which was good because Rocket would never out his source. All that mattered was when they needed the shit, it was there.

Weapons were even easier to obtain. The club had plenty of those stashed in an underground vault beneath the clubhouse.

"I got eyes on two rooftop guards. No one on the ground," Rocket said.

"Copy. Same," Zach replied as the old cabin came into view. The building pretty much fit Toni's description to a tee. One story, boxy log cabin in a clearing. Nothing fancy. According to Toni, the place had four bedrooms. It was used by the higher ups in the gang. A place for them to party and engage in some of their more questionable recreational activities.

Shark's great grandfather had died a few months after Toni started dating Shark. At the time, he'd been working to prove himself to the gang's leadership and he offered the house up for use by the inner circle in exchange for a seat at the table.

The property wasn't listed anywhere as owned by Shark or the gang, which explained why so few people knew its whereabouts. Low level gang bangers weren't even allowed on the premises, per Toni. They had to be initiated into the inner circle or some shit before they were invited. Unless they were guarding the place.

For men in the gang, getting a golden ticket to Shark's love nest meant offing someone of his choice. For women...well, it meant being fucked by the top three leaders in the gang. If a man wanted his woman to be invited to the compound he had to give her up to the leadership.

Made Zach's stomach turn to think of Toni going through that. Not because he was ashamed of her or her past. Fuck no. But because the thought of her being used, of her childhood need for love and affection being exploited like that made him want to toss a match at the place and watch it fucking burn.

With everyone inside.

"All right," Copper said through the com. He was not the type of president to sit on the sidelines. "Let's move in. Like we planned. Wait until the guards move to the back of the roof. Zach, Rocket, Jig, Screw, and Dope, you five head in and get to the basement."

Toni had sketched out as much of the interior layout as she could remember. Most of her time spent there she'd been wasted or high, so her memory was fuzzy, but she recalled the way to the basement.

A basement she'd seen Shark and his piece of shit cronies coming out of bloodied on more than one occasion. Looked like the house was used for more than just the Dragons' fuckfests.

Probably where Mav was being held.

If he was there at all.

He had to be. There weren't any other leads. So, if Maverick wasn't there, they were all fucked.

The five chosen men inched their way out of the woods and toward the dark cabin. The other five stayed scattered at the edges of the woods, backup in case it all went to shit. Which there was a very high possibility of. They'd specifically chosen to go in the middle of the night because of the potential for fewer Dragons being present.

As he made his way toward the side door Toni had described, the back of Zach's neck itched. Never one to ignore his gut, he checked his six before continuing. The heebie-jeeebies had to be coming from knowing Toni was nearby, waiting. Sure, she was guarded by a prospect, but Zach hadn't wanted her anywhere near this shit.

She'd threatened to castrate them all if they shuttled her home. Zach hadn't cared. He'd give up his dick and each of his brother's dicks to keep her away from any more of this shit, but Copper had overruled and said she could wait in the truck parked a mile out of the woods.

As pissed as he'd been, Toni's triumphant grin made him laugh.

He was fucked in the head where she was concerned.

Nodding to Rocket, who reached the door first, Zach checked his surroundings once again.

Something wasn't right. It was no longer a little scratch at the back of his neck, now it was full-on dragon-lady nails raking over his skin.

Rocket gave a quick shake of his head and started to inch away from the door.

Fuck.

He felt it too.

Together, they silently circled the building. Neither rooftop guard was in sight when they came around to the front.

As he turned to check behind him once again, Zach's sight bloomed-out. Everything in his entire field of vision turned bright green.

Which could only mean one thing.

Someone turned on some lights.

They were fucking outed.

In one simultaneous move, Zach ripped his head gear off with one hand and raised his rifle toward the roof with the other while backing away as quickly as his legs would carry him. About fifteen feet away, Rocket did the same.

He could hear the muttered curses of the rest of his brothers, all reversing toward the woods, weapons at the ready.

Giant flood lights illuminated the open space between the woods and the cabin, making it as bright as fucking day.

The two guards on the roof stood at the edge of the building with their guns trained down on the Handlers as they all convened in the center of the clearing.

Zach's first instinct was to take out the guards. Two or three bullets would be all he needed. As he steadied his rifle, a slow clap accompanied by a mocking laugh filled the air.

"Fuck me! You found me!" Shark stood in the open doorway of the house's entrance. "You assholes cost me three hundred bucks just now. Did you know that?"

What the fuck?

Out of the corner of his eye, Zach caught Rocket shift his gun from the guards to Shark.

"Uh uh." Shark tsked and wagged his finger back and forth like a parent scolding their toddler. "I wouldn't do that if I were you. I got somebody here I think you'd all like to see, and my men have orders to shoot on sight should anything happen to me. So, let's just keep the trigger-happy fingers nice and still, okay?"

No one responded, but then Shark couldn't really expect anyone to. He just wanted to run his trap, show he was the big swinging dick in charge at the moment.

"As I was saying," Shark went on. "Me and my men had a little bet going." While he spoke, he pointed to the guards over his head. "I said there was no fucking way a bunch of dirty ass, shit-for-brains bikers would find my playhouse. I bet three hundred fucking dollars on it. Someone's gonna pay me back."

Enough listening to the asshole. "The fuck you want in exchange for our man?" Zach called out.

Shark's gaze swung wildly as he tried to locate the speaker. He had the crazed, glassy-eyed look of someone hopped up on something. That would be to their advantage if it slowed his reflexes, but it could swing the other way if it made him impulsive and rash.

"Who the fuck's interrupting me?" Shark's voice grew shrill and it sounded like the banger was nearing an all-out hissy fit.

Zach

"I fucking interrupted you, asshole." Zach stepped forward from the group. If he could divert some attention to himself, maybe his guys could figure out a way to end this.

"Zach." Copper's warning voice filled his ear.

Shark started to pace in front of the open door. "You want to know what I want in exchange for your friend. You mean this friend?" He reached in the door and yanked a very roughed up Maverick outside.

Zach's finger flexed against the trigger, but he couldn't pull it because Shark shoved Mav in front of him human-shield style and held a wicked looking knife to his throat.

God damnit.

"I'm thinking you wasted your time coming here, bikers. I've had a shitty week and Maverick here has been great. He let me work all my frustrations out on him." Shark cackled like some kind of witch as he jerked Mav from side to side. "I'm not ready to give him up."

Both Maverick's eyes were bruised and swollen to twice their normal size. His head lolled to the side, blood dripping from both his nose and mouth. Shirtless, his torso looked like it had been used for a punching bag. For a moment, Zach wondered if he was drugged, but it looked like he was just in severe pain.

Shark was a big man, and he held Maverick up with ease. The knife at his throat dug into Mav's flesh, leaving a shallow gash dotted with blood. It was impossible to assess the extent of his injuries, but they appeared severe.

"See his fucking arm?" Rocket whispered through the com link.

"Fuck me," Copper said. "Shark's a fucking dead man. No matter what happens in the next few minutes, Shark dies today."

Zach couldn't agree more. Maverick's left forearm was one of the few parts of his body free of ink. He left a wide space of clear skin around his Hell's Handlers brand. That skin now looked charred and infected. Whatever Shark had taken to it had completely destroyed the brand and the surrounding skin. If he had to guess, it was a fucking clothes iron.

Zach's heart clenched in his chest. The brotherhood of the club was everything to Mav, who grew up bouncing from one miserable foster home to another his whole childhood. No matter how grave his other injuries, the destruction of that brand would be the most devastating.

Rule was, no brand, no club membership.

Somehow, an exception would have to be made.

"Enough bullshit," Zach called out, taking three steps toward Shark. If he could piss the gang leader off enough to distract him and get him to loosen his hold or remove his focus from Mav for a moment, one of his brothers could take Shark out. "You don't fucking need him and we aren't leaving without him. Why not hand him over before we shoot you in the face and burn your palace to the ground, princess?"

Shark laughed again and Zach clenched his teeth. Hopefully, Shark would survive long enough for them to have a little payback fun with him.

"The interrupter. You know, I still didn't get to finish what I was saying. Hey, Mav? You think I like being interrupted?" He shook Maverick like a rag doll, scraping the knife across his neck and making a second shallow cut.

"Fuck," Jig said into the com. He was somewhere behind and to the left of Zach. "We need to move this along. He ain't looking good. One wrong move and he slits our boy's throat."

"Just get on with whatever the hell it is you want to say so bad," Zach yelled.

A creepy smile curved Shark's mouth. "I couldn't fathom how I lost the bet. How did a bunch of idiots find me out here, off the grid?" The smile grew. "Then I got my answer. And I feel better knowing that you are all, in fact, a bunch of stupid fucks."

"What's the answer then?" Zach asked.

"It's coming."

Zach

In the next second, Zach's entire world came crashing to a halt as Toni walked out of the woods and into the clearing.

Actually, it was more like she was dragged out of the woods literally kicking and screaming.

With a gun to her head.

CHAPTER TWENTY-FOUR

"Can't take it anymore, babe. Get your ass out of the car." Special K, the prospect assigned to babysit Toni while the rest of the men rescued Maverick, shoved his door open and exited the truck.

He stomped around and yanked the passenger side door open, as well. "Seriously, babe. You're making me fucking crazy," he said, motioning with his arm for her to get out.

Toni scowled but slid from the very high pickup's seat until her feet hit the road. It wasn't her fault she couldn't sit still. She was nervous. "Sorry," she grumbled.

For the past fifteen minutes, since Zach and the rest of the men disappeared, she'd been bouncing her heel on the floorboard and drumming her nails on the dash. Yes, that probably got a little annoying after the first few minutes, but come on. If ever a situation called for a nervous tick, this was it.

"Here," he waved his hand in front of the truck. "Pace or some shit like that. Just be quiet about it." The kid couldn't have been older than twenty. With a sexy black beard and thick black hair, he was hot as hell and Toni could appreciate it in a look-but-don't-touch kind of way.

Maybe Zach was right and she should have gone back to the clubhouse. At least she could have tapped her nails in peace there. Or gotten wasted with Shell.

But she'd *had* to be present. She and Zach had driven around for almost two hours under her terrible navigation until a farm

206

stand on the side of the road finally jogged her memory and she'd recalled the maze of dirt roads leading to a turnoff in the middle of the nowheresville that led to Shark's old cabin. Once she'd identified the spot, Zach called the cavalry and had a prospect drive her a mile out to wait.

Very impatiently.

But she refused to leave until she saw Zach walking out of those woods with her own eyes. Hopefully next to Maverick.

"Tell me something about yourself," she said. They'd left the truck's doors open and it provided just enough light to see his face.

Special K shot her a look that said he ate nails for breakfast and wore puppies as slippers, so he couldn't be bothered with inane chatter. "Quiet." Hand on his very scary gun, he scanned the area all around their vehicle.

"Come on," she said, trying very hard not to whine. "I'm going out of my mind here. If you don't want me to start singing to myself—and trust me, you don't want that—I need a distraction."

He just stared at her.

"Give me something here, buddy. How about your name. Why do they call you Special K?"

His lips quirked. "My name's Ken."

"Seriously? That's it? Your name starts with a K and you're special? No offense, but that's so lame." Toni paced back and forth in front of the car, kicking a rock with her foot. On one pass, she got a little overzealous and sent the rock flying into the undercarriage of the car.

"Shit, woman!" Ken stalked over to her. "If I tell you where my name comes from, will you park your sweet ass against the truck and stop moving?"

Victory. At least she could listen to him talk instead of obsessing in her own head. With a tentative smile, Toni walked to the car and leaned her bottom against the grill. "Okay, I'm parked. Start talking."

He folded his arms across his chest, letting the gun hang crosswise in front of his torso. "I have a reputation for being skilled at something. Guys found out about it and gave me my handle."

She scrunched up her nose. "Well what is it?"

"Something for the ladies."

Really? This was the perfect distraction. "That could be anything from holding purses while they use the restroom, to foot rubs, to…"

His lips curved in a sexy grin.

"Special K…" she muttered. "Oh my God!" Toni jumped away from the car with a laugh. "Please tell me that doesn't stand for Special Kisses."

The grin grew even bigger.

Toni slapped a hand over her mouth in a fruitless effort to stifle the laughter. "That is too much," she said. Then she stopped laughing and thought. "What do you do that makes you so good?"

Ken snorted. "Not telling you that, babe. You think your ol' man would be okay with me describing my technique to you?"

He had a point. Zach would probably flip his shit.

Wait. "I don't have an ol' man."

"Whatever you say, babe."

If she wasn't so curious, she'd be pissed at his dismissive attitude.

"Just tell me one—"

"Shit, you don't ever shut up, do you?"

"Hey!"

"Okay," he said, as he scanned the area once again. "I'll just say this. Under four minutes. Every time."

Toni's jaw dropped. "No way! Every woman you've ever… you know to has come in under four minutes?"

"One hundred percent success rate. And the sample isn't small." He smirked.

Zach

"Well, color me impres—" A quick succession of three *pops* coincided with Ken's body jerking three times. He gasped and brought a hand up to his chest. "Ken? Oh fuck! Ken?"

He drew his hand away and stared down at his bright red palm while red bloomed across his chest soaking his gray shirt in an instant. His legs gave out and he crumpled to the ground, sprawled out on his back. A terrible whistling sound came from his chest with each attempted breath.

The entire thing seemed to happen in slow motion, as though hours were passing when in reality it couldn't have been more than five seconds.

Toni dropped to her knees beside him. "Shit! Ken? Please hang on." She patted her pockets. "Where the fuck is my phone?"

"Run," Ken rasped out, the sound gurgly and muted.

Toni shook her head as tears started to fall. "No. I'm not leaving you." She pulled off her sweatshirt, completely impervious to the chilly night air. After balling it up, she jammed it against his chest and put her full body weight into it.

"No u-use. I'm fucked." Ken said, his eyes closed and face pale as a ghost already. "Th-they're com-coming. Run." His voice was barely a whisper.

"No, no, no. You're gonna be fine, Ken. Focus on something good. Think about all the ladies who still need to experience your talents." Oh my God, she couldn't do this. Couldn't watch a man die. A man who she'd been joking with and driving crazy just seconds before. A sob lodged in her throat, coming out like a wounded animal sound instead.

Ken coughed making blood erupt from his mouth and trail down his cheek.

Another rapid clip of gunfire sounded and this time a bullet whizzed by her head.

Toni shrieked and tried to keep pressure on his wound and inch toward the car at the same time.

The heavy trod of footsteps crunching over gravel sounded way too close for comfort.

"Run, woman."

"I c-can't just l-leave you." She was sobbing now. How could she leave a dying man on the side of the road? One who was dying because his job was to protect her.

"The o-others…" He coughed one last time then his body went limp.

Toni's breath seized in her lungs. The others! Shit, if Shark knew they were coming, they'd be walking into an ambush. Without thinking about the fact that she barely knew which way to point a gun, Toni pulled a pistol from the holster on Ken's hip and stuffed it in the waistband of her jeans. It was hidden by the oversized T-shirt she'd stolen from Zach.

As the footsteps grew closer, Toni sprang to her feet and ran about fifteen feet before a male voice shouted. "Stop running, or I'll shoot you in the fucking head."

Her feet stopped so abruptly she nearly toppled ass over head.

"Hands up!" the voice barked.

Trembling like she was naked in a snowstorm, Toni stuck her hands in the air. Her eyes drifted closed and she tensed, waiting for the pain of a bullet to rip through her skull. When the barrel of a gun was rammed between her shoulder blades, she couldn't help but screech in shock.

"Walk into the woods."

Into the woods? At night? With no light, no jacket, and all kinds of hungry darkness-loving creatures? No way. No how. Her legs were shaking so hard she'd probably fall flat on her face with the first step.

Her captor nudged her forward with the gun. Inside her chest cavity, her heart pounded so fast she felt lightheaded. It took everything she had to keep from hyperventilating. She had to get herself under control. Zach's life and the lives of his brothers might depend on her ability to keep her shit together.

Zach

With a stuttered breath, she took small steps toward the woods. At least there was a chance the animals in the woods wouldn't kill her. The guy behind her had already proven his willingness to end a life.

She whimpered as she thought of Ken.

Running would never work, so without any smart alternative, Toni tromped through the woods. The hike seemed to last forever and she tripped and stumbled in the darkness more times than she could count. Without light to guide her way, Toni smacked into trees, and branches ripped at her bare arms. She'd be a bloody mess of scratches by the time they reached their destination. For some reason, whether it was cold, shock, or the fact that her mind was clogged with fear, the pain of tearing flesh didn't even register.

After another few minutes of trudging through the growth, some distance up ahead, through the dense mass of trees, the forest suddenly flared up with light. What would she find when she reached the light? Would Zach and the rest of the men even be alive. Suddenly paralyzed, she came to a complete stop. Her stomach churned and she swallowed down the need to vomit.

"Keep moving." The gun hit her between the shoulder blades yet again.

The lighted area grew closer and closer until she could finally see what was waiting for her. And then she recognized five of the men she'd traveled with standing in the center of the clearing, guns aimed at the building.

Oh, thank God. They were all alive.

When she was just five feet from being out in the open, she heard Shark's voice and nearly lost her stomach contents. The rush of negative memories was so powerful, her vision blurred and a buzzing kicked up in her ears.

Shark was too dangerous. This wasn't going to end well for the Handlers.

"No," she said and stopped walking again. "I'm not going any farther. Shoot me if you have to."

Her asshole captor laughed and grabbed the back of her neck, dragging her forward.

She fought. Kicked, screamed, attempted to bite and scratch, but it was useless. In the next thirty seconds, Toni blinked and realized she was now in the clearing, staring at Zach's shocked and outraged face.

"Antonia," Shark said, making her cringe. She hated the name since leaving him. He'd always called her by it. At first, she'd thought it was so sweet. Now, the memory made her want to vomit.

On Shark's grave.

"You've made some new friends in the years you've been gone." He was holding Maverick, who looked so battered Toni wanted to weep for him. "I see you remembered how to get here. The place must have had a big impact on you." The way he said it made her think he was recalling the hours spent with her there. Hours she found revolting and panic-inducing but he seemed to relish. "But a few things have changed since you've been here. Like the cameras I've installed all over my woods."

Shit. It was a risk Zach and the boys had identified earlier in the day. Had Mav been with them, he might have been able to do some computer voodoo and discover the cameras, or so Zach claimed. As it was, they didn't want to waste the time finding someone else they could trust. So they'd taken the risk. And failed. What would happen now? Would Shark kill them all? Take them prisoners?

She caught Zach's gaze just before he turned away. God, how she wanted to run into his arms. But she stayed still. And silent. Shark would not get to her.

"Okay, Shark. Gang's all here. We get it. You have the upper hand. What the fuck do you want?" Copper yelled out. Toni looked around but didn't see him. He must have been in the woods, waiting for an opportunity to take a shot.

Shark looked the same as she remembered except for the crazy in his eyes. He wasn't overly tall, a few inches under six feet, and broad. Built like a rectangle, he had long blond hair that reached his shoulders and hazel eyes that, depending on what he was wearing, could look green as the grass. It boggled her mind now that she'd once found him attractive.

"Well," he said. "I had a plan." His gaze shifted from Zach to Toni and she shivered. "But plans change. I'll make it very simple. A trade. Mav for Antonia."

Her knees wobbled and threatened to buckle.

"Not fucking happening, Shark." Zach said, the anger in his voice a living thing.

"No?" Shark walked forward, dragging Mav, until he was halfway between the building and Zach. "I guess I'll just have my guys shoot Maverick right no—"

"I'll do it!" Toni screamed. She'd survived Shark before and could again. This time, she had the Hell's Handlers behind her. They'd come for her. Rescue her, eventually. The alternative was Maverick's death on her conscience, and that was something she couldn't live with. She'd already have to find a way to deal with Ken's.

"Toni, no!" Zach yelled. "Fuck no!" He started toward her but Rocket caught him with an arm around his chest. "Brother, get the fuck off me."

"Come on then, Toni. Let's get this reunion started." Shark stared at her.

As she walked toward Shark, she locked eyes with Zach and tried to convey to him that it was okay. She'd survive. She had a plan. Somewhat. When she passed him, he whispered, "Please don't do this, Toni," and reached for her, but Rocket held him firm.

"It's okay," she whispered and kept walking.

When she reached Shark, he said. "Get behind me."

She obeyed without a word.

"Here's how this is going to go," he said. "Mav will walk toward you and Antonia will come around and take his place.

You shoot my guys on the roof, and I'll slit her throat. We'll stand here until you are gone. If you don't leave, she's dead."

Zach made a choked sound that had Shark laughing. "Guess we know which one of you she's been fucking."

"Hope you can stay on your feet," Shark said to Maverick as he removed the knife from his neck. "Walk straight. No funny shit or she dies."

"Antonia, after he takes five steps, you slip around front. When they are gone, we'll go inside and get reacquainted."

She shuddered and bile rose in her throat. She'd sooner die than have his hands on her again.

This time, instead of fighting the unpleasant memories, she let them come. Let them fuel her hatred and anger. She embraced the feeling of being a needy unloved seventeen-year-old girl yearning for attention and affection. She let the old feelings of shame, humiliation, and fear wash over her and power her next move.

She knew what she had to do. Could live with it.

She just prayed it would work.

CHAPTER TWENTY-FIVE

Zach struggled against Rocket's unbreakable hold. He was going to kill his brother the second they were free of this fucked up situation.

The only reason he didn't let his rage fly and take Rocket down was that he couldn't put Toni at risk any more than she was already.

She had to be terrified, standing behind Shark, knowing what would happen to her the moment Maverick reached the group. Blood ran in small rivers down her arms and face from what looked like dozens of scratches. They'd better just be from the trees in the woods. If the fucker that brought her from the car had laid a hand on her, he'd be dying a slow death as well.

"I'm cool," he said to Rocket who loosened his hold. That was a damn lie. He was about as hot as it got, but his hands were tied. Used to being in a position of power, being rendered impotent and unable to help his woman was torture. There might not be anything he could do in that moment to save Toni. But he damn sure could end Shark's life when this was done.

As he watched, Maverick took a staggering step forward then stopped to catch his breath. After a few seconds, he managed another step that looked agonizing.

Mav would need to be transported straight to the hospital. For a second, Mav's gaze found Zach's and Zach worried his friend would turn and charge Shark. He wouldn't survive it and

Toni might not either. He gave Mav the smallest head shake he could manage.

Mav struggled forward another step and then a loud bang rang out. Shark made a strangled noise, clutched his abdomen and fell to the floor.

Zach gaped at the gun hanging limply in Toni's hands and her dazed expression before all hell broke loose.

Zach and Rocket both charged forward. Rocket grabbed Mav around his waist and swung him toward the building. Zach plowed into Toni. He tackled her to the ground and shielded her with his body while the pop of assault rifles sounded around them.

It didn't take long before quiet ensued. Zach lifted his head and did a quick count. Ten Handlers were milling around. Mav was over Rocket's shoulder in a fireman carry that must have hurt like a sonofabitch but was the easiest way to get him out. The two rooftop guards weren't anywhere to be seen but were probably dead on the roof, and the man who'd escorted Toni out of the woods was dead as a doornail. Shark lay unmoving just feet away in a pool of his own blood.

The only thing Zach regretted was not being the one to dish out a little MC justice before killing Shark himself.

Beneath him, Toni squirmed. "Let me up. Are you hurt?" She pushed against his chest until he sat back on his knees. Scrambling to her knees as well, she ran her hands over his body. "Did you get hit anywhere?" Her voice was one breath away from hysterical.

Zach grabbed her hands, stilling her frantic search for bullet holes. "Baby, I'm fine. Not a scratch on me, though I can't say the same for you." He ran his finger over an angry gouge running up the side of her porcelain neck.

Toni didn't even seem to notice she was bleeding. "Is everyone else okay?" She tried to shove him away with thrashing arms, but he yanked her close and held her head against his pounding heart. "Everyone is okay. You did good,

Zach

baby. You are fucking amazing. Shit, I can't believe you had a gun."

"Oh my God. I shot him. I had to do something." Trembling in his arms, she burrowed as close as she could get without climbing into his skin. "The guys on the roof! Did they kill anyone? Should I have waited? Oh my God. Did I get someone killed? Let me see. Please, I need to see everyone."

She shrugged out of his embrace and Zach helped her to her feet. The red, ragged scratches covering her skin looked worse up close. Her hair was a snarled mess, falling out of its band and with twigs scattered throughout.

"Wait," he said, lifting one of her arms. "Baby, you're scratched to shit. I promise everyone is okay and you can see them in a minute. I just need to know you're okay. Scared ten fucking years off my life just now."

She met his gaze and he saw that she wasn't quite as good as she claimed. Hell, she'd just taken a life. But being the fierce woman she was, she didn't fall apart. She shoved it down and straightened. Later, in private, might be a different story, but Zach planned to be there for every tear, every second of guilt, every worry, and he'd soothe them all away.

"I'm good," she whispered.

Zach cupped her injured face and pressed his lips to hers. He'd come so close to losing her. To losing the fragile connection they shared but had yet to define. That was going to change. Once this was over, he was locking that shit down. No more running. No more games. She was going to be his if he had to handcuff her to her bed and make her come until she was too exhausted to fight anymore.

"Z, we need to roll, brother. Mav ain't good." Copper stood behind him. "Your truck is closest. I'll ride with you, and we'll bring him to the hospital in Townsend."

Zach nodded. "You okay to walk, Toni? We have flashlights."

"Yes, I can walk it," she said.

"Where'd you get that gun, baby?"

Toni gasped and grabbed his arm. "Oh, Zach!" Her eyes flooded. "It was Special K's. He was k—I mean they sho—" She shook her head and pressed a fist to her mouth. "I can't even say it."

Zach felt it like a sucker punch to the gut.

Copper nodded, his face impassive.

"I'm so sorry," Toni said, tears falling freely now. She shook her head and a sob broke free. "I tried to stop the bleeding. And I didn't want to leave him, but they found me."

"Not your fault, babe," Zach said, rubbing a hand over her back. "You didn't do anything wrong."

Copper just turned and started through the woods. "Get movin', you two. We need to catch up."

"It's okay, babe," Zach said as he caught Toni's stricken look. "He doesn't blame you for a thing. He blames himself."

She nodded and took a deep breath, straightening her shoulders. "Let's go."

They made their way back to the truck at a rapid clip. Toni shielded her eyes from the blood spot on the ground where Special K's body had been. His brothers must have moved him to one of the trucks farther out.

Her eyes were solemn as she climbed into the pickup. With Copper and Rocket's help, they were able to maneuver Maverick into the back seat with her. He lay across the bench with his head in Toni's lap.

Copper drove like there was no such thing as a speed limit. The car was quiet but for Toni's occasional whispered words of comfort to Mav. She stroked her fingers through Mav's hair as she spoke, telling him they all loved him and they'd take care of him. That with a little time, he'd be good as new. He didn't move and his breath whistled in and out of his lungs.

She'd just been injured, watched one man die, killed another, and was probably out of her mind with stress, yet her only concern was for Maverick's comfort. If he hadn't fallen for her before, seeing her care so much for Zach's brother would have done it.

She was a gift he sure as hell didn't deserve but was selfish enough to keep.

They made it back to Townsend and to the small hospital in record time. Copper ran in through the Emergency Department entrance while Jig and Rocket darted over from their SUV to assist in getting Mav out of the vehicle.

Zach helped Toni out of the truck. "I want you to get those scratches checked," he said, gently running a hand over her arm.

Toni shook her head. "No. It's just scrapes. All I want is to go home."

Zach considered her. A few of the gashes were angry and ragged, but she was right. They were just scratches. Some soapy water and Neosporin and she'd be just fine. "Okay, but you can't go home. I'll have Jig take you to the clubhouse and show you to my room. You can hang out there. Shell and Beth should be there."

She rubbed her arms as though cold, so Zach shrugged out of his black hoodie and draped it over her shoulders. "You're not coming?"

"I'll be there as soon as I know Maverick is stable."

"Okay." She stepped close and stared up at him. "Zach, I—"

He placed his hand over her lips. "Shh. We'll talk later. Everything is going to work out, baby, I promise."

She nodded then raised up on her tiptoes, parting her lips. Despite all the shit of the past few hours, happiness filled Zach. Toni was hurt, scared, feeling guilt, and trying to hide it all. And she was turning to him for comfort, reassurance, care.

He pressed his lips to hers, planning on a chaste kiss, but she gripped his T-shirt and held him close. He deepened the kiss and tasted her until she moaned. A throat cleared nearby making Toni jump and pull back.

"I needed that," she whispered, then turned and disappeared into the SUV with Jig.

Once inside the hospital, he quickly found Copper and Rocket looking like giants in flimsy plastic waiting room chairs. The six or so other people waiting around all stared like his brothers were leather-clad chimps at the zoo.

"Outside," Copper said when he saw Zach. He and Rocket followed Zach back out the way he came in.

"What are they saying about Mav?" Zach asked.

Copper pulled out a cigarette and shoved it between his lips. "Not a fucking word," he said, throwing Zach a pissed off glare. "They took him for a bunch of scans. We'll know when they know or some shit like that." He inhaled and flew a long stream of smoke into the sky. "Fuck. Fuck!"

An elderly woman being wheeled in to the hospital in a chair shot Copper a disapproving glare.

"Gimme one of those fuckers." Zach held his hand out to Copper. "We got guys on clean up?"

Copper handed him a cigarette and his lighter. "Yeah, guys are gonna torch the place. Mav said something about a girl being held prisoner, so we're gonna search for her first."

Zach couldn't have been more shocked if Mav came walking out the door dancing a jig. "Seriously? Think he was delirious?"

Copper shrugged. "Fuck if I know. While the nurses were moving him to a bed he kept mumbling some shit about someone named Stephanie. Then he grabbed my hand, looked me straight in the eye, and begged me to save her. Last thing we need is some kidnapped teenager all up in our business, but I can't let the girl burn to death either, can I?"

Rocket shook his head. "Shit," was all he said.

They headed back inside and an hour later were told Mav was asking for them. Copper's phone rang just as a nurse in hot pink scrubs came to retrieve them. Rocket had gone off in search of caffeination, so Zach made his way in by himself.

"Hey, brother," he said when he reached the bed.

Zach

Mav turned and grabbed Zach's arm with his left hand. The right one was bandaged from wrist to elbow where Shark burned off the Handlers' brand. "You find her? The girl?"

"Shit, Mav, you look like hell. What did the docs say?"

Mav shook his head and squeezed Zach's arm with a surprising amount of strength. "The girl."

"All right, man, calm down. Cop is sending men to look for her. We'll get her."

Sagging against the pillow, Mav licked his chapped lips and nodded. "She'll need help."

"We're on it, brother. Just worry about doing what you gotta do to get sprung from this joint. Now what'd the doc say?"

"Broken ribs, bruised all to fuck, infection in my arm." He lifted his bandaged arm and grimaced. "It's fucking gone, Z."

"Don't worry about that now, Mav. We'll work it out."

"How's LJ?"

"Fucked up. He's home now, though. I'm sure he'll be in tomorrow."

Zach stayed with Maverick until Copper and Rocket joined, then took off to meet Toni back at the clubhouse.

As he drove the truck back to the clubhouse he couldn't help but replay the night's events over and over.

And with each passing mile the part that stuck in his brain the most was Toni selflessly offering herself up to Shark in exchange for Mav.

By the time he reached the clubhouse he'd gone from irked, to mad, to fucking furious.

CHAPTER TWENTY-SIX

"Well, I think that's the last of 'em," Shell said as she capped the tube of antibiotic ointment and sank to the bed next to Toni. "Looks like you went three rounds with an angry cat and lost, but I don't think any of them need stitches."

"I feel like I should be making a pussy joke right now, but I got nothing."

Shell giggled. "I'll excuse you just this once since it's late, you had a traumatic night, and you're scratched to shit, but you owe me one pussy joke."

"Got it. Hey, thanks for doing this, hon." Toni rotated her arm back and forth. They'd decided to only put bandages on the deepest of the cuts, so she had about three or four on each arm and one on her neck. The few lines on her face were unattractive, but superficial and already scabbing over.

"No problem." Shell had been in the rec room of the clubhouse when Toni returned, watching infomercials and drinking coffee, unable to sleep. She hadn't said it was because she was waiting up for Copper specifically, but she didn't have to. It was written all over her face. "So how are you really?"

Toni sighed and flopped back on the bed, her feet still on the floor. "I'm not sure. Kinda feel numb right now. I'll probably lose my shit at some point. Wanna place a bet on when it will happen?"

Zach

Squeezing Toni's hand, Shell shook her head. "You feel free to break down whenever you need to. If that man of yours isn't around to catch your fall, you can always cry on my shoulders. They may be small, but trust me, they can hold a lot of weight."

Her man. Reminding Shell that Zach wasn't her man would be fruitless. "I may take you up on that."

Shell laid back on the bed next to Toni. "God, I hope Mav's okay. Shark may be dead, but Copper's not gonna stop until the whole gang is six feet under."

A chill skittered down Toni's spine. Shell stared at the ceiling. She grew up in the club, would know much better than Toni how things worked, so she didn't doubt Shell's statement for one minute. Copper's expression had been murderous. Shit was about to get real.

With a groan, Shell pushed up onto her elbows. "Well, I'd better get back. Beth is sleeping in one of the spare rooms." She sat up straight and peered down at Toni, who didn't have the energy to see her friend out. "I'm so sorry for what you went through tonight. But I'm so grateful to you for what you did for Mav and the rest of my family. So, thank you. Regardless of what happens between you and Zach, you have a sister for life."

"Thanks, Shell."

"Feel free to raid the kitchen or rec room. Make yourself at home." She winked. "And I'm sure Zach wouldn't complain if he came back to find you sleeping in his bed."

After dropping a kiss on Toni's forehead, Shell was gone and closing the door softly behind her. Copper had a damn good woman waiting for him when he finally got his head out of his ass.

Quiet filled the room. Used to living alone, Toni usually adored the silent peace of being solo. Not tonight. Tonight, the lack of noise and companionship just allowed her to replay the past day like a film loop in her head.

Everything about that day, from waking in Zach's arms, to receiving the video file, to spilling her guts about the past filtered through her brain. Especially the part where she murdered a man.

Fuck. She'd killed someone.

Killed someone.

Killed...

Granted, the man she killed would have raped her for sure and probably tortured her before possibly killing her, but still... She'd taken a life. Ended it. There was a person who would no longer get to live on earth thanks to her.

It was a lot to process.

Too much.

Toni toed off her shoes and climbed under the brown comforter in Zach's very utilitarian bedroom. No pictures, no color, not much of anything besides a bed, bookcase, and big screen TV.

Boring.

But it smelled of Zach, which was comforting, and she had high hopes she would just pass out and begin the process of putting the events of the day behind her.

An hour later, she'd counted to three hundred and twenty-four, rearranged her closet in her mind, and planned her outfit for the next day. Oh, and she'd obsessed.

Suddenly, the bedding was smothering her, shrinking down around her and cutting off her air. She threw back the covers and climbed out of bed. Maybe some kind of snack would settle her nerves.

The clubhouse was easy to navigate, with the kitchen being at the bottom of the stairs and to the right. It was deadly quiet, almost creepy. No one was partying. Most of the men were probably dealing with the fallout of her killing Shark, while the rest waited for news of Mav. A few were left there to guard the clubhouse, but they were on post outside.

Just as she reached for the freezer in hopes of finding some ice cream, footsteps sounded behind her. Toni gasped and spun, her back hitting the refrigerator and her hand flying up to her racing heart.

"Zach," she breathed. "How's Maverick?" One of the things she'd been obsessing about.

"Fucking beat to shit. Infected arm. But he's getting good care. He'll be okay."

She nodded. "Good. That's good."

Zach didn't say anything else and apprehension crawled through Toni. He looked exhausted, hair mussed, circles under his eyes, clothes a mess. But there was a tension about him that had her uncertain how to proceed. Holding himself rigid, he clenched his jaw and the blue eyes she loved so much had darkened with what she could only assume was displeasure.

"Um, do—"

"What the fuck, Toni?" he suddenly roared, making her jerk and smack her head on the freezer.

"Zach?"

He stormed toward her, stopping only when his palms slapped against the freezer on either side of her head.

"I swear to Christ, woman, if you ever do that again, if you ever offer yourself up to some fucking psycho, I'll take you over my knee and tan your ass until it's redder than your pussy."

Toni's eyes widened and she gasped. But not in fear or horror. Was it sick if her core clenched and the cheeks of her ass tingled in anticipation? Because if it was, she'd never tell a soul, but if not…

"I had to," she whispered. "I saw Maverick and just…had to."

Zach groaned and dropped his head into the curve of Toni's neck. When he sighed, his warm breath ticked her collar bone. "I get it, baby. I do. But shit, when I saw you walking toward him and Rocket held me back…" He rolled his forehead back and forth across her shoulder. "Fuck."

Toni threaded her fingers through Zach's hair. "I'm okay," she said. "And Maverick will be okay. And no one else got hurt. Except Ken. God, I'm so sorry about Ken."

"Shhh." His tongue licked out and trailed up the side of her neck, making her tremble with need. When he reached her ear, he nipped the lobe and Toni's eyes fluttered closed. The tiny bite of his teeth on her sensitive flesh did crazy things to her. "I don't think you're ready to hear how much I fucking care about you, Toni. Promise me you won't ever put yourself in danger like that again. Please, baby. Just say it."

There was anguish in his voice, as though he was in real pain. Protecting the club was everything to him, but this seemed so much more. His hands dropped to her hips and he kneaded her flesh. This was more than his responsibility as the enforcer. It was intimate, it was deep, and it reached inside and wrapped itself around her soul.

So dangerous.

But in that moment, she didn't care. All she could think of was soothing him. Finding a way to show him how much she cared for him as well without having to bare her soul and say the words.

And she knew exactly how to do it. Without a word, she reached for Zach's belt and had it unbuckled in seconds flat. The zipper of his worn jeans was next, followed by a push of the denim and his boxer briefs over his hips. She worked fast and was on her knees before his jeans hit the ground.

"Toni, what are you—oh, fuck."

She wrapped her hand around the base of his cock and licked up the slit, capturing a drop of precum with her tongue. He may have been pissed at her for endangering herself, but that hadn't put a damper on his desire. He'd been steel-hard before she even touched him.

"Shit, babe, you don't need to do this. You should be resting."

Clearly, she needed to up her game if he was still able to think about her scratches. Flattening her tongue, she ran it from the base of his dick, straight to the head and followed it up with a slow swirl around the tip. Then she opened wide and sucked him in.

Zach

"Shit. Fuck. Okay, babe, you win. You do need to do this. Every fucking day."

Pride flared in Toni as she giggled around his shaft. The vibrations must have been working for him because he cursed again and dropped one of his hands to her head. He gathered her hair away from her face and gazed down at her.

Still full of him, she raised her eyes and stared up at his face.

"So fucking beautiful," he said, stroking over her cheek before bracing himself on the freezer once again.

Toni grabbed ahold of the backs of Zach's thighs and drew her lips back until just the tip remained. She sucked hard then took him deep again. His fingers tightened in her hair, holding her steady, but not stealing her control. Sometime that would be fine, him taking over, but tonight she wanted and needed to be in the driver's seat.

Taking him to the back of her throat, Toni breathed through her nose and fought the clench of her gag reflex. She swallowed and was rewarded by the jerk of Zach's hips and low growl.

As she worked her mouth over him again and again, Toni completely lost herself in the act. His manly scent, salty flavor, the feel of his hardness against her tongue, his grunts and hisses of pleasure, the sting of her hair pulling against his hold. It all worked to drive her nearly as insane as she was making him.

She was torn between the desire to see this to completion and the need for him to fuck her. She desperately wanted to feel him inside her. It was the only thing that would end her spiraling thoughts.

Then suddenly, as she cupped his balls and gave the gentlest of tugs, the decision was ripped from her.

Zach's entire body was on fire with the need to climax. Locking his teeth together, he battled coming too soon as Toni sucked like he'd never had.

Damn, the woman's mouth could start wars.

The moment he felt her soft hand cup his balls, he knew he was out of time. He shoved his hands under her arms and heaved her up. "Need to fuck you."

Shit. It was like she'd sucked his brains out through his dick and all that was left was a caveman grunting demands.

Toni didn't seem to mind. Her lips curved into a sexy grin and she winked. "Something else you have to do first." Then, she blew what was left of his mind by turning and stepping to the side of the fridge.

All she had on was one of his T-shirts and she drew the hem up and over her ass revealing two flawless globes separated by the vanishing string of her thong. Zach swallowed hard.

I'll take you over my knee and tan your ass until it's redder than your pussy.

She wanted it. She wanted his hand on her ass.

Fuck me.

Toni was going to be the death of him.

"Bend over. Arms on the counter," he ground out, worried his voice would crack and reveal just how affected he was by her trust.

Toni did as he asked, bending at the waist and resting her forearms on the counter. Her gorgeous ass was on full display before him. Starting at her neck, he ran his hand down the length of her spine and over the right cheek of her ass, lingering when she sucked in a breath. She knew what was coming. Fuck, she'd asked for it, but the anticipation was making her edgy.

He withdrew his hand and heard another intake of breath. This time she held it in. Zach breathed as well, then counted to ten in his head. Toni whimpered. He hadn't even touched her, but anticipation was doing its job. Making her antsy, needy.

Without making a sound, he lifted his hand and brought his palm down with a crack across her ass. She jumped and gasped then let out a low moan. Pink glowed across the cheek. Zach pulled her thong to the side and slid his fingers through her folds.

Zach

Just as he suspected.

Drenched.

He slapped her ass again, in the same spot, then once on the other side. Each time his hand connected with her, Toni gasped and grew a little wetter.

"Zach," she said on a moan the next time his open palm landed on her.

"Never again, right, baby?" he asked.

Slap.

"No." She moaned. "Never."

Slap.

"You like this, don't you?"

Slap.

"Yes."

"Gonna make you come?"

Slap.

"Yes."

"Not until I'm inside you." He shoved her panties down and thrust until his hips met her ass. Some unintelligible sound flew from her and she pushed back against him.

It took a moment to figure out why her pussy felt hotter and wetter than he'd ever experienced. "Shit, condom." How the hell was he supposed to pull out of her when there was a good chance he'd unload the second he moved.

"Pill. Clean," she said.

"Hell, me too."

"Then fuck me, Zach. Now!"

Zach didn't need to be told twice. He drew back, then snapped his hips forward until she screamed his name. Three thrusts were all it took to have her clamping down on his cock and coming with another shout of his name. That spanking really worked her up. The orgasm seemed to go on and on.

He kept pounding into her for probably nothing more than an embarrassing forty-five seconds, but since she'd already come like the world was ending, he didn't feel too bad about it.

Gripping her hips so hard she might end up with a bruise or two to go along with her scratches, he rammed home and exploded.

Coming bare inside her was the most intense experience of his life. Pleasure spread from his dick through his whole body until he growled out her name and spots danced in front of his vision.

Shit, Zach couldn't imagine never feeling the sensation of her pussy on his naked cock again. In fact, it was going to have to happen again within in the next half hour.

"You okay?" he asked as he helped Toni stand, once he had control of his limbs back.

She gifted him with a slightly fuck-drunk smile and nodded. "That was, um…unexpected."

Zach laughed. "I'll say." He wrapped his arms around her and pulled her in for a kiss. He explored her mouth, taking everything she had to give.

She owned him. But did she want that? All evidence in the past pointed to no. But after the day they'd had, their connection had grown. She trusted him. She'd proven that to him.

The trick would be getting her to realize that.

Toni was the first to end the kiss. "Um, Zach?"

"Yeah, baby?" He rested his chin on her head.

"We're in the kitchen. Of your clubhouse. Anyone could walk in at any time, and our assess are kinda bare."

He'd never tell her, but there was a good chance someone had heard them and they may have even had a prying eye peek in.

After a quick kiss to her lips, he righted his pants. "Come on, babe. Let's get some shut eye." He bent down and tucked his shoulder into her stomach before lifting her in a fireman's carry.

"Zach!" Toni shrieked and scrambled to grab hold of the waistband of his jeans. Her panties were still around her ankles so Zach peeled them off and stuffed them in his pocket. He was starting a collection.

"Wait! You can't carry me through the place like this!" Her voice was a high-pitched panicked sound, but laughter killed her attempted at anger.

Zach

He jogged up the steps. "Everyone's asleep and if you'd stop screaming like a banshee, they'd stay that way."

Toni growled and pinched his ass, hard. He couldn't help but burst out into laughter as he reached his room.

Good fucking end to a day that could have ended quite differently.

CHAPTER TWENTY-SEVEN

Two days after she'd killed a man she used to sleep with, Toni was in full-on freak out mode. She felt like an unstable tower built haphazardly by a toddler. Each mismatched block represented one stressor. And the tower was wobbling back and forth precariously close to collapse.

She'd watched a man tasked with protecting her die.

She'd killed a man.

She'd almost been that man's hostage.

There was a very scandalous sex video hanging over her head.

She had a douchebag ex to deal with.

Maverick was in the hospital.

She hadn't seen Zach in two days.

She had a whole host of complicated feelings for a man to sort through.

She had a job waiting for her in Chicago and a business in Tennessee.

And to top it all off, she walked into the diner at six a.m. on a rainy morning to find a hole in the roof and a trickle of water that seemed to grow to a stream in no time. Well, great. What the hell was she supposed to do now? The diner was slated to open in an hour, and staff should be arriving within the next thirty minutes.

Zach

She grabbed a mop bucket and placed it under the falling water. At the rate it was pouring in, she'd need to replace it in twenty minutes.

Toni's lower lip quivered and she stared up at the ceiling while blinking to ward off the impending tears. Last thing she needed was to bring any more water to this party.

The bell over the door jangled and Shell walked in. "Hey, To—oh, shit."

"Couldn't have said it better myself. Watch your feet, it's a little slippery."

Ever the amazing friend and employee, Shell dropped her purse and jacket in a booth and booked it behind the counter. "I'll grab some rags and get the lake cleaned up while you make some calls."

The muscles at the base of Toni's skull seemed to tense on the spot, causing a throbbing headache. "Any idea who to call in this situation?"

"Rocket has a construction company. I'd start there. If he's not the right person, I'm sure he'll steer you in the right direction," Shell said as she spread some large rags on the floor to soak up the water. "Actually, call Zach. With that bunch, they tend to get testy if their woman calls another man for help. Even one of their brothers."

"You can't be serious?"

Shell laughed. "Don't look at me like that. Just trust me. Call Zach."

"I can't bother Zach with this, Shell, he's got too much going on. I haven't even seen him in two days." Toni ran a hand through her disheveled hair and tried not to scream in frustration.

"He hasn't checked in?" Michelle looked up from where she was bent over wiping up the mess.

"I didn't say that. He's texted about a million times to see how I was doing. He just hasn't been able to escape. Poor guy must be exhausted." Zach had spent those two days bouncing between the hospital and the clubhouse, dealing with the fallout of Maverick's rescue. It turned out Shark had been holding a woman captive, a woman who was in almost as bad shape as Maverick. The club had gotten Stephanie to the hospital and per Mav's request, was taking responsibility for her, so now there was another thing on their overflowing plate.

"They all are." Shell sighed. "Hate seeing them stretched so thin, but these guys are the definition of tough. They'll get it all sorted."

"And Zach is not my man, Shell. You know that."

With a snort, Shell rung the rag out over an empty bucket. "Sure, girl, you just keep telling yourself that one."

As she opened her mouth to fire back a sassy retort, the door bells jangled once again and this time *not-her-man* strode in, in all his masculine glory.

"Fuck, baby. Why the hell didn't you call me?" Zach didn't wait for an answer. As he walked toward her, he pulled his phone out. Holding it to his ear, he gave her a quick kiss then turned away. "Hey, man, Toni's diner's got a fuck of a leak in the roof."

His voice faded as he stepped farther away.

Shell shot her an I-told-you-so grin.

"Shut up," Toni muttered to Shell's laughter.

"Rocket will be by in twenty to put a temporary fix on the leak, and once the rain stops his team will take a look and see how bad the damage really is," Zach said as he returned. "Shell, stop cleaning. Got some prospects coming by who will get this taken care of."

"Zach—"

"Oh good," Shell said. "This would have taken the two of us forever."

"Zach—"

"Yeah, babe, they'll get it done fast so you can open up. You might be thirty minutes late or so, but you shouldn't have to shut down for the entire day."

Zach

"Zach!" Toni yelled, clenching her fists at her sides.

He tilted his head and gave her an adorable grin that she was tempted to smack off his face. "What's wrong?" He sounded completely baffled.

"I don't need you to manage this for me. I'm perfectly capable of taking care of this myself." While that was true, he'd cut down on the stress and time suck by at least a factor of ten. She should be grateful. She was grateful; it made perfect sense for him to be the one to coordinate this. He had the connections; he had the contacts. It would be stupid for her to turn down his help.

It was just easier to blame it on his taking control rather than say, *I'm terrified because I'm falling for you and I don't trust my judgment when it comes to men. Please don't do nice things so I'll become more dependent on you than I already am.*

No. She would not be saying that out loud to Zach or anybody.

"It's really no big deal," he said. "I've got Rocket on speed dial and he doesn't mind." Zach shrugged. "Easy fix."

"Okay, but make sure he tells me how much he charges for an emergency call."

Zach snorted. "Sure, baby. I'll do that." His phone rang so he kissed her on the forehead and walked off, completely unaware she was about two breaths away from a nervous breakdown.

One hour and fifteen minutes later the floor was dry as a bone, the roof was patched, and Rocket had refused a single penny from her for this or his upcoming appointment to install a more permanent fix. When she'd asked his rate, he'd given her the stink eye and muttered something like, "Family don't fuckin' pay, babe."

Bikers!

All a bunch of macho alphas who drove her crazy. It might have also been true that the gesture warmed her heart and gave her all sorts of fuzzy family-love feelings. By now, it was no secret to the club that she'd had a less than stellar family life growing up. Being so accepted by Zach's MC family was a really wonderful feeling. She found herself wanting that connection as much as she wanted Zach.

They were getting ready to open, just thirty minutes late as predicted, when Zach found her in her office. "Good to go, beautiful," he said as he plopped down in the empty chair on the opposite side of her desk, sending a thrill through her traitorous body. What woman wouldn't love being called beautiful by a hot biker?

He looked delicious, as usual, in his leather cut and faded denim. His T-shirt was dotted with rain from helping Rocket, but thankfully the storm had waned to a drizzle.

"How's Maverick today?" Toni had visited him twice and he seemed stronger each time.

"Better. Giving the nurses hell, but being that he's Mav, he manages to make them all fall in love with him while he's being a giant ass pain." Zach kicked his booted feet up on her desk and crossed his ankles. "How are you doing?"

"Good. Good. I'm good." Toni shuffled some already organized papers around on her desk and looked anywhere but at Zach's hypnotic blue eyes.

"Baby," he said, in a tone that let her know he didn't believe her for a second.

He could read her so easily and it both excited her and scared the pants off of her. Which at least explained why she couldn't seem to keep them on around him. "Really. I'm doing fine."

"Ah, fine. Women's favorite word and man's worst nightmare." He winked as he spoke.

Toni couldn't help but laugh. He had a point.

"I've got an idea. I shouldn't be any later than six tonight. How about I bring my woman some dinner from Vincenzo's and we eat it in bed? Naked." He bobbed his eyebrows up and down.

His woman.

There it was again. That phrase seemed to haunt her at every turn. They hadn't discussed anything about their relationship, yet everyone assumed they were a couple. Assumed she was his.

Zach

She couldn't be his. Nine-to-five, safe automobile, picket fence, sophisticated wine tasting parties. That's what she was searching for. An alpha biker who worked with his fists, rode a Harley, and went to parties where people fucked against the side of a building was not what she was looking for. It was too dangerous. Too close to the past.

It was not happening, no matter how much her body craved what she'd only ever experienced with Zach.

That didn't mean she couldn't find it with someone else, right? Just because she was looking for a sedate and serious man didn't mean the sex *had* to be boring, did it?

"Oh, I'm not sure, Zach." It sounded like the perfect way to close out the past few shitty days. Good food, plenty of wine, and Zach. Not much more a girl could need.

"No? Not in the mood for Italian? How about Mexican?"

"No, that's not it. It's just, um…" Excuse time. "I've got so much to do here. So much to get in place before I leave."

"Before you leave?"

"Yeah, you know that. School starts up again in Chicago in a few weeks."

"Leave Tennessee? To go back to Chicago? Where your asshole ex is? Fuck, Toni, we haven't even had a chance to discuss how to deal with him yet. And you're still planning on leaving?"

Per Zach's instructions, she'd written to Chris and told him she'd be back by the three-week deadline he'd given her. At the time, Zach told her it would give them enough time to come up with a plan to keep that video off the web without her having to go back to Chris.

"I can handle all that by myself, Zach." *Liar, liar.* She didn't have the first clue how to get herself out of that mess. "Now, more than ever, I want to help kids like me. Kids with screwed up families that are on the verge of making horrible life altering choices."

"You've never once even considered the idea of staying, have you? So, I was just, what? A little something to amuse yourself with while you were on an extended vacation?"

"No, Zach, that's not—"

He shot to his feet and rounded the desk. After yanking her to her feet he sealed his lips over hers in a kiss that almost made her forget everything she'd just said. Her nipples puckered and her panties were soaked five seconds in. She needed him like she'd never needed anyone else, and that alone was enough to make her break the kiss and step back.

"Tell me," he said, his face a mix of lust and fury. "Tell me that you feel anything close to this with one of those pencil-pushing suits you date and I'll let you go."

She couldn't, of course. She'd never felt anything close to it with any man.

"Zach, that isn't the point. The plan has always been for me to return to my life in Chicago." She scrunched her nose as it began to tingle, warning of the incoming flood of tears.

"Why? Because you're too chicken shit to admit you want me. Too scared to take a risk. You're so afraid I'm going to turn into a monster like Shark that you can't even think about giving us a shot?"

She staggered back a few steps as his verbal slap stunned her. God, the truth hurt. And even worse, it sounded ridiculous. But he was right. She was scared. So scared.

"That's not it, Zach," she lied. "My life is in—"

He cut her off with an outstretched hand. "Just stop, Toni. If I have to hear you say your life is in Chicago one more time I'll lose my shit." He stalked toward the door. "Go. Go back to Chicago. Go back to a job that's not what you thought it would be and your boring fucks. See if I give a shit."

The door slammed behind him and Toni sank into her desk chair. He seemed to take all the life out of the room with him.

Why was she fighting this so hard? Toni wasn't weak. Ever since Mark dragged her away from Shark's gang, she'd worked her ass off to become a strong woman. Being able to handle any situation thrown at her was something she prided herself on. Yet, here she was, running away from something that could be amazing. It was like she was still that seventeen-year-old girl, fleeing from her mistakes.

But she wasn't that girl anymore. Hadn't been that girl for a long time. And Zach certainly wasn't Shark. In fact, it was pretty damned insulting of her to even consider the two similar in anything beyond the fact that both had dicks.

It was time to get real and stop bullshitting herself. She wanted Zach. Hell, she was halfway in love with him.

From her desk, her phone started ringing. It was Mark's ringtone. Her uncle just might be part psychic, somehow knowing she needed an ear.

"Hi, Uncle Mark."

"Sweetie, what's wrong? What the hell did that biker do to you?" Mark sounded as though he was getting ready to charge through the phone.

Despite her somber mood, she chuckled. "Why do you think something's wrong? All I said was hello."

"Sweetie, I know you better than anyone. You think I can't tell your mood by your voice? You'd be wrong. Now, what'd he do?"

With a sigh, she slumped back in her office chair. "He called me on my bullshit. Made me think about what I'm doing with my life. And he asked me to stay with him."

Her announcement was met with silence.

"Uncle Mark?"

"If you tell anyone I said this, I'll deny it to the death, but I think I'm starting to like this biker of yours. You need someone to give you a swift kick in the ass."

This time, Toni's laugh was loud and full, but it turned into heaving sobs in a flash. Before she knew it, the whole story tumbled out, including the video and threats from Chris. It took quite a bit of convincing, but Mark agreed to let her handle it herself as long as she swore on her life to come to him if she needed help. By the time she finished recounting the story, Mark was looking at plane tickets and Toni felt pounds lighter.

"Well, I wanted to hate him, but I don't think I can do that. Toni, he sounds like a good guy."

"He is."

"So, what's really holding you back? And don't say it's working with troubled kids, because you know what? There are troubled kids in Tennessee, too. You should know."

Toni snorted out a laugh at his snarky comment.

"I'm serious, sweetie. You don't have to be a counselor. There are plenty of other avenues to explore if you want to play a role in helping at risk youth." She could hear the click-clack of the keyboard as he made good on his promise to visit soon.

He had a really good point. Later, when her mind wasn't stuck on thoughts of Zach, she'd dedicate some serious thought to finding other avenues of working with at risk youth. "It's not the job. At least, the job isn't the major reason. Zach's right. It's fear."

"You need to talk to him, sweetie. Let him assuage those fears for you." Andrew's voice filled the line. He was such a gentle soul. Kind and patient. Good for her dominant and often impatient uncle.

"Isn't that why I'm talking to you? So you can rid me of my fears."

Both men laughed. "Sure, we could say all the right words, but you need to hear them from your man. And from inside yourself. So, get off the phone and start introspecting," Mark said.

"Thanks for the non-advice," she said as she kicked her feet up onto the desk. "Bye guys. Love you."

"Love you too," they said at the same time.

After hanging up, she closed her eyes and breathed, trying to find some peace. She owned a thriving diner, with a fantastic staff working for her, had made some great new friends, and owned a home that had a view of the most gorgeous sunsets. And that was on top of having a really great man who clearly wanted her. What was really waiting for her in Chicago? A job she'd hoped would be so much more than it was, a shoebox apartment that cost more than her mortgage, a few friends she'd never really let in, and a psycho ex-boyfriend. Mark and Andrew didn't even live there anymore. They'd moved away six months ago when Mark opened a new branch of his law firm in New York. Sure, he still traveled to Chicago frequently, but he could just as easily make a trip to Tennessee.

Even without all the great reasons to stay, Zach should be reason enough.

She dropped her feet to the ground as the magnitude of what she'd just done hit her.

Shit. Had she just ruined everything?

CHAPTER TWENTY-EIGHT

As the day wore on, Zach's guilt mounted until it was a ten-foot monster chasing after his bike. He'd been a real shitheel to Toni. Throwing her fears back in her face. Of course, she was afraid he'd take advantage of her. She'd dated a man with a somewhat similar lifestyle and he'd violated her trust and fucked their relationship in the worst of ways.

It wasn't like she'd caught her high school boyfriend making out with the head cheerleader under the bleachers. No, she'd essentially been pimped out and abused by someone who should have taken care of her. Before she was even out of her teen years. And Zach had rubbed her face in it like it was nothing.

In his defense, he'd been blindsided by the casual way she'd dismissed him and informed him she was leaving, but he should have seen through her bullshit to the deep-seated terror at the core.

Giving up wasn't his style, so he planned to attack this from another angle. Most of Zach's problems could be solved with the help of Louie or his fists. He wasn't used to having to work for anything when it came to women, but Toni was well worth the effort.

Armed with dinner from Vincenzo's Italian restaurant—and Toni's favorite dinner if Shell was correct—he turned his bike onto her driveway. The rain had subsided hours ago while the hot July sun burned off any lingering clouds, leaving behind a gorgeous blue sky and photo-worthy sunset.

One Toni would never miss watching. It was like mother nature was giving him the thumbs up. Sure enough, she sat in her usual rocking chair on the porch watching him as he walked up. A glass of wine dangled from her fingertips and an unopened bottle of beer sat on the small table that separated the rockers.

For him.

That had to be a good sign, right?

She kept her gaze on him as he approached, but she didn't smile. She looked serious, lost in thought. And hotter than sin with a black ribbed Hell's Handlers tank top and itty-bitty shorts. Shell must have given her the shirt. It was the first time he'd caught her in any of the Handlers' gear and seeing his club's logo scrawled across her tits had his cock begging to be released.

He climbed the three steps to the porch then leaned his shoulder against a white column. "Country?" he said, indicating the music playing on a cell phone resting on the table. "Really? Didn't peg you as a country fan."

Her unpainted lips turned up in a half smile and she tilted her head. Her hair was down, but un-styled, like she'd let it air dry after a shower. She looked young, fresh, and he wanted to drag her in the house and to her bed. "You can't be raised in Tennessee and not at least have some appreciation for musical twang."

"You have a point. Blake Shelton, right?"

That got her chuckling. "See, even you know your country artists."

He shrugged. "Guilty as charged."

Silence fell between them. Not uncomfortable, but full of unacknowledged emotions. Zach stepped forward until he was just two feet from Toni. He held out his hand. "Dance with me?"

Her laugh was disbelieving. "Seriously?"

"Seriously," he said with a nod.

She studied him for a moment before placing her wineglass on the table and giving him her hand. With a gentle tug, Zach drew her up and against his body. He circled her hips with one arm, holding her against him. The other hand held hers and tucked it against his chest, between their bodies.

For a few moments, they swayed to the low sound of Blake Shelton as the sun dipped behind the trees. She stared up into his eyes as they moved to the music and he saw everything she tried so hard to hide.

Vulnerability.

The need to be loved and accepted.

Fear of being hurt.

He'd had fear too, and maybe he should have talked to her about it. Maybe it would have helped her to know she wasn't the only one. His fear stemmed from his worry that having a woman would take him away from the club. From his family. From his responsibilities.

But, hell, Toni blended with his family as though she'd always been there. She cared for his brothers, cried with them over Special K's death. She'd risked herself to save Maverick. Having her in his life wouldn't detract from his commitment to the MC, it would enhance it because she would be a part of it too.

"It's okay, you know," Zach said in a low voice.

"What's okay?" There was an uncertainty to her question.

"It's okay to want me. To need me."

She tried to look away, but he raised their joined hands and turned her chin back to him.

"It's okay to want what's between us." He leaned forward until he was speaking next to her ear. "It's also okay to want to act out your every dirty thought and naughty fantasy with me."

"Zach." She stiffened a bit but he wasn't having it. It was vital for her to understand she could trust him with her mind, heart, and especially, considering her past, her body.

Zach

He pulled his head back so he could see her again. "I'm serious, Toni. You can't even begin to imagine all the things I want to do to you. With you. Only you, baby. Deep down, you know what I'm about to tell you, but I'm going to say it anyway."

She blinked and the arm around his back tightened. "What?" she whispered.

"I will never ask you to do anything you are uncomfortable with. What we do together, no matter what it is or how kinky we get," he winked and squeezed her bottom, "it will only ever involve two people. You and me. I will never allow another man to see or have what's mine. You don't have to be afraid of repeating your mistakes, because I promise you, I'll kill any man who tries to touch you. Brother or not."

Her eyes grew wet and a tear tracked down her makeup-free face. Zach rubbed his cheek against hers, wiping it away.

"You're right, Zach. My heart did know all of that. But I've been having a hard time getting my brain with the program. It keeps injecting me with this paralyzing fear of making the same mistakes I have in the past. I needed to hear what you said though. To calm my brain."

They'd pretty much stopped dancing at that point and just stood holding each other on the porch. Darkness surrounded them, except for the glow of an overhead light. "I want you to be mine, Toni. Not my fuckin' friend. Not my *fucking* friend. My woman. My ol' lady. And I don't give up easy, baby, so you should just give in now and save yourself the trouble."

Toni smiled up at Zach. A lightness she hadn't felt since she left Chicago filled her insides. Even though she'd already decided to go all in, his words were exactly what she needed to hear to know she'd made the right decision.

Maybe she really could have it all. A good man who adored her, would protect her heart and body, and set that body on fire every night. "Hmm," she said. "Maybe you should chase me a little bit more."

"Woman," he said giving her a squeeze while he laughed. "So, I've been thinking. Chicago isn't thaaat far."

"Zach—"

"You go back to your job and your life. We long-distance it for a while. I'll come up every weekend."

"Zach—"

"Hold on, let me tell you my idea. When you feel good. One hundred percent safe and confident in our relationship, then we revisit the idea of you moving here."

She smashed his lips between her fingers. "Zach. Stop bossing for one second and listen."

He tried to talk despite his clamped mouth and Toni laughed at the unintelligible sound.

"I quit my job today. And gave my landlord thirty days' notice. Since I'm your woman, I guess that means you're going to have to make a trip to Chicago to help me pack my stuff."

Zach slid his hand from her ass up to her head and gripped her hair, tilting her head back. "You nagging me already?"

Toni laughed and it felt amazing. Freeing to be able to express herself with him. "You sure you want an ol' lady?"

"No. I don't want an ol' lady. I want you," he said as he kissed her. It was slow and sweet, but no less deep and potent.

"Zach," she whispered, after he'd scrambled her brain. "Take me inside, please."

"What for? To eat the dinner I brought you?" he asked moving his mouth to her neck.

"Mmm." She tilted her head to give him better access. It didn't matter where he kissed her. Anywhere his lips landed seemed to have a direct connection to her sex. She needed him horizontal and inside her in the next two minutes.

Well, vertical would work too.

"Sure, we can eat the food. After you fuck me."

Zach

He nipped along her jawline then rubbed his stubbly cheek along the bite, making her tremble with need. "Fuck yeah. That's my girl."

Zach kissed her again and somehow managed to maneuver them into the house while their mouths were joined. They made their way toward her bedroom kissing, laughing, and removing clothes.

While trying to hop on one foot to remove her shoe and keep her lips on Zach, Toni tripped. Zach caught her and pressed her to the wall. He trailed kisses down her neck, over her collar bone, to the tops of her breasts. He dipped his tongue between her breasts then pulled the cups of her bra down, revealing her tightened nipples.

"Fuck, I love your tits." He sucked a nipple into his mouth and Toni cried out. "I could suck them for fucking hours."

God, that sounded like heaven. "Yes. Please," she said.

Zach licked a path to the other nipple and drew it into the warm depths of his mouth, pressing the nipple to the roof of his mouth. Toni's back arched off the wall and she moaned.

"Next time," he said. "I need pussy."

Well, she certainly wasn't going to argue with that. After ushering her into her room, Zach gave her a push and sent her sprawling onto her bed with a laugh. His mouth met hers yet again while he worked her shorts off her legs. There was an urgency about him, a desperation in his actions that had him almost ripping at her shorts. Then he went to work on his jeans, treating them to the same impatient removal.

When they were both completely naked, Zach lowered himself over her and dropped his forehead to hers. "Fuck," he said, suddenly calm. "You have no idea how much I needed to feel your skin on me."

His bulky body pressed her into the mattress and prevented her from moving. Her breasts were mashed against the strong hardness of his chest. His belly, much firmer and defined than hers, rubbed along hers, all the way down past her hips. And his cock, so hard it was almost pulsing, rested against her thigh.

"Promise I'll do right by you, baby," he whispered against her lips.

"I know you will, Zach. I'm not worried. And I'll do right by you," she promised.

"Already have. Baby, you saved my best friend's life. And your own."

A flash of the moment when Shark dropped to the ground threatened to destroy the happy moment. "I don't want to talk about that now," she said. "I just want you to fuck me."

He didn't respond for a moment and Toni held her breath. If he made her deal with it right then, she'd break down and cry. Slight mood killer.

"Okay, but we're hashing it out later. Gotta make sure my woman is taken care of."

She gave him a saucy grin. "So, take care of me, big guy."

"My pleasure."

CHAPTER TWENTY-NINE

Zach stared down at the gorgeous woman spread out beneath him. Her brown hair fanned out across the pillow with the golden highlights catching the light and shining. The beautiful green of her eyes was deeper than usual, darkened by lust and something else. Openness, vulnerability.

For the first time, Toni was truly open to him. She was giving him her full trust and had dropped all her defenses. He wouldn't let her down.

Zach had never made love before. Fucking was as far as it went, even with Toni. But tonight felt different. Significant in a way it never had before.

His brothers would rib him to his death if he admitted this out loud, but it had to do with the way he felt about her. He wanted to protect her, make her laugh and smile, make her moan and scream, but he also wanted to wake up with her, share coffee with her, listen to her complain about a rude tourist making everyone at the diner miserable.

He wanted a life with her.

And that meant more than wild sex.

It meant forging a bond that was more than just physical.

For now, he would honor her wishes to avoid talking about what went down with Shark, but they would revisit it.

And soon.

"Eyes open," Zach said as he rubbed his unshaven cheek against the plump curve of her breast. She shivered and he kissed her breast to soothe away the slight rough sting of the stubble.

His cock was so hard, it hurt. The skin felt stretched and so sensitive, just the brush of her thigh had precum beading at the tip. Every primal instinct he possessed was screaming at him to shove into her and fuck her until she couldn't crawl out of bed.

But the rest of him, brain included, wanted this to last. Wanted her just as out of her mind with need as he was. So, he bit the inside of his cheek, hard, to try and regain some control over his cock. The squirming Toni was doing didn't help anything.

"Zach," she said in a breathless voice as he briefly sucked a nipple into his mouth then blew across the damp skin.

He held her hips, anchoring her to the bed to keep her from rubbing all over his aching cock. Then he took a slow journey down her body, pressing an open-mouth kiss to each rib. Toni threaded her fingers into his hair and gave a little tug each time his lips landed on her body.

Did she even realize she was doing it? She seemed so lost in the sensation, it was probably an unconscious reaction. Regardless, he loved it. Even more if it wasn't done on purpose. Just showed how caught up she was.

He licked his way over the slight swell of her stomach, pausing to circle her navel. With a soft gasp, she breathed out his name again. The entire time, she was trying to move, writhing against his hands, but he held her still. When he reached her hips, he sucked on the prominent bone that jutted out and Toni cried out.

"Shit, Zach. You're killing me. Please. You're so close to where I need you."

"Hmm," he said against her skin. "Where exactly do you need me? Here?" He pressed a kiss to her inner thigh.

"Very funny." She sounded hoarse.

Zach

"Not it? Let me try again." He kissed right in the crease of her groin. Her tangy aroma hit his senses. "Here?" If he wasn't careful he'd be done in by his own game.

"No, damn it," she said as she slapped a hand against the sheets.

He chuckled. "Okay, give me one more chance." This time his mouth landed on her pubic bone, directly above her mound and she growled, eliciting a laugh from him.

"Zach! I swear to God…" Still gripping his hair, she shoved him down and lifted her hips. "There," she said. "No more guessing. This is where you belong."

Zach couldn't help it, he burst out laughing. This was what it was like, being with someone he cared about, respected, someone who was a friend and lover instead of just a release. They could laugh, tease, have fun as well as hot as fuck sex. "I get it now. Thanks for the help."

Toni giggled but it quickly turned into a gasp when Zach licked directly over her clit. He didn't bother teasing her anymore but set out to blow her mind. He sucked, nibbled, fucked her with his tongue until she was straining so hard against him his arms actually grew tired holding her down.

"Zach," she said on a moan after he'd felt the first quiver of impending orgasm around his tongue.

She tugged on his hair. "Zach, I'm so close. I don't want to come until you're inside me. Please." She tugged again.

Far be it for him to deny his woman begging for his cock. After one last flick over her clit, he rose over her and planted his hands on the sides of her head. Toni needed no instruction. She wrapped her small hand around his dick and immediately guided him to her soaking wet entrance.

They stared into each other's eyes as Zach pushed in one agonizing inch at a time. Toni gasped, then bit her lip, giving her sexy-meets-innocent look that drove him wild. He wanted that mouth against his but couldn't bear to break their visual connection.

Somehow, the blistering heat and strangling tightness of her surprised him each time. Even though he remembered it was fucking amazing, that first thrust was still a shock to his starving system.

Their usual was a fast, hard, almost brutal fucking, and while they both loved it, this night was different. Zach pulled out and pushed back in keeping the same slowness he'd started with.

In.

Out.

In.

Out.

The pace was leisurely, and after a few seconds, there was almost a hypnotic quality to it. Toni's knees were bent and her hips rose to meet his every thrust. He'd assumed it would take awhile this way, without the hard pounding they were used to, but it wasn't long at all before she squeezed him with trembling thighs.

"Oh, God, Zach." She grabbed his ass, digging her nails into his skin. Fuck, he hoped she'd leave marks. Branding her man. Claiming him.

"I'm coming," she whispered. "Oh, my God, it's so intense."

Her body bowed and her pussy clamped down so hard on Zach's cock he saw stars. Needing an even deeper connection, he captured her mouth and absorbed her cry of completion. The next time her pussy pulsed, Zach was lost. He hooked his hands under her shoulders and held her tight against him as he plunged in as far as he could and shook with the force of his orgasm.

Ripping his mouth away, he cursed and stared down at her. Satisfaction was written all over her face.

"Jesus," he said, dropping his forehead to hers.

"Well said." She chuckled. Their chests rose and fell against each other as they tried to calm themselves.

Zach dropped to his side and wrapped his arms around her, turning her to face him. After a few minutes of just gazing at her beauty, when he felt able to speak without panting, he brought them both back to reality.

"No bullshit, baby. Tell me how you're doing." There was no point in delaying it. The longer they avoided talking about what happened, the longer it had the opportunity to grow and fester in Toni's mind.

He certainly didn't give a shit that she'd killed Shark. Well, not beyond the fact that it would upset her. He only wished he'd been the one to do it. And after a few hours of alone time with the shithead. And he fully meant to speak ill of the dead.

"I'm…" She paused and shook her head. "No bullshit?"

"No bullshit."

She traced over a tattoo on his chest, remaining silent for a long moment. "I'm processing. All of it. I know he wasn't a good man. Even more than that, I know he was an evil man. And if I'd have been left there with him, it would have been really bad for me. And Stephanie. I don't regret what I did. It's just… I don't even know what I'm trying to say."

"It's just that you killed someone and that's not something you ever imagined would happen in your life. Regardless of the fact that he was a scum sucking bastard who actually got off easy."

"Yeah. I think that's it. My brain just isn't sure what to do with that yet, and I've alternated between being okay and freaking out."

"He was never going to survive, Toni." Zach stroked his hand up and down her back. The repetitive motion comforted him as much as he meant it to soothe her. "After seeing that video, I was going to be the one to take him out, and trust me, it would have been a lot less humane than the way he went." It was a risk, admitting such premeditated violence to her, but he wanted her to know him. Because if anyone ever hurt her again, he'd let his beast free and she had to come to terms with that. It was who he was and that part of him would never change.

Toni fell silent, still rubbing her soft fingertips over his chest. At one point, she raked a short nail over his nipple and his cock sprung back to attention. The damn thing was going to have to be a little patient, because this conversation needed to be had.

"Do you feel like I robbed you of the chance to go after him?"

He considered that question for a second. "No. To be honest, you had the right to kill him more than I did. I just wanted to make him suffer. I regret that you have to live with it."

"I think I'll be okay, eventually. Just bear with me if I have the occasional freak out, okay?"

He kissed her. "Baby, I'd worry if you didn't freak out. Just promise you'll keep me in the loop. I can't help you get through this if you don't tell me what you're thinking."

Toni kissed his chest, then his jaw, his chin, and finally his lips while she pressed her hips against his erection. "I promise. Now what do we do about Chris?"

Christ, he loved hearing the word *we* fall off her lips with such ease. Loved that she wasn't pushing him away but turning to him in her time of need.

He rolled until she was on top of him and she sat up, straddling his stomach. "How about we limit the discussion to one asshole per night, huh?"

Toni shimmied her hips until she was over his once again throbbing cock. No one would ever believe he'd come hard only moments ago.

"That's the best idea I've heard all night."

With a raised eyebrow, Zach reached up and thumbed her nipples. "The best?"

"Well second best. Hey, Zach?" She lowered herself onto his shaft while he played with her tits.

"Yeah, baby?"

"Thanks for making me your ol' lady," she said as she swiveled her hips and rose up and down on his cock.

"Shit, Toni." His eyes rolled back in his head. "Best thing I've ever done."

CHAPTER THIRTY

"Are you really going to sit there like that when he walks in?" Toni asked as she folded her arms across her chest and attempted her best pissed off glare. Hard to do when the nerves she was trying to hide trumped irritation.

"Fucking A, baby." Zach's eyes immediately landed on her breasts where they plumped over her crossed arms.

Men. So predictable.

So frustrating.

So damn hot, it drove her crazy.

"Don't you think this is all a little overkill?" She threw in a foot tap to go along with the overlapped arms and squinty-eyed glare.

Looking like a man without a care in the world, lounging on her couch with his legs wide, arm on the arm rest, and posture all relaxed, Zach said, "No, baby, I don't think it's overkill. Overkill would be taking a good ole Babe Ruth style swing at his head the moment he walks through that door. But Louie here promised not to do that. Unless the suit pisses him off, then I can't predict how Louie's going to react."

Louie. The man named his bat. The bat he used as enforcer for the Hell's Handlers to scare the pants off…well, she wasn't really sure who, but to scare the pants off of people the club didn't like, apparently.

Named his bat.

And apparently, that bat had a mind of its own and communicated its plans to Zach. Childish much? "Bikers!" Toni threw her hands in the air and stomped toward the apartment's tiny kitchen.

"Aw, come on, baby, don't be like that. Louie and I are both going to be on our best behavior. You'll see." The laughter in Zach's voice as he called after her did nothing to douse her fiery temper.

Okay, in truth? She was glad. Thrilled even, that Zach had accompanied her from Tennessee to Chicago and was now sitting in her apartment ready to shield her if need be. But that was a big if, and she'd have much preferred he waited in her bedroom and only made an appearance if things got out of hand with Chris, who was due to arrive any second.

She'd even come up with a plan. A code word she'd say loudly if the conversation wasn't going well. Zach had laughed, *laughed* in her face, kissed her, and plopped in the chair with that blasted bat. If he wasn't careful, she'd snatch the thing and use it on him.

It was exactly two weeks to the day since she'd agreed to be Zach's ol' lady, and aside from the looming threat of a sex scandal hovering over her head like a bird about to shit, the fourteen days had been amazing. Zach was fun, spontaneous, attentive, protective, and it turned out the man could cook and was relatively neat. They'd seen each other every day, whether it was just him stopping in for a quick coffee at the diner or a full-on date out on the town. He took her dancing, to a movie, and to more than one party at the clubhouse.

Toni loved his brothers and they all seemed taken with her as well. More often than not, she'd sent a mountain of food to the clubhouse when the diner closed and had quickly earned the nickname of Aunt Jemima, which was immediately shortened to Jem. Everyone seemed to call her by the name except Zach and Shell, who stuck with Toni.

Zach

It was easy, re-fitting into Townsend and slipping into Zach's world. She'd been accepted as is. No questions asked. And that was a great feeling. Somehow, her relationship with Zach was both comfortable and exciting at the same time. The way they interacted, how she could completely be herself around him, and the way he accepted her was the comfortable part. The way he lit her body up with just one look was more exciting than anything she'd ever experienced.

The doorbell rang, and Toni jumped as though the tinny *ding-dong* had been attached to a live wire placed under her skin. She raced out of the kitchen and back through the small living room.

"Babe, wait," Zach said from the chair. How was it he could sound like the person at the door was doing nothing more than selling magazines for their high school basketball team? Hell, he'd probably sound more pissed off it was a solicitor. "Come here before you answer it."

Toni shifted her gaze from Zach to the door and back again. He crooked his finger and she sighed. "I have to get the door, Zach."

"The suit can wait for a minute. Come close."

She walked until she was directly between his spread legs, her knees butting up against the couch.

"Closer," he said. "Bend down and give me those lips."

She did as he requested, and he caught her by the nape of her neck, dragging her mouth to his for a kiss that was as sweet as it was gentle. Not exactly the norm for them, since they usually flared out of control the second their lips touched. But now, without anywhere for it to go, tenderness was the name of the game.

And it was better than a fistful of valium for calming her.

He pulled back after a second, kissed the tip of her nose, and held their foreheads together. "Everything will be fine, Toni."

"Thank you," she whispered. "I've been a wreck."

"I know, baby. Now get the door so we can get this over with and I can take you to your room and eat your pussy. I'm feeling the need to leave my mark on this apartment."

Jesus. And saying those words wasn't even the dirtiest thing he could do with that mouth. He released her and she stumbled back a few steps. Could he tell how his promise affected her?

Probably.

Zach seemed to be able to read her like a book.

With her mind full of the filthy things her new boyfriend wanted to do to her, she opened the door and admitted her old boyfriend into her apartment. Before she even had a chance to greet him, he was wrapping his arms around her and holding her way too close for comfort.

"I'm so glad you came to your senses, Toni."

The moment his arms closed around her, she went completely stiff. Like a two-by-four, instead of the soft, pliant woman she became whenever Zach's hands were on her. The too-intimate hug needed to end before Zach, or worse yet, Louie, got angry and stepped in.

Toni shoved against his chest to no avail.

Damn it.

She couldn't even be stronger than Chris? Time for some weight training.

Instead of picking up on her subtle as a pissed off bull cues, Chris lowered his head as though he was going to kiss her.

Zach decided *that* was the perfect moment to clear his throat.

Chris froze, but only for a second before gripping her shoulders and holding her an arm's length away. "What the fuck is he doing here?" The word *he* sounded more like Chris was speaking of the devil than one lone biker.

"Chris—"

"Guess you want the world to see it, huh? See you whoring yourself out for some gangbanger's fuckfest. Your choice, sweetheart." As he spoke, he shook her, only once, but it was so hard her neck snapped back then her head wrenched forward before she had a chance to get control of it.

She needn't have worried about what to do next since her role there had apparently ended.

Zach shot out of the chair and pinned Chris to the back of the closed door so fast, Toni lost her footing as she was released. After staggering a few steps, she regained her balance and stared slack jawed at the scene before her.

Gone was the Zach she'd fallen so hard for over the past few weeks. The man who could make her laugh, smile, swoon, and lose her mind all in the span of a few minutes. Instead, she was wholly in the presence of the Hell's Handlers' enforcer.

And had she met this man when she first returned to Tennessee, she'd have run fast and far.

Because he was scary.

No, scary was a movie with creepy music and ghosts popping out at unexpected times. Scary was a Freddie Kreuger Halloween mask showing up at her door. Zach? Well, Zach was terrifying.

His blue eyes had darkened to a midnight color and there wasn't a hint of warmth. They were so cold, they were almost inhuman. Robotic.

His jaw was clenched so hard, the muscles ticked and his neck corded. He had Chris against the door with Louie across his neck. Chris gasped and sputtered for breath, his face growing paler by the second.

She'd never seen Zach this enraged. Not when he first saw the infamous video. Not when she volunteered to take Maverick's place. And not when she tried to push him away and end their relationship.

No, this was a new level of anger and uncharted territory for her. There was a good chance if she didn't step in, the man she loved was going to kill her ex who wasn't even worth a few sore knuckles, let alone a prison sentence.

Yes. She loved him.

No doubt about it.

"Zach," she said, working hard to keep the tremor out of her voice. "I think you need to ease up before you k-kill him." Holy shit. Was she really advising her boyfriend to avoid killing someone? What the hell happened to her boring life?

Sick as it was, she felt a little thrill knowing the troubles she currently faced actually came from that boring life. Not the motorcycle club she'd taken up with. Not that she needed it any longer, but the realization kind of reaffirmed her decision to be with Zach.

It was strange to see such a violent scene playing out right beside a bright wall hanging of happy yellow sunflowers. A print she'd purchased at the botanical gardens. "Zach, please. I don't want you to get in trouble for hurting this asshole. He's not worth it." She took three steps forward and put a tentative hand on Zach's shoulder.

He didn't speak, but moved the bat from Chris's throat to his chest, allowing a choking Chris to inhale.

"Th-thank you, Ton-Toni," Chris said as he sucked in air. "God, Toni, he's a maniac. Can't you see that?" He coughed and inhaled a whistling breath. "He would have killed me if you weren't here." Color was returning to his face, but he still couldn't move due to Louie's continued presence across his chest.

Zach snorted.

"Shut the fuck up, Chris. I didn't tell him to stop because I don't want you dead. I said it because you aren't worth going to prison for. You aren't worth shit. Zach, let's just do what we came to do and get out of here. I want to go home."

He reacted then, turning his head until his mesmerizing gaze bore into hers. The corner of his mouth turned up.

He liked her calling it home.

In that moment, she wanted nothing more than to tell him she loved him. In fact, she had to clench her lips between her teeth to keep the words from spilling out. Because she'd be damned before she'd spill something so important in front of her stupid ex.

But she'd tell Zach later.

She'd tell him every day.

CHAPTER THIRTY-ONE

Zach had an overwhelming urge to tell the gorgeous, brave, feisty woman trying to keep him from a murder rap that he loved her. Fuck if he'd thought that would ever happen, but in just a few short weeks, the woman had turned his whole world on its ass and he couldn't imagine ever being with another.

The thought of losing her, of not seeing her every day, of not touching her, tasting her, hell, of not just being in her presence made him physically ill. If that wasn't love, he didn't know what the fuck was.

Toni probably wouldn't appreciate him telling her he loved her for the first time while he was two minutes away from offing her ex. He almost laughed out loud at the thought. Time to move the show along.

"Here's how this is going to go," Zach said, putting just enough pressure on Louie to have Chris nervous but not struggling to breathe. "You're going to give me your computer and any flash drives or discs that might have a copy of that video."

He had to hand it to the suit, for such a pretty-boy, the guy had balls. "Fuck you," Chris said. "I'm not giving you shit. Everyone's going to know what a slut she is. See if she ever gets a job again."

Zach sighed. Why couldn't Chris just make things easier on himself. Zach hefted Louie in his right hand and swung it like an axe toward the door. It landed with a crack an inch away from Chris's head, splintering the wood and eliciting a high-pitched scream from the man whose balls just shrunk two sizes.

"You're going to give it all to me, dickhead, and not just because I'll bash your fucking head in if you don't. As we speak, thirty thousand little green pieces of paper are being deposited into your bank account. If anyone checks, they'll notice the money comes from one LBT Corporation. Huh." Zach dug the tip of the bat into the carpet and leaned against it. This was going to be his favorite part by far—since he'd promised Toni he wouldn't beat Chris bloody.

"Funny thing, isn't that the same corporation your firm is involved in a class action suit against? We are talking big bucks, aren't we?" He kept right on talking, not giving Chris an opportunity to answer any of his questions. He didn't give two shits what the fucker had to say. Playing with him was just a little bit of fun. And thankfully, Toni remained bug-eyed but quiet throughout.

Her silence showed she trusted him to handle this for her and that meant the world to him.

"So, if someone you worked with, say Toni's uncle, were to find a deposit from them, it would be a bad day for you, huh? It would look like you were taking bribes to blow the case." He tsked. Time to bring it on home. "Don't bother trying to move the money. It will make you look even more guilty. Do I need to keep going here, or are you catching on yet?"

Fury blazed from Chris's eyes, but he was at least smart enough to realize he had no options. While Zach would love nothing more than to throw down with Chris, he'd made a promise to Toni. One he now regretted, but that was beside the point.

He tapped Chris on the shoulder with Louie. Chris was gonna be sore as shit tomorrow. Fuck yes.

"You want the video in exchange for canceling the money." Chris's voice was tight, fear-filled.

"Aww, baby, he isn't as stupid as you told me." Zach grinned at Toni, who rolled her lips inward seemingly to suppress her own laughter. Why, he'd never know. Laughing at the guy was the least she owed him. If she was willing, he'd hand Louie over and let her have at it.

And he never let anyone touch Louie.

"Can't speak to the rest of what you told me. Remember, babe? About how much he sucked in bed?" They'd never spoken about any such thing beyond the time he walked in on Toni yelling about Chris's poor fucking skills.

This time she chuckled and a sly smile lit her face as she shrugged. "Nobody compares to you," she said with a wink.

"Damn, baby, you're the sweetest." Shit, this was fun. He could play this game all day, except that he had a wet pussy waiting for his mouth. She was always wet for him, so it wasn't a stretch to think she'd be so now, watching him dominate her ex. "What'd you come, three times in an hour and a half last night? Fuck, it was hot."

"Four."

Zach's dick twitched as he recalled the events of the previous night. Toni had been so nervous about the trip, he'd set out to melt her mind.

And he'd succeeded in just ninety minutes.

"Hell yeah! Four. Almost forgot the one where I—"

Toni cleared her throat.

Zach wanted to burst out laughing at the pretty blush on Toni's cheeks, but he refrained. "Too much?"

Chris must have forgotten he had no power, because he mumbled, "Slut," under his breath.

Quick as lighting, Zach jammed Louie against Chris's chest again, loving the grunt of pain he emitted. "Every single copy. Or I'll ruin you. This ever finds its way onto social media, I'll ruin you. You come near Toni again, you so much as breathe the same air as her, I'll ruin you. You're also going to find a new firm. You're done working for her uncle. Or, guess what?" He leaned his body weight into the bat.

"You'll ruin me." The words were so strained, they were barely audible.

"Ding, ding, ding." Zach stepped back and released Chris without warning. The other man's knees gave out and he almost hit the floor before his quads kicked in and kept him upright. "Looks like we're done here. Unless you have anything." He turned to Toni and extended his hand.

She took it without hesitation and he pulled her against his body. And fuck if she didn't snuggle into his side like she couldn't get close enough. Christ, he loved her.

"Where did you get it? The video," she asked, slipping her arm around Zach's lower back. Her small fingers hooked into his belt loop on his opposite hip.

Chris didn't answer right away, so Zach choked up on Louie.

"I'll tell you." Chris raised his hands in a position of surrender. "Found the file on Mark's computer."

Toni gasped and Zach squeezed her close. "Why don't you go call him and I'll see our guest out."

She nodded and walked toward her bedroom without so much as a glance in Chris's direction.

As soon as she was out of earshot, Zach tapped Louie against Chris's shoulder. The asshole jumped like he'd been electrocuted. "Drop your computer and any flash drives you have here before ten a.m. tomorrow. You do that, you'll never see or hear from us again. You come anywhere near my woman, and I'll make a beating from my bat look like a day at Disney. Get me?"

Chris nodded.

"Good. Get the fuck out of here."

The door slammed shut behind Chris and Zach dropped into the chair he'd been in when the man arrived. After cracking his unsatisfied knuckles, he rested his head on the back of the chair.

A few minutes later, a soft weight landed in his lap. "Better move it along missy. My woman is one possessive wench. She'll rip the hair right out of your scalp." He spoke without opening his eyes.

Normally, Toni would at least give him a chuckle for a joke like that so when she didn't so much as huff, he popped his eyes open. She was staring at him, a stricken look on her face.

"What'd Mark say, baby," he asked, tucking her hair behind her ear.

"He was looking all over for me. Back then. And found me during…" She swallowed and closed her eyes for about five seconds. "He walked in on that scene and there was a camera. Shark's men were seconds away from throwing him out and probably beating him bloody when he offered one hundred thousand dollars for me and the recording." She dropped her head into her hands. "Oh my God, Zach, he paid one hundred thousand dollars for me. How on earth will I ever repay that?"

"Baby." With a gentle tug, he removed her hands from her tear-stained face. The sight of the wet tracks on her smooth cheeks hit him like an arrow to the heart. "There's a reason you never knew about any of this. And it's because you don't owe him a damn thing. He doesn't want your money."

"I feel so guilty. How did I not know any of this? It makes so much sense now that I actually think about it. Shark never would have let me just walk away."

"Listen to me, Toni. Mark did what he did because he loves you. And he made sure you were in the dark for this very reason. He knows you and knew you'd feel guilty and want to pay him back. And it's not necessary."

"But—"

He held her face between his palms.

"But it's so much—"

"Yes," he said. "It's a lot of money. But you're worth it, baby. You're worth ten times that."

"Zach," she breathed.

Zach

"Hold, up. Let me say something."

She closed her mouth and nodded, green eyes solemn.

"Never thought I'd have an ol' lady. Just didn't give a shit about letting a woman into my life. Never wanted to know a woman beyond—" a delicate growl came from Toni and Zach laughed— "Yeah, okay, you get it. Anyway, what I'm trying to say is that I want you, Toni. I want you in my days and I want you in my nights. I want you when you're happy. I want you when you're pissed. I want you at your best and I want you at your worst. Thank you for deciding to leave this behind and give us a chance."

Her lower lip wobbled and her eyes shone glossy with unshed tears. "Zach, I have no idea why I fought it so hard at first, but I'm done fighting. I want you. I want us."

Whether she was about to say more, Zach would never know. He sealed his mouth over hers and kissed until they were both breathing like they'd run a marathon. "Come on," he said as he stood with Toni in his arms.

She shrieked and flailed her arms before settling against his chest with a smile.

"I need you naked and spread for me in the next two minutes."

"Hmm," Toni said, tracing a tattoo where it peaked from his shirt sleeve. "I love that plan."

He kissed her once and stared into her eyes. All sorts of feelings he'd never be able to properly express to her were bouncing around in his chest. So, he'd show her. Hell, he'd spend all night, every night showing her just how much he needed her in his life.

Before he was done with her, she'd be drowning in pleasure so deep she wouldn't be able to fathom leaving him.

EPILOGUE

"You done yet, babe?" Zach shouted into the diner's kitchen.

"Keep your pants on," Toni murmured as she shoved her arm into the gorgeous leather jacket Zach had given her a week ago.

"You know you don't mean that. I do my best work with my pants off," Zach said the moment she stepped into the dining area. He bobbed his eyebrows and smirked.

"How did you even hear me?" She grabbed his outstretched hand and allowed him to draw her close.

"Don't you know by now, baby?" He kissed her for a good thirty seconds. "I know all."

With a snort, Toni followed him out of the diner. Arrogant man. Of course, he had the goods to back it all up, but still...

He snatched the diner's keys out of her hand and secured the building. He had a thing about being the one to lock the house if they left together and the diner when he was taking her home, which was pretty much all the time. Said if he wasn't the one to lock it, he stressed over whether or not it was done properly. Not that he didn't trust her to take care of it, it was just a thing for him.

So, she indulged his quirk and let him lock the doors. Such a small concession for his peace of mind.

"Where're we going?" Toni asked, accepting her helmet.

"Foothills Parkway." After another kiss, Zach straddled the bike and waited for her to climb on.

Zach

"My favorite."

"I know."

"I forgot to tell you," Toni said as she swung her leg over the bike. "I received an envelope from Mark in the mail today. On the back it said not to open it unless you were with me."

"Huh. Guess we'll open it when we get there." Zach sounded almost disinterested in whatever it was she'd received from her uncle, but Toni got the impression that wasn't actually the case. It sounded more like he already knew what they'd find when they opened the package.

What were those two up to?

She settled in behind him and took a moment to enjoy the feel of Zach in the circle of her arms. The strength of his firm back and shoulders. The hills and valleys of his abs beneath her fingertips. The smooth feel and earthy smell of his leather cut. Combine it all with the power and rumble of the bike between her thighs and it was a sensory experience to be savored.

As Zach maneuvered the motorcycle through town and out onto the Foothills Parkway, the view changed from storefronts and businesses to the gorgeous scenes mother nature gifted the area.

The farther from town they rode, the more a feeling of peace spread through Toni. There were a few weeks in there that she'd worried she'd never climb out of the darkness that had slowly enveloped her after she killed Shark. It had only been within the last seven days that she'd been able to sleep through the night without nightmares and stopped experiencing a heavy, almost suffocating, sense of guilt throughout the day.

There was no blowback on the club, or her. The Handlers saw to it that the evidence would never lead back to them, so she hadn't really been worried about any legal repercussions. Taking a life in and of itself had messed with her head in a way she never saw coming. Even though there was a good chance she'd saved not only her own life, but Maverick's and Stephanie's as well, it had been hard to move past.

Zach was amazing. Patient when she needed to talk it out. Calming in the middle of the night when she woke up shouting and gasping for breath. Tolerant when she just needed some space to process. He'd been the epitome of a gentleman, except in bed where he tended to be more of an animal.

Just how she liked it.

After about forty-five minutes, Zach pulled off to an overlook they'd yet to visit. Viewing the sunset from different locations had become their thing over the past few weeks. This was a new one.

"Just in time," Zach said as he dismounted and helped her remove her helmet.

The giant auburn glowing orb was just hitting the horizon line.

"Wow," she said as she grabbed Mark's letter and walked away from the bike. "It's beautiful tonight."

Zach sat on the ground with his knees bent, legs spread. He snagged her and drew her down between his thighs. "Sure is," he said. "Second most beautiful thing here."

She leaned back against him, loving his strong arms around her. "Quite the silver tongue you have there."

"Damn straight. But that shouldn't be news to you." He tightened his hold on her and ran his tongue up the side of her neck.

Toni shivered and snuggled deeper in his embrace. With the altitude and setting sun, the air held a chill. "No, it's not. I've been a fan of your tongue for a while now."

"You know what day it is?" Zach brushed his nose along the shell of her ear.

"Yes, it's Wednesday. Why?"

He chuckled. "It is Wednesday, that's true. It also would have been the first day of school for you."

"Oh, wow. I can't believe I didn't realize it. Guess someone's been keeping me distracted." How different her life was from the

Zach

first day of school last year. Night and day. "I'm so glad I stayed," she whispered.

She turned her head and stared up at Zach. "Really, Zach, I know it took me a while to come to my senses, and I know I've not been the most fun person to be around the past few weeks, but not once since I decided to stay have I questioned or regretted that decision."

A full and true smile from Zach was one of Toni's favorite things and it didn't disappoint then. "You're missing your sunset. Probably the most beautiful one we've seen yet," he said.

"That's okay." She kissed his chin. "It's not nearly as important as making sure you know how much I care about you."

How much I love you.

Was it too early to admit those feelings? Because they were strong and on her mind almost every hour of every day.

It was at that moment, with the sun lowering below the horizon and the man she loved wrapped around her, Toni experienced complete and perfect happiness for the first time in her life.

Six months ago, if someone had told Zach he'd be sitting in the dirt with his arms wrapped around a woman he loved, watching the sunset, he'd have driven them to the hospital. Psych ward.

It wasn't that he hadn't wanted it, he'd just never given much thought to having an ol' lady. Who needed it when there were willing women hanging around the clubhouse with no goals beyond helping the club members get off?

Turned out, he did.

And he'd found it with Toni.

"Open the letter," he said as he nuzzled her ear.

"Okay." Without hesitation, she ripped the envelope open. "I've been dying to know what it is all—holy shit," she whispered. "Zach what the hell is this?" She held up the slip of paper with two fingers like she was holding a scorpion by the tail instead of a check for one hundred thousand dollars.

He chuckled. "Looks like a check to me."

"Yeah...but...what..." Her mouth opened and closed at least four times.

Giving her a squeeze, he said, "Why don't you read the note."

Toni's hands trembled as she unfolded the short note accompanying the very large check.

Toni,

I apologize for assuming Zach would be a repeat of your past. Clearly, I couldn't have been more wrong. You seem happier now than I can ever remember you being. This gesture brought tears to my and Andrew's eyes, but it is completely unnecessary. Keep it. Zach has a wonderful idea for its use. Hang on to him.

With so much love,

Mark and Andrew

Toni turned in his embrace, her brow furrowed, and the check still in her hands. "I'm more confused after reading the note."

"I know how much it bothered you that Mark paid so much money to Shark. You told me how guilty you felt. How you feel like you owe him." He shrugged. "I've worked for years with only myself to support and minimal expenses. I have money. So, I re-paid Mark." He couldn't help the smirk that formed. "I'd rather you owe me. I can think of some very inventive forms of payback."

As he spoke, he squeezed her waist. His words were meant to lighten the mood. Keep her from becoming too emotional and making a huge deal of it. Because it wasn't that big of a deal, at least not the financial part of it. He had the money. Who better to spend it on than the woman he loved?

Tears immediately filled Toni's eyes. "I can't believe you would do that for me, Zach. It's so much money. Why would you do this?"

He wiped an escaped tear off her smooth cheek. "Who else would I do this for, baby? You're the only one who matters."

Zach

"I take it Mark wouldn't accept it."

"Nope."

"Well, here," she said holding the check out to him. "This belongs to you then."

Zach folded his hand over hers and nudged it into her lap. "I want you to have it."

"What? No, Zach, I can't possibly take this. I don't even have a use for it."

"Yes, you do."

"I do?" The cute furrow was back on her brow.

"I was thinking you could use it to start a work program for troubled teens. You know, training them, giving them skills they can use in the real world. You have a lot of opportunity with the diner. Cooks, servers, management, human resources, those kinds of things."

The words were barely out of his mouth when Toni catapulted herself into his arms. "Oh my God," she squealed as she crushed him in her embrace. "You are the most wonderful man," she whispered against his ear. "It's perfect. Absolutely perfect."

He wished he could say it was all for altruistic reasons, but the reality was, he was selfish. He never wanted Toni to regret her decision to stay in Tennessee or consider leaving again. What was the one thing she was missing from her life in Chicago? The ability to help troubled teens. Well, not anymore. This was the last piece of the puzzle. She'd have no reason to ever search for greener pastures. Zach would see to it.

As he hugged her back, he said, "I was thinking I should sell my house." He held his breath while he waited for her reaction. She'd only been his ol' lady for a little over a month. Some might think it was too soon to move in together, but fuck that. He hadn't slept at his house once in the last month. Toni was it for him, so why waste a bunch of fucking time just because other people might give them the side eye.

He'd been getting that from people since he first put on his cut.

"Oh really? Where are you thinking of moving to?"

Zach pinched her waist and she giggled until she snorted. "Oh, that's cute," he said, eliciting another round of giggles. Damn, it was nice to see her so lighthearted and free. The past few weeks had been rough and he'd done his best to keep her from getting pulled under by the unnecessary guilt. The world was a much better place without Shark.

That didn't make killing him easy. Especially not for someone as good as Toni.

"I want you to move in with me, Zach. I've been thinking it for the past week but I was afraid it was too much too soon." She wiggled in his lap until she had her legs wrapped around his waist.

Fuck if he wasn't the luckiest bastard in the world. He brushed her hair off her shoulders. "Not too much, baby. I want to crawl into bed with you each night and fall asleep with you in my arms after pleasuring you for hours. I want those beautiful green eyes to be the first thing I see each morning. I want to make a life with you, Toni."

"Zach…" Her eyes shimmered with unshed tears.

"And I want to keep discovering new places to watch the sunset every evening until we're absolutely certain we've found the best place."

"I think this is it. Even if the sun burned out and turned gray, this moment would make it the most beautiful." She played with the hair at the nape of his neck.

"Guess we'll know for sure in fifty years or so, after we've seen thousands of sunsets together."

Toni almost knocked him on his ass with the most gorgeous smile he'd even seen. "That sounds like the perfect plan."

He leaned in to kiss the lips he couldn't get enough of but stopped a breath away from her mouth. "One more thing," he said."

"What?" Toni asked, her voice a breathless whisper full of need.

Zach

"I love you." He closed the distance and kissed her.

"Zach," she said against his mouth. "I love you too." The words were muffled by his lips and they both chuckled.

Zach slid his hands into her hair and worked his mouth over hers until she moaned. Then he shifted and guided her to her back in the dirt.

"What about the sunset?" she asked when they came up for a breath.

Zach sucked on the skin of her neck hard enough to leave a mark. "Fuck the sunset. We've got thousands ahead of us. Missing one won't matter. I've got much more important things to do, like make the woman I love scream."

"Well, don't let me stop you. Love you, Zach."

"Love you, Toni," he said as he set about driving her crazy. Making love to his ol' lady with a gorgeous sunset backdrop. Hands-down the best moment of his life.

He couldn't wait to try to top it.

Thank you so much for reading **Zach**. If you enjoyed it, please consider leaving a review on Amazon or Goodreads.

Other books by Lilly Atlas

No Prisoners MC Sereis
Hook: A No Prisoners Novella
Striker
Jester
Acer
Lucky
Snake

Trident Ink
Escapades

Hell's Handlers MC
Zach
Maverick
Jigsaw
Copper

Join Lilly's mailing list for a **FREE** No Prisoners short story.

www.lillyatlas.com

Join my FB group Lilly's Ladies for early cover reveals, teasers, and exclusive contests!

Maverick Preview

The world existed in only two states: right and wrong.

At least that's how Stephanie Little had always seen it.

A clear divisive line separating saints from sinners kept life manageable.

Good and evil.

Truth and lies.

Rule followers and rule breakers.

Criminals and law-abiding citizens.

All the murky gray areas and half-truths were just excuses and loopholes for people who weren't willing to make the right choices.

Stephanie always chose right after careful consideration, or at least she tried to. And if she didn't, she owned it and faced the consequences of her actions.

The split between right and wrong was what drew her to law enforcement straight out of high-school. Well, that and the fact that she grew up with the police chief for a father.

Born and raised in Pittsburg, she'd hardcore hero-worshiped her father through her childhood. He'd received countless commendations for his amazing work reducing the murder rate and crime rate in general.

Stephanie had wanted that. Craved the opportunity to leave that kind of mark on the world. Rid the planet of some darkness and inject good back for those who deserved it. Those who followed the rules and lived in the light.

So, at twenty-one with a shiny new criminal justice degree, she'd joined the police academy. Dreams of confiscating drugs, saving kidnapped children, and locking up murders powered her to the top of her class.

On the eve of graduation, her father showed up at the apartment she shared with another female cadet. In a matter of twenty minutes, he'd shattered Stephanie's perfectly compartmentalized world.

"Steppy," he'd said in the way her younger brother used to say her name. Jake had trouble with the F sound until he was four, but by then the name stuck and she'd been Steppy to her family from then on. "I know you're excited to graduate and eager to dive into your first position with the PPD, but I need to tell you something important."

She'd frowned and leaned her head on her father's broad shoulder. "What's that, Dad?"

"The world doesn't always work the way you think it does, Step. You see black and you see white. Well, honey, in the real world, those colors don't even exist. It's all a grayscale. You need to know that, really know it, in order to survive the life you've chosen for yourself. There may be things you're called on to do that don't fit neatly into the boxes you've created."

That conversation was the beginning of the end of her relationship with her father. She'd smiled, nodded, and told him what he wanted to hear, but rolled her eyes the moment he left. He was older, nearing retirement, out of touch with the way the world worked.

Such youthful arrogance and ignorance.

But Stephanie managed to hold on to her ideals through the first year of work. Even when her father lost his position in a shameful bribery scandal that earned him five years in prison she hadn't budged.

He'd done the crime, he deserved the time.

Then, somehow, she made it through two years working for the FBI before her perfectly divided world was smashed to bits. And it wasn't smashed with a sledgehammer either. No, a damn wrecking ball in the form on an undercover assignment crashed through the glass house she lived in, launching millions of sharp shards at her delicate skin.

And it hurt.

God, did it hurt.

"One more chance, bitch. What the fuck are you doin' here?" some crazy-eyed brute asked her about five seconds after his fist connected with her face.

For the second time.

The second punch disoriented her for a second. Long enough to lose her sense of vertical and meet the ground.

On all fours, with palms and knees throbbing from the bits of gravel and dirt embedded in the skin, Stephanie spit out blood that had pooled in her mouth from the split lip. "Hiking," she said, the sound a bit muffled from her swollen lip. "Got lost."

And…damn…who knew talking with a split lip would hurt so freaking much. Tears pooled in her eyes, but she'd rather die than let one of those suckers slip free. She wasn't the toughest of chicks out there…physically at least. A few arrests during her time as a beat cop had resulted in physical altercations with significant bumps and bruising. She'd always put on a tough mask in front of her fellow officers but bawled like a baby in the privacy of her own home.

Crazy-eyes threw back his head and laughed before looking at his buddy, a guy so overweight, Stephanie was pretty sure she could outrun him even if they broke both her legs. "You believe this bitch, Top?" he asked the larger man.

Top grunted and shook his head, his many chins wobbling like Jello. "Fuck no. No reason for a bitch to be hiking out here, Shark. Ain't even any fuckin' trails."

Like he would know?

Stephanie bit back the smart-assed remark on the tip of her

tongue. Silence was her best bet. Plus, this little gangbanger pow-wow gave her a second to reorient and breath through the pain.

"What about you, King? You believe her?" The man called Shark asked the man on his right and Stephanie held her breath.

This was it. Her way out. Sure, there'd be hell to pay later for the rookie-level mistake of getting busted snooping in the woods outside their compound, but she'd take an ass chewing form her boos over being beat to shit or worse by pissed off gang members.

All her partner, Eric, or King to these pieces of shit had to say was that he believed her. Saw her tromping around like an idiot. Spotted her looking lost and stupid in the woods. He could volunteer to drop her somewhere and scare the piss out of her so she wouldn't talk.

Shark and the Top dude were scary as fuck and she wanted gone in the worst way.

"No I don't fuckin' believe this, bitch," King said, lifting his military grade rifle and stomping forward until the weapon was pressed dead center against her forehead. "I say we just waste her now. Bury her and get back to those bitches we left naked and needy."

What. The. Fuck.

Stephanie had never worked so hard in her life as she did to keep the shock off her face and the vile words in her mouth.

Calm down.

King wasn't serious. He couldn't be. Her partner was a veteran FBI agent for crying out loud. There had to be a plan to get her out bouncing around in his head.

That knowledge helped her relax despite the fact one twitch of King's finger and her brains would be splattered all over the Tennessee woods.

"Nah," Shark said. "Where's the fun in that? Let's take her with us. A few hours hanging with the boys and she'll be ready to talk."

Fuck. Fuck. Fuck.

She stared hard into King's eyes trying to send him a mental message. This was as bad for him as it was for her. They'd torture her for information and she'd crack.

Everyone cracked.

Especially if they had only a rudimentary training in enduring torture.

"Who gives a fuck why she's here? Let me kill her and be fuckin' done with it."

Stephanie was in serious danger of puking all over the forest floor. As she stared at her partner of two years—the partner who taught her everything she knew about working for the FBI, the partner who teased her endlessly for her opinions on the black and white nature of the world—his lips quirked.

And her viewpoint was validated.

There were no shades of gray.

She'd been right all along.

Only black. Only white.

And King had officially been swallowed by the darkness.

He'd always told her working undercover would change her perception of the world. That undercover agents often had to live the life of a criminal and learn to deal with living in the shadows for the sake of doing good. But this wasn't a case of doing what he had to maintain cover. This was a monster who wore human skin for a time and managed to fool even the most skeptical.

"What the fuck did I say, King?" Shark asked. "I want her at the compound. You can kill her eventually, but it's been a shit week. The boys need some fun first."

Stephanie swallowed. Boys? Fun?

There weren't too many ways to interpret that.

The gun fell away from her head and she sat back on her heels.

Why? What was so appealing about this lifestyle that a decorated FBI agent would do a one-eighty and betray everything he once stood for.

Money?

Frustration with the system?

Stickin' it to the man?

It seemed too dramatic to be making a point.

The ultimate hissy fit.

"Let's roll," Shark said, turning on his heel and strolling toward the building she could see through the trees in the distance.

The fat one leered at her for a second more before waddling after his master like an overfed but well-trained dog.

Somewhat alone with her partner, Stephanie rose to her feet. Whatever was about to happen, it wouldn't happen while she was on her knees in front of him. He'd have to look her full in the eye. For one second, she had the insane urge to call out to Shark. To yell as loud as she could and let the scumbag know his precious King was an undercover FBI agent.

It wouldn't matter if he pledged his loyalty to Shark forever. He'd be killed. That's how it worked with gangs.

Nothing less than he deserved at that moment.

But she didn't give into that urge. Because it would be wrong. And she always chose right.

"Why?" she whispered when Shark was out of earshot.

King grunted and shook his head. "So fucking naïve, Stephanie. You always have been. It's all gray out here."

No. She refused to believe it. This situation was clearly not on any gray spectrum. King was evil. Plain and simple.

"No, Eric, I'm not naïve. But you sure are a fucking traitor."

"You'll never get it. And you'll never survive this world. Wake the fuck up," King said as he thrust his right arm forward and rammed the butt of his rifle into her head.

His murderous expression was the last thing she saw before her vision blacked.

About the Author

Lilly Atlas is an award-winning contemporary romance author. She's a proud Navy wife and mother of three spunky girls. Every time Lilly downloads a new eBook she expects her Kindle App to tell her it's exhausted and overworked, and to beg for some rest. Thankfully that hasn't happened yet so she can often be found absorbed in a good book.

Made in the USA
Middletown, DE
28 May 2021